A Haven in Ash

Ashes of Luukessia, Volume One

Robert J. Crane

A Haven in Ash
Ashes of Luukessia, Volume One
Robert J. Crane
with Michael Winstone

1st Edition

1

Alixa Weltan watched the sky from a mossy boulder.

Behind her, Jasen Rabinn crept up. The breeze kissed his skin softly, not strong enough to cover his steps. It sighed through the mountains, cooling him in spite of the growing heat. Midday had come, not that you'd know from the blanket of grey spread out overhead, and the day was getting warmer.

He slunk, quiet as a mouse … and then drummed his fingers on the top of her head.

She flinched, as he'd intended. He only did this to annoy her.

"Cousin," she greeted him, tone flat. "Stop it." And she batted at his hands, ducking out from below his fingers. A curl of hazel hair twisted out from behind an ear. Gracelessly, she pushed it back into place with her palm.

"Why do I always find you with your head in the clouds?" Jasen asked.

"I was greeting the sun," she retorted.

"What sun?"

She cast him a disdainful look. "It was here until you arrived. Likely your ugly face scared it off."

Jasen shook his head and sat down beside her. "You're so charming, cousin."

She turned up her nose and made a disgusted sort of noise low in her throat, but said no more.

Their village, Terreas, lay behind them. It was the sort of place the elder villagers tended to describe as "quaint," a word Jasen thought implied more charm than the little town actually possessed. It was small and uninteresting, notable only in that it lay sprawled at the foot of the mountains. The nearest one towered above the little town, high and close enough that on wintry mornings the low sun would draw a vast shadow across the village that seemed never to end.

Jasen and Alixa had parked themselves at the edge of the Weltan farmland, itself toward Terreas's southern boundary. A vineyard, Alixa's mother's, lay behind them. Nestled in the earth beside the farmland was a boulder that grew a thin carpet of green moss every spring. The moss provided a soft cushion for them to perch upon and watch the mountains.

The closest mountain coughed a thin plume skyward, barely visible against the cloud-carpeted sky.

Jasen pointed. "The mountain breathes again this morning."

"You're too concerned with that rock," Alixa muttered. "I hope one day it takes notice of your attention, stands up, and eats you whole." She was teasing, of course, though it was hard to tell by the dryness of her voice.

Jasen tilted his head back, running his hands down the moss at his side. He squinted.

In spite of the heat, an ethereal cloud of fog had condensed around the base of the small mountain range. Jasen's eyes roved across it, searching for dark shapes moving within.

Finding none, he turned a scrutinizing eye on his cousin. "The mountain will come eat me? Not the scourge?"

She paled, not even able to sputter at his casual mention. Though the scourge hadn't ever visited Terreas, the pallid beasts were known to take refuge in the fog, in packs that wandered close to the village borders.

Alixa shook her head. A curtain of hair slipped over her shoulder, masking one side of her face. She pushed it back, brushing at it distractedly. "Don't..." Her composure returned. "You need not mention those things."

"Did you weave?" Jasen asked, feeling a breath of contrition run down the back of his neck. "With Sidyera?"

"*Aunt* Sidyera, and yes."

"She's not *my* aunt."

Alixa frowned. "My fingers ache."

"Do you want to take the rest of the morning off? Go looking for scourge tracks?"

He did not expect a no, unless Alixa were being awkward. She knew well his desire for adventure, but she was in a surlier mood than usual today, or perhaps a little more bitter, no doubt from the endless lectures Sidyera delivered while Alixa wove at her side.

She closed her eyes; this time she did not pale at the mention of the scourge. She seemed to draw a long breath, and finally, for the first time that she broke into a smile. "Let's go," she said, giving a very earnest nod and clambering to her feet.

Jasen leapt up, not quite believing it but not willing to question his luck. Falling into step—she was half a head shorter, at fifteen years to his sixteen, and slighter, though he too was slim, yet to fill out like his father kept saying he would—he pointed ahead. "Let's walk by the boundary. Might be tracks on the other side."

Alixa looked uncomfortable. "Really?"

"We've done it before."

"Yes, but … my shoes aren't appropriate."

It was an excuse. Jasen raised his eyebrows skeptically in response.

"Fine," she conceded begrudgingly. "Wait here." And she backtracked, half-running in the direction of the vineyard and the house beyond it.

Jasen dawdled, eyeing the range, and fiddled at his neck. A flat amulet of polished stone hung there, just below his shirt. He lifted it free and considered it. A morose twinge clenched his stomach, and with a huff he stowed it, then swiveled and put on a burst of speed to catch up with Alixa on her way to the house.

The Weltan cottage was well-kept, sturdy, and covered in moss at the rear, which rounded into view first from the direction Alixa and Jasen approached. It managed to squeeze a bigger family into it than Jasen's would've—but then, it had to: Alixa had three brothers and her parents, not to mention Aunt Sidyera, who seemed to take up a disproportionate amount of space and fill much of the rest of the building with hot air. Jasen thanked the ancestors daily that she was not *his* aunt, too—because after his mother passed, he would have surely ended up with her, listening to lectures for hours and hours on end as she spun that awful creaky wheel.

There were also a multitude of scents vying for attention. The smell of grapes in the vineyard was quickly muted by the herb garden's many smells, all vying for dominance. The fresh smell of upturned earth lingered in the air too: a harvested patch needed repurposing, the soil turned in preparation for new seedlings.

Alixa made her way to the back entry. She kept her "roughing" boots there, as she called them, repurposed from a pair of riding boots.

She shoved through the back door, letting it swing heavily, and quickly swapped shoes. She gripped Jasen for leverage as she yanked at one heel.

"You could've just used the step," he said. "Or actually gone in."

"Then we might run into someone who'd keep us," she murmured back.

She certainly meant Aunt Sidyera, the crone.

Straightening her skirt and her blouse, she stepped back out, shutting the door behind far more carefully than she had opened it—again, avoiding the attention of her aunt. Then Jasen fell in alongside her, heading for the trail toward the mountains.

The dirt pathway had been created as a result of hundreds of footsteps trampling it down over time. It skirted up to the boundary and then beyond, splitting off into goat trails that snaked the lower portions of the mountains. Today, Jasen could not pick them out; the mist obscured too much.

"What do you say we climb up the unfinished mountain?" he asked. "We might finally see the little cottage that's nestled inside." Smoke regularly puffed from the dip at the mountain's peak, and Jasen and Alixa often joked that someone had built a cottage there, and the smoke was from their chimney stack.

Alixa directed him a look from the corner of her eye. It was a sidelong glance Jasen knew well. It said that she worried about his brains and the sorry state of them.

Sorry in her mind, of course; they were perfectly acceptable brains as far as Jasen was concerned.

"Jasen, scourge are out there. We aren't going to search for danger."

Jasen pouted, tilting his head down. Copper curls drooped over his eyes. He sullenly ignored them.

Alixa prodded him. "We'll go up there eventually," she said. "When we have one or two days free …" Her tone lacked conviction.

"And the nerve for it," Jasen murmured.

Alixa glared at him, cheeks blossoming scarlet. "I have plenty of nerve."

"Fine," said Jasen. "We'll spend the afternoon by the boundary then, shall we? Perhaps if we call loud enough, one of the scourge will come right up to us."

Alixa's glare pivoted into a semblance of dismayed pity. "That's it. It's finally happened. You have lost your mind."

"What's the problem?" Jasen pushed. "No scourge have ever crossed the boundary. A hundred of them could come to my shouts, and still the boundary would protect us."

"So let's challenge that by putting ourselves out like bait, hm? Summoning them like dogs?"

Jasen didn't respond, just looked at her with raised eyebrows. So Alixa huffed a breath. "Fine. Let's go then." And she stomped ahead, ignoring Jasen's victorious grin.

The boundary was a stone wall, about as high as Jasen's waist. It clutched Terreas in a semi-circle, cupping it where the mountains left off. Blooming with moss, stones uneven and in places fallen away, it served as a warning more than anything. The scourge, which ruled the rest of the lands of Luukessia as far as anyone in the village knew, had never dared to cross it. Instead the wall warned the village's youngest residents: *Do not pass this line.*

Or perhaps...*Death waits beyond.*

Jasen avoided a shudder at the grim thought, but only barely.

Alixa's smile had long vanished. Now her mouth was a thin line, downturned at one end. She clenched and unclenched her fingers, working nails against her palms—Jasen could see the knuckles whiting, and many times had seen the crescents she dug in.

"You're getting twitchy," he observed.

"You're projecting your fears onto me," she shot back, but she immediately ceased her nervous movements.

"Please," Jasen said. "You'll run the moment we see so much as a scourge toe print."

Alixa rolled her eyes at him. "Watch me." And she strode the last short distance to the boundary, stuck out a hand—did he see it quiver?—and laid it across the top of the wall.

"There," she said defiantly. "How's that for twitchy?"

"You wouldn't cross it," Jasen challenged.

Alixa hesitated. She was a determined girl who didn't like to back down from a challenge—but crossing the boundary? That was, perhaps, a challenge too far for Alixa.

Truth be told, would it not have been a challenge too far for him too? He had considered it, of course, thought about it plenty: what it would be like in the world out there, how it might feel, where he might go … but to actually vault it, as he was daring Alixa?

"I have no reason to cross," she said. "And neither do you," she added, more fiercely.

Jasen looked out. Fields took up root on the other side of the boundary, open and softly waving in the breeze. This was rye. The heads were just coming in, green and frail. As the summer stretched, those heads would grow, turn fat and golden, blanketing for miles to see—the carpet stretched well beyond Terreas on either side, disappearing over hills.

No sign of the scourge. No mist, and though the rye had grown taller just this past week alone, the scourge would struggle to sneak through it, unless they pressed low and slunk. And they didn't have the brains to conceal themselves … did they?

"Let's walk," Jasen said and directed Alixa along the boundary.

They went in silence, Jasen looking out, Alixa not so much. She'd positioned herself farther from the wall than he, and as his gaze swept the rye field, and out over the hillocks extending beyond Terreas, he thought he could feel her gaze move over him. Keeping an eye on him, probably, lest he do anything rash. Well, he wouldn't.

Not today, anyway.

Sometimes, he and Alixa chattered about what might be out there. Today, Jasen mulled that over to himself, the only sound between them their feet on the earth and grass.

Alixa's father, Jasen's uncle, had told stories when they were little of what lay beyond—before the scourge had come to Luukessia and taken its land for themselves. Somewhere lay ocean, a vast body of water that extended a hundred, or a thousand, times farther than the rye field Jasen's eyes wandered over now. He'd tried so hard to picture it, many, many times, frowning so hard his face almost folded in on itself, and still he couldn't.

Maybe he never would.

Alixa broke their silence. "Quiet as ever." She was solemn, yet sounded pleased.

The wind gusted, changing direction and blowing hard all at once. A rancid smell came with it, like rot.

Alixa turned her nose up. "Ugh. I hate when the wind shifts like that."

Jasen's face had twisted in disgust too—but he paused. The wind had brought vile scents, yes, but it had also carried …

"Do you hear that?" he asked, squinting the way it had come.

Alixa stared at him in bewilderment then followed his gaze over the fields.

The rye swung, bobbing with momentum from the wind—

Where it parted, a small figure, its arm raised skyward—

And nearby, something shifted, unnatural … wrong.

Jasen spotted it at the same moment Alixa did.

He broke into a sprint.

"Jasen!"

He barely heard. All his focus had drawn in on the space where he'd seen that person—a child, he was sure, in the part of his brain still actively processing for him where the rest worked on pumping his arms and legs. Without thinking he flew for the boundary, gripping it with one hand, and swinging over—

Another cry from Alixa, lost to him.

Then he was hurtling through rye.

The grasses weren't at their full height, but the earth was rich with minerals that the mountains had disgorged over time. The rye was thick and tall, right up to Jasen's shoulder already. Sprinting through it was more like wading, and for a moment Jasen thought that this was what being in water was like—only the grasses fought against him, stinging, and one particularly sharp barb whipped at his neck. He grunted against the bite of pain—then he was past and it was gone, not clinging like thorns but simply giving up—

The wind gusted again, from another direction this time. The stink of rot assailed him, and it seemed somehow stronger, as though it came from the very fields themselves, whickering, whickering—

A flurry, and the rye parted—

Jasen almost slammed into the boy, avoiding a hard collision at the last second.

The boy gasped, eyes wide with fright. Pale skin gone blotchy from tears, he'd been fighting his way through the rye with his hands out in front of him. Blonde hair had gone awry, like the grasses had mussed it for him.

Jasen came to a jerky halt. "Tery?" He groped for the surname, suddenly lost into mists like the scourge stalking the mountains' base. Malori? That was it. Son of the village butcher.

Tery grasped onto Jasen's middle and bawled. "I g-got lost!"

"Why are—?" Jasen began then cut himself off. Questions could come later. For now, they needed to get back to the boundary. Gripping Tery's shoulder with a firm hand, Jasen steered him around, swiveling to find the wall. Just barely visible, cut off by the expanse of rye behind, Alixa stared in horror.

"Jasen!" she yelled.

"I've got him," he called back. To Tery: "Come on. It's this way."

"Th-thank you," the boy sniffed.

The wind blasted again. The stench of decay hit Jasen hard like a slap to the face. He recoiled from it, gagging.

It was so *close*.

Muffled by the gusting air came another noise. It wasn't the rye, bending to the wind's whims … but something moving through it.

Something close.

Jasen gripped Tery's shoulder tighter. Hurting him, probably, but he had to keep hold.

"Can you run?" he asked the boy.

"I don't know," Tery whimpered. "Why do we need to—?"

Then the question was answered. From behind, back the way they'd come, the rye parted as though the very earth had exploded beneath it.

Jasen twisted, eyes almost all whites—

A scourge.

Up close, it was worse than Jasen could have imagined. Lumpy and grey and wrinkled, it was like the worst parts of a frail old man combined them with an ill, oversized, hairless dog.

It yawned a roar, black eyes like endless pits on Jasen and Tery—

"Run!" Jasen instructed and muscled the kid around.

Tery cried something Jasen didn't catch. It was lost to Alixa's scream from the boundary, a scream that *maybe* someone might hear back in the village proper. But even the closest houses were two miles away; the fastest among the villagers would never get here in time.

It was up to Jasen alone to save the Malori boy—and himself.

And he had scant seconds to do it.

He shoved through rye, hand clasped as tightly as it could on the boy's tunic. Tery's legs to barely seemed work, and he tripped and stumbled, gasping strangled breaths. Jasen tugged him up every time, dragging him desperately through the grass—

The scourge bounded behind.

Ancestors, the *smell* of the thing. Like an old carcass, it came straight for them—

We'll be corpses too, Jasen thought, and then smashed the image down. He just had to focus on the boundary, had to push, one foot after the after, closing in on Alixa's screaming face—

The scourge loosed another of its awful noises, and Jasen twisted. The thing seemed so *large*, larger than its true size surely was—they weren't much taller, wider or longer than big dogs. But it was ungainly too, and where Jasen and Tery could slip through a channel in the rye, the scourge was tangled every leap—

Good. Let it get stuck and die in it.

It snarled as if hearing his thoughts, and careened forward in a renewed mad burst.

Jasen yelped—

The rye parted. Grass. A few yards of it. Then the boundary, Alixa—

Jasen twisted, gripping Tery in both hands. He swung him up for the boundary, shouting to Alixa, "Take him!" Then, Tery released, he planted a hand on the wall and vaulted—

Cloying death hit the back of his throat, and he felt the scourge mere inches behind—

Then he was over, landing hard with a thump, and the scourge did not follow.

Alixa had collapsed under Tery's weight. She lay sprawled under him, but thrust herself up, kicking backward from the boundary with terrified eyes. One arm clung around Tery's waist, and he gripped her like he'd gripped Jasen in the field, as though he might never let go again. Alixa did not look as though she were likely to let go any time soon, either.

Dirt had caked Tery's face in the sprint, and tears cut tracks through it.

Alixa wiped at his face. "What were you *doing* out there? Are you okay?"

"I-I got lost," Tery whined. "I couldn't find my way."

She fussed, checking that he was not hurt.

Jasen remained flat on his back, panting up at the sky. There were breaks in the clouds now, gaps where Alixa might hope to see sun should they be back on the rock by the vineyard.

Ancestors, if they'd stayed … If Alixa had declined to come …

Jasen shut the door to those thoughts. The only thing to focus on was the way things had actually gone. No what-ifs or pretend histories or presents or futures. They'd come out here, and he'd saved Tery from that thing.

He eyed it, pushing up. The scourge remained on the other side of the boundary, dead black eyes looking in. Its mouth was wet and hung open as it breathed.

It could scale the boundary easily. Yet it stayed.

Why did it stay?

"We should go," Jasen said, clambering unevenly to his feet. He stuck a hand out to Alixa. "Come on." His voice was rough.

"Yes," Alixa said shakily. "Yes, we should. Come, Tery." She hoisted him up as Jasen helped. He clung, making it difficult; some seven years separated them by age, but Tery was tall for his age, and Alixa was short. His head came most of the way up her chest.

As one they made their way back to Terreas. The walk was mostly quiet, Alixa fussing with Tery, his cries growing softer as they put distance behind them.

Jasen was silent. He couldn't keep from looking back over his shoulder, at the scourge standing just beyond the boundary, watching them disappear until, finally, when Terreas was closer than the wall, it slipped back into the rye and disappeared.

2

"This breach of tradition is an *outrage*!"

Hanrey Smithson slammed his fist hard down on the thick wooden table he was seated at. Old and stubby, he had a dwarfish look to him, almost as broad as he was high. Alixa had sometimes said that if ever a scourge were to attempt to eat him, it would spit him out for being too tough and leathery.

Cowering from the *crack!* delivered via the table, Jasen couldn't help wishing a scourge were here now to at least *attempt* it.

"Oh, take that stick out of your behind, Hanrey," said Eounice Bevers. Perched across from the grumpy codger, just as old but somehow even stouter, she punctuated her words with a dramatic eye roll.

"There's no stick up my backside, Eounice!" Hanrey barked back.

"There most certainly is."

"It has been understood since this menace invaded our lands—"

"And it rides up farther every bloody year."

Hanrey raised his voice to speak over her, "—that passing beyond the boundary is forbidden. And so for this *boy*—" He jabbed a gnarled old finger out at Jasen, "—to cross it so brazenly—"

"This *boy* has a name," growled Jasen's father.

Hanrey rounded on him. "Your boy—yes, *boy*—failed to honor one of Terreas's most key tenets."

"He crossed a *wall*, you barmy old goat," snapped Eounice.

"To save a child, if I'm not mistaken?" That was Alixa's mother, and Jasen's aunt, Margaut. The resemblance between mother and daughter was uncanny, even down to the clothes; the same blanket of hair, the same tight expression, identical probing eyes. Rushed to this meeting, as they all had been, her hands were still caked with dirt well past the wrists, and she gripped Alixa's shoulders at the sidelines.

Alixa, looking somewhere between tense, ashamed, and petrified, was still as a post. Jasen wondered if she'd even noticed the soil upon her clothes. Probably not; she'd have been much more fussed if she had.

"Another breach," Hanrey grumbled. "That boy let our village down too."

"He's a *child*, Hanrey," Eounice retorted. "Remember that? About seven centuries ago?"

"Don't you spit barbs at me, Eounice. Crossing the boundary will only invite scourge. That these children trampled over something so sacrosanct—"

"The Rabinn boy went out to save Malori!"

"That boy should never have been out there in the first place."

"But he was," Eounice said. She leaned over the table, threatening to shunt it forward. "And this one here went out to rescue him. *Successfully*. He saved a life today."

Hanrey harrumphed.

Eounice puffed up. "Oh, that's the attitude then. And what would you have done? Let me tell you now, Hanrey, if you say that the Malori boy should've been left in that field to die, I will come over there and slam this stick of mine right across the back of your head. Knock some sense into that bony skull of yours," she added, muttering under her breath.

Hanrey's cheeks flooded with red heat.

"Listen here, you old battle axe," he started, and he shoved up to his feet—not much of a change in height—and turned that knobbled finger toward Eounice instead.

He opened his mouth to spit something suitably vile—Eounice was already clambering up, drawing her small frame to the most its feeble height could muster—

"That is *quite enough*."

This came from the last person in the room, and thus far the most quiet, except for perhaps Alixa, whose few utterances had been fragmentary and strangled. Griega Marks rose from the middlemost, and farthest back, table in the dimly lit room where the assembly had gathered for this emergency meeting. Younger than both Hanrey and Eounice by at least two decades, but still greying, Griega was a severe woman who observed constantly and spoke rarely. She was thin and tall, and as head of Terreas's assembly, her position was denoted by a rather shapeless dress dyed the dull purple of beets, and a headdress in the same color, speckled with polished ore fragments. With the shutters drawn and candles lit, those tiny stones twinkled gently.

Jasen and Alixa and Tery had been accosted quickly after their return to the village proper. They had told their story over Tery's bawls—although he had done most of the job, shouting and crying for his mama and papa between wails of the scourge stalking him in the rye—and before Jasen knew what was happening, his father and Alixa's mother had been summoned, and everyone had been bustled in here for this meeting, which was on the verge of turning into a full-on altercation, the way Eounice and Hanrey were going.

Jasen and Alixa had told the story, not that it had felt like much of one. And since then, Jasen had quivered, directly in the crossfire of these two warring elders—it was he who had passed the boundary, after all—awaiting judgment.

His head spun.

The noxious scent of candles—why did they have to be so pungent? In fact, why did the shutters have to be pulled closed at all?—made it worse.

And now Griega's eyes were on him, and oh, he was going to be so sick.

"I have heard your story," Griega said slowly. "Both of you." A brief flick of the eyes toward Alixa. Though Jasen didn't look around, he could feel her flinch, even positioned on the sidelines as she was.

And Griega said no more.

Fortunately, Eounice was there to pick it up.

"This boy should be commended," she said, directing a pointed glare at Hanrey. "If this one hadn't been there, I dread to think what would've happened to the Malori child."

"It's a damned good thing the fool didn't let an army of scourge inside," Hanrey growled.

"That *fool* is my son," Adem said.

Hanrey rounded on him instantly. "And he *is* a fool! Traipsing out into scourge territory. It's a wonder he didn't get himself—and the rest of us—killed."

"*He saved the Malori boy!*" Eounice cried. "Are you too dim-witted to wrap your meager brains around that?"

"The Malori boy shouldn't have been out there either. In fact, why aren't his parents here now? They ought to be reprimanded for their short-sighted, imbecilic—"

Eounice snorted.

"—failure to keep an eye on their boy. And let me tell *you*, Eounice, if you think that I am out of line—"

"Before you disappear up your own backside with the stick, like you've been threatening to the last fifty years," Eounice cut over, "on this, and for once, I actually *agree* with you."

Hanrey hesitated.

"Don't look so surprised," Eounice muttered. "The Maloris failed to adequately safeguard their child. I trust—" she looked to Griega "—that they will be brought in for a discussion once the shock of this morning's events has settled."

"They will," Griega confirmed. "As for these two …" Her gaze had not shifted from Jasen's face—he had been terribly aware of it, and desperately avoiding it—and now that he met eyes with her again, her look seemed to grow only more piercing.

Adem had stood just behind and to the side of Jasen, much as Margaut was stationed behind Alixa. A heavy hand lay across Jasen's shoulder. Now that Griega seemed to be preparing her judgment, the fingers tightened. Later, Jasen would find a row of red marks still lingered there. For now, he barely felt it, so unable to move was he under the assembly matron's stare.

"Our rules and traditions bear remembering," Griega began slowly. "The boundary clasping Terreas's rim exists for a reason. The scourge do not cross it—"

"Haven't yet, anyway," Hanrey muttered.

Eounice picked up her stick and thrust it at him. She was just long enough to whack him in the side of the leg.

He began a retort, but was silenced by an icy look from Griega.

After ten long seconds, Griega turned back to Jasen, and picked up as though she had not been interrupted.

"—and in return, we do not cross it either. In remaining on our side, we keep ourselves safe: the individual, and the collective."

"What the Matron of the Assembly means—" Hanrey began.

Another dramatic eye roll from Eounice. "Oh, here we go."

"Is that such traditions are not to be trampled on. To spit in the face of this rule—to endanger *all of us*—is cretinous, moronic, dim-witted, short-sighted—"

"That's my son," Adem repeated.

"Consider yourself lucky you have a son left," Hanrey snapped. "Crossing the boundary is asking to be devoured by scourge."

"Jasen did wrong," Adem muttered. "I am aware. I will be reprimanding him myself, thank you very much."

"He needs more than scolding," grumbled Hanrey, but he didn't elaborate on what Jasen did need, exactly.

Jasen bit his lip and frowned down at his feet. How had this happened? He should be feeling exuberant. He had longed for adventure, wished for it with all his heart. Today, he'd come as close as he had ever been. And all right, he had only run partway into a field and back—but Eounice was right: he had saved a life! There was no doubt of that; he'd seen the scourge burst from the rye with his own two eyes, felt its thundering behind him as he muscled Tery back to safety.

He should be ecstatic.

Yet here he was, in this dark room, throat choked by those overpowering candles, under attack from all sides.

All he felt was hollow.

And, like Alixa, pricked with guilt … and fear.

This was not how he'd pictured today going.

"This has gone on long enough," Eounice pronounced before Hanrey could begin another repetition of his spiel. "They've heard enough: do not cross the boundary. We have more pressing matters to occupy us today. There are … accommodations to be made."

Jasen swallowed the hard lump that had suddenly formed in his throat. He knew this time of year well; knew exactly who those accommodations were being made for.

Baraghosa. Just the name sent a shiver up Jasen's spine.

"This is a pressing matter," Hanrey said.

"Disciplining children who do not need disciplining is not a 'pressing matter,'" Eounice answered snippily. "It's a pointless exercise."

"It is not—"

"Oh, shut up for once in your life, for goodness sake," Eounice cut across. "You've said your piece. Four or five times, if I recall correctly. This young man has heard. Now, unless you've got something new to say, can we dismiss these children and address the issue of Baraghosa's arrival?"

Hanrey muttered something, but Griega held up a hand. "We ought to attend to Baraghosa." To Jasen, though Griega's eyes had not left him: "You may leave. And Miss Weltan."

"Um … thank you," Jasen choked.

Aunt Margaut relaxed. She guided Alixa toward the door, murmuring. Jasen caught, "You did well," before his father's grip shifted to bring him around, and he was forced to come eye to eye with him.

His father's gaze was something else entirely. Jasen had only met it once today, when he and Alixa had been brought in for questioning. Then Adem had seemed angry. Now he looked positively enraged. His entire face was hard, impenetrable—but then, what did that matter? There would be nothing behind it but more of that same anger. Like an onion: the same at every layer, right to its core.

Jasen fought not to cower from him.

"I'll speak to you tonight," Adem said gruffly. "Now go."

Jasen nodded, and turned.

As he neared the door, open now where Alixa had been let out by Margaut, who waited on the sidelines for the next stage of the council's meeting, Adem called, "And don't stray from the village today. If I hear you've been anywhere near the boundary …"

He didn't say more, nor did he need to. Jasen had heard loud and clear.

He exchanged a meek smile with Aunt Margaut, then exited the building.

Twisting at the last moment, he got one last view of his father's stony eyes on him before the door closed.

3

Alixa lit into him immediately.

"You!" she cried, and she jabbed him sharply in the chest before he'd even fully turned in her direction. "You are—you are—*argh!!*"

Jasen caught her hand before she prodded him again. "Hey, hey, stop it! For someone so small, you have a lot of punch."

Alixa's eyes grew wide. "We just had to face up to the assembly!"

"You think I don't know that?" Jasen said.

"We were just on *trial,* Jasen!"

"Stop being so loud. People are starting to look."

They were. Would've been anyway, of course; the assembly hall was close to Terreas's roughly constructed square, and as midday approached villagers had been going about their business when the whole affair had been kicked into motion. Plenty had heard Tery's cries, plenty more had seen Jasen and Alixa marched in for their hearing—and now Alixa was doing her part to make sure that every man, woman and child who *hadn't* previously known were now aware that the Rabinn and Weltan kids had been called in for questioning.

"Perhaps leave off for a bit," Jasen added, glancing back at a shuttered window. "Let's get farther away before you tear me a new one, why don't we?"

Alixa blustered, but allowed Jasen to lead her off. She muttered ceaselessly, one hand tugging at her clothes, as though straightening them might undo the past half-hour. Jasen had seen wild cats once, bandy-legged little things that fought far more dramatically than seemed necessary. The victor had skulked away, leaving the loser parked upon its backside for close to an hour, cleaning every inch of its fur. If not for the novelty, Jasen would have grown bored long before it slunk away, disappearing—probably to be snapped up by one of the scourge.

Out of the assembly hall, Jasen squinted slightly. The sky was still overcast, but even so the mid-afternoon light was almost blinding after the dark hall. The air was fresh again, although the scent of perfumed candles seemed to have caught somewhere deep in Jasen's chest, and a whiff of it lingered. He coughed, trying to loose it.

Alixa harrumphed. "Cover your mouth, you animal."

"Sorry."

"Typical." She rolled her eyes, much like Eounice had, an exaggerated motion that seemed to fill her whole being. "You don't do anything properly, do you?" It was an insult rather than a question; she turned her nose up accusingly.

"Not covering my mouth when I cough …?"

"Crossing the boundary!" Alixa exploded.

"Oh."

"It's just like Mr. Smithson said. We've been told since we could walk—since we were *born*—not to cross over. And you did it anyway!"

"Tery was out there!" Jasen said, voice growing louder.

But Alixa went on as if she didn't hear him. "I knew I shouldn't have gone out with you today. You've been trying to trample that tradition for as long as we've been friends—longer, even, because I remember you talking about it before Pityr went."

"I was joking!"

"Were you?" She rounded on him, and Jasen stopped dead in his tracks to meet the fire in her eyes head on. "It seems you've been looking for excuses to go out of Terreas, as if you forget there are scourge out there."

"I don't *forget* about them," Jasen bit back. "Ever. That's exactly *why* I jumped over the wall this morning. Tery was out there—did the smell of that bloody place addle your brains, or did you forget the scourge that chased after us when I got him? That wrinkly grey thing with the black eyes—remember? The beast that would have *eaten* Tery if I hadn't gone out there to save him?"

They were drawing a fresh round of stares now. They'd stopped just shy of the shoe-mender's, where fragile Mr. Timmons was working outside, sitting on the stoop. The shoe he'd been working was forgotten in his hands, and he stared open-mouthed at the two arguing teenagers. Two doors down, the baker, Mr. Hughes, had stuck his head out to see what the commotion was all about.

Alixa seethed. "It's not safe out there."

"No, it's not," Jasen said, and he worked to keep his voice low again, to encourage this slice of Terreas to just stop watching. "That's why I went." And he set off at a march again, not much caring whether Alixa followed or not.

She did come, hurrying her legs to fall into step at his side.

"That was horrible," she started.

Jasen gritted his teeth. Here she went again. "And there I was thinking you'd enjoy a run-in with the Matron of the Assembly."

"That's not what I meant," Alixa said. "Although it *was* horrible, thank you very much. I mean breaking the tradition."

"What's the problem? It's not like *you* did it. Everyone in there heard that."

"It's still not right, Jasen," she snapped. "My mother was disappointed. I could see it in her eyes." She shook her head, idly fingering her hair. "You know what that feels like?"

"My father was disappointed too." Or just angry. Although, with parents, wasn't that more or less the same thing?

"It felt like a hot poker to my very soul," Alixa finished dramatically.

Jasen pursed his lips. Not that he didn't understand the feeling, but the description was much too poetic for Alixa. For all her complaints about Sidyera, Alixa had begun to mimic some of the crone's flamboyant turns of phrase just lately. Jasen said nothing, but filed away the growing resemblance should he need to break it out sometime Alixa's castigation got out of hand.

"We oughtn't to have gone," Alixa said. And then: "I oughtn't to have agreed."

"We went. And in doing so, we were able to save Tery's life."

Alixa made a noise of discontent.

"Don't act like that. Come on." It was Jasen's turn to round on her, and now he found he suddenly didn't care about the passers-by whose eyes would inevitably turn to them. "You're so full of disapproval and dead set on propriety. What's your alternative? Should I have left Tery out there to die?"

"No," Alixa answered, sounding put out.

"So why are you so down in the mouth?" Why was *everyone*, himself included? "Why can't you accept this for the good thing it is, instead of chastising me at every turn? Don't you think I got enough of it back there from Smithson?"

Alixa groped for a response. Finally, she burst out, "It's just wrong, okay? I'm glad Tery is all right, but—but it doesn't mean I feel it's okay to scorn our traditions like that! Both of you made a mistake today in crossing that wall—"

"It was a mistake to go out and save him?"

"It's—*yes*," she said. "It's not wrong to have saved him. But it's … you shouldn't have … the tradition … it's not right to just—"

"Fine," Jasen said, holding up a hand. "Done with it." And once again he stalked away, a little self-conscious after all under the gaze of a middle-aged woman who peered at him as he passed.

He'd hoped Alixa would take that as her cue to go … but very soon her hurried footsteps followed, and she was once again at his elbow, marching to keep up.

"It's difficult," she ceded.

"Sounds like you find admitting that painful."

"I do," she said. "I struggle with it. It's not just black and white now."

"What a shame."

"I *like* black and white, Jasen."

They lapsed into silence for some time.

Only when the outskirts of Terreas approached, where the Weltan home was positioned, Jasen's another half-mile north, did Alixa break their quiet.

"Baraghosa is coming."

Her words were low.

Jasen suppressed another shiver.

After a moment … "Maybe Pityr will be back with him?" Alixa said hopefully.

Pityr—boyish-faced, dark-haired, tall and slightly doughy round the middle in spite of the ceaseless energy pouring from him. Jasen had been friends with him since he was barely old enough to walk. Alixa had been his friend too, and it was really through Pityr that the cousins had come to be as close as they were.

He'd be sixteen now.

Jasen missed him.

Alixa's question hung in the air, hopeful: *Maybe Pityr will be back with him?*

Jasen shook his head. "He won't be."

And again they fell into quiet.

The Weltan house came into view, set back from the path, a small walkway of cobblestones set into the earth winding to the door. Margaut had turned the front garden into a miniature spot of farmland. Summer squashes lined one plot, then sprouting heads that might belong to carrots, and finally a row of runner beans. The opposite plot, on the other side of the path, was bushy and low: fruit, just now budding. Those flowers would turn into fat little strawberries, and take much too long in doing so.

"I've weaving lessons with Aunt Sidyera," Alixa said. "See you." And she ran off, leaving Jasen dawdling by the path.

After she'd gone in, he huffed and kicked a stone. "What am I going to do then?" he muttered to himself.

Maybe home was best. His father would be done with assembly meetings before long. He'd probably hope to catch Jasen and deliver this latest in a long line of reprimands. And much as Jasen longed to avoid it, it was like removing a thorn or a sliver of wood from the sensitive home it had made in skin: the quicker it was done, the better. So he ambled home, hands in pockets, kicking a clod of earth until it disintegrated.

Jasen's home, in comparison to Alixa's, was smaller. It had once held three, now just two, and neither of its occupants seemed to make great effort to fill it. Outwardly much like any of the other homes in Terreas—wood and stone and thatched roof—the warmth in it seemed to have evaporated. Same with the light. No matter how wide the shutters were thrown, or how far the curtains were pulled back, no matter if every lamp was turned on in the place, and the fire roaring in the hearth—it never seemed bright. Just dark and dingy and sad.

Jasen stopped by the path to scrutinize it.

Home.

Didn't feel like much of one. And today less than ever.

He breathed a sigh, kicked loose a new clod of dirt and sent it careening away with the side of his foot—anything to avoid going inside, and waiting—and meandered to the door.

As he was about to push it open, his father called, "Jasen!"

He looked back.

His father came up the way. Still looking hard, as he had done since … well, for a long time. But there was less rage in his face now.

"Father," Jasen greeted.

"Is Alixa at home?"

Jasen nodded. "Probably weaving with Sidyera, being bored to death."

A curt nod was all his father gave.

At the stoop too now, he stopped and looked Jasen over—properly, as if seeing him for the first time.

Jasen wondered what he saw. An echo of himself? Not quite; Jasen's father was taller, though Jasen was promised he'd grow to the same stature. Adem Rabinn had muscle too, though, and Jasen didn't have a lot of that. Nor did he have the same dark hair, unruly and awkward to tame. He'd inherited his mother's copper curls, and softer

features to match. None of that hardness lived in Jasen. In Adem it had taken root, sending those tendrils deep, like a tree's, too deep to be chopped out.

Was he disappointed in him?

If he was, Jasen couldn't read it. Couldn't read anything from his father. He was closed, shut tight.

"In you go," his father said at last.

Jasen obeyed, in dread already.

Inside, the house was plain. Except for aging furniture, a battered table, and a row of wooden trinkets on the mantel, the main room was mostly bare, same as the rest of the house. The only real feature it had, that made it theirs, was a musty scent that they'd never been able to rid it of.

His mother's things had been squirreled away, and even those had been reduced to a handful of keepsakes.

"Sit," his father said, and took up his usual armchair.

Jasen lowered into his seat. It was hard, difficult to sit on for long without a cramp driving down his leg from his backside.

And he waited.

Adem crossed one leg over the other. He laid a hand upon it, just staring at his knuckles for a long time.

At last, he breathed a sigh, and met his son's look.

"Being a councilman is … difficult," he started.

Jasen carried on waiting. He'd not interrupt his father—not now, not ever, if he could help it.

"We have to make tough decisions," Adem went on, slow, a trifle stilted. "That is our job. It's not an easy one, and some people don't see us as being very fair. But we try our best to be balanced, and make the choices we do as decently as possible, using all the information—objectively, and properly."

Jasen didn't say anything.

Adem ran his thumb and fingers across opposite cheeks, downward from under his eyes, meeting together just below his bottom lip, which he gently pinched. It was his thinking face, one of the few parts of his father that Jasen *could* read.

"Take Baraghosa, for example," Adem said. "I am in favor of our dealings with him. But many others are not. And can you blame them? It is a devil's bargain … yet necessary to keep our village safe."

His eyebrows wrinkled at that, and he appeared to think to himself for a few moments.

"Anyway. In spite of what I'd like, we have to take account of the world as it is, not how we'd like to see it. If we set foot beyond

Terreas, the scourge will descend upon us. So," he sighed, "it is better to make our trade with Baraghosa; let him bring the seed, and make the exchange we have made for so long."

There were so many questions that Jasen wanted to ask. The most pressing burned the back of his throat, threatening at the end of his tongue:

But what of the price?

He kept his mouth shut, and so for another day those questions would go unanswered; for Adem certainly had none, and this story, in this musty little room that was almost as dull as the assembly hall, had nothing to do with any of those things, Jasen sensed.

"The point I'm making," Adem said, "is that we have to look at the world as it really is. Not as we'd like to see it. Like you." He leaned forward. "You wish for adventure. I know you do, Jasen," he said, as though Jasen had been about to speak, though he had not been. "I hear word around the village. You've long had a wish to leave this place and rove beyond. Today, you clutched at that. Just the barest sliver of it, but you did.

"You *cannot* clutch at it again. For your sake, and for the sake of all of us. You did a good thing by saving the Malori boy, whatever Smithson says. But do not chance beyond the boundary again. You might think there is a life of adventure out there, a world to uncover—but there is not one. Only danger. The scourge infest these lands, and if one should gets it teeth around you … that's the end of your tapestry, Jasen—out there, alone, knowing in your last moments that you were wrong.

"Rules exist for a good reason, son. I'd like for you to continue following them."

That was that; Adem's tone said as much. So Jasen nodded solemnly, pulling his lips up in a brief ghost of a smile.

Adem rose. "I've got to go back to the assembly hall. You be good today and stick to the village, you hear?"

Another nod.

Adem granted Jasen a pat on the shoulder. Then through the door he went, and was gone.

For a long time, Jasen sat, and pondered the future.

No adventure out there. Not for him. Not for anyone, with the land so filled with scourge.

So what lay in store for him? What future did he have? He had no skill; unlike most of the children in the village, he had no apprenticeship. The Rabinns had no land to farm. There was no store for him to mind. His father was an assemblyman, a position he would inhabit for a long, long time, one that Jasen might inherit only when he was old himself.

What did Jasen have to point toward? To look forward to?

Most pertinent of all, and the one question for which Jasen could not find an answer, had never been able to, no matter how his mind went around and around—

Where in this world did he belong?

4

Moping could only last a person so long before they tired of it, and today Jasen tired of it much sooner than usual. Still, midday was long past by the time he left the house again, and the afternoon hours were piling up like logs beside a chopping block.

The first breath outside was still tainted with a stale tang. Mustiness clung to him. It always did, in Terreas. The freshest air he had ever breathed was beside the boundary wall … at least until the sickening rot of scourge came to linger in the air.

He could return to Alixa's, busying himself in the herb garden, or perhaps the vineyard. Those pungent smells would mask the scent on him easily enough. But Alixa was still weaving, and should he show up and Sidyera catch a glimpse of him loitering through the window, he had no doubt that she would try to ensnare him too. Once in a thousand times, when he felt particularly bored and listless, he would allow her to do so. Today, having been lectured more than enough for the year, he decided the Weltan place was not where he wanted to be.

He idly tracked up the path. Toward Terreas's outskirts, his house was perched toward the edge of the gentle slope that angled down and away from the clustered village buildings. Other houses and pathways were laid out beyond, but the descending earth gave him a long view out to the mountains and the wide stretch of land that stretched to the boundary.

Another time, he might have wandered down by himself, spending the afternoon stalking back and forth beside the perimeter. But this afternoon he couldn't even stand to look out there, to search for scourge around the base of the mountains now the sun had turned the mist to only a faint wisp. Nor did he want to fall back the way he always did, whiling the day away by constructing stories about the adventures that lay beyond. Why bother? It was just childish hope anyway. Nothing but scourge out there by the thousands, roaming this defiled land.

Folly. All that filled his head was folly.

He thought, *You'll be lucky if you don't get shunned.*

He pursed his lips at that … and then a thought struck him, and he turned on his heel and headed in the other direction.

Terreas faded, houses quickly becoming fewer. The ones out on the edges were like Jasen's: small and pokey. But they had a wide swath of land around them—would do, of course, until eventually new ones were erected—and Jasen thought they were probably fine enough places to eke out a life. Perhaps a mite lonely; these paths were rarely trodden. The village children didn't come out here very much … As the house Jasen headed toward came into view from behind a straggly-looking tree, he thought he knew why this part of Terreas was ignored.

Shilara Gressom. Her house was little more than a box, and a rundown one at that. The wood was going rotten, great chunks of it missing in places. The thatch roof was tatty, looking like Jasen's hair did when he woke up after a particularly poor night's sleep. If she had ever cleaned the windows it had been well before Jasen was born, because they were all misted with dirt, and alive with cobwebs. Jasen had never seen inside, but he had no reason to think it was in any way different from the exterior.

There was no properly demarcated yard, because why bother when the next buildings were some two hundred feet to east and west? Gressom's plot was clear enough though, because littered amongst the unruly grass were relics of war: shields, spears, a log on its side with a row of daggers embedded along its length.

To Terreas's teenaged boys, these objects should be fascinating. Yet no one came to see—for these were Shilara Gressom's things, and few were those who wished to fraternize with the village outcast.

She sat in front of the house. She'd hefted out an armchair, the fabric full of holes. And she lolled in it, sunken low, and swigged from a ceramic bottle.

A beady eye fixed Jasen as he approached. She lifted a hand. "Hail."

"Pleasant sunning," Jasen greeted.

Shilara peered skyward. "Wouldn't call it sunning myself. Atrocious weather for summer." Another sip at her bottle. "Well, come on by then, lad, sit yourself down. I know you've not happened upon me by coincidence. One moment." And she thrust upward, heading back into the house with a *bang* of the front door, bottle still in hand.

Jasen obliged, stepping off the path and navigating the overgrown patch leading to her. As well as her weapons, plus years' worth of broken spears, a log pile spilled out from one edge of the house. There were also, here and there, straw dummies, crudely fashioned but recognizable enough. Most were half-rotted, and had gone to die where they fell. A couple remained standing, staked into the ground. One was relatively fresh. Another, a wood block surrounded by a thick wad of wool and covered in leather, had seen much better days: most of its stuffing lay in the grass at its base.

Shilara returned with a footstool. "There." She shunted it out of the door, which she slammed behind her.

Jasen winced. No wonder the place was on its way to dilapidation; she was doing a damned good job of shaking the house apart.

Shilara took up her seat again. "Sit down there, why don't you?" She pointed to a spot on her right, which put him closer to the front door and, beyond it, that row of split logs.

Jasen obliged, pulling the footstool to where she'd indicated. It was wood, and banged up; plenty of nicks had been made in the legs and seat.

He lowered onto it. Not comfortable.

Shilara took a swig from her bottle.

Jasen watched her from the corner of one eye. Shilara was a reedy woman, and fit—it was rare not to see her practicing thrusts with her spear, or swipes with her daggers, or footwork as she squatted behind a shield, taking intermittent swipes at some imagined foe. But her habit of daytime drinking had put a pouch around her middle and a layer of fat about her neck that reminded him of a bullfrog. Maybe it had contributed to the greying of her hair too; she was only in her fifties, but the color had been robbed of it for years.

She extended the bottle to Jasen. "Want a nip?"

"Uhm." He considered, more tempted than he would ever let on to Alixa. Poor girl, if she were here she'd probably have a heart attack at Gressom's offer. Having said that, Alixa would probably have had a heart attack at the sight of the woman's house. Jasen didn't think she'd ever come this way—much too improper for her.

"I'll pass," he said at last.

"Suit yourself." She took another tipple. Jasen watched enviously.

For the best, he reminded himself. Smelling like grain alcohol when his father returned would be yet another mistake today to add to the list.

"You aren't on guard duty today," Jasen said to make conversation.

"If I am, I'm doing a ruddy poor job of it." Shilara shook her head,

lips puckered. "Only one here with any experience, and they'll take me for a half-day each week. Disgusting."

Jasen didn't say anything. Not much to say. Shilara knew the village barely tolerated her presence, her *ways*, and he knew it too. What else was there to say?

The silence here was a different sort to the others today. Not companionable, like when he spent time with Alixa, each relegated to their own thoughts. Nor was it a thoughtful one, as when Adem chose his words and Jasen waited, expectant, for his father's wisdom. This one, Jasen couldn't find a word for. It was not uncomfortable, but not particularly friendly.

Shilara was the one to break it. "Foggarty's been talking about replacing me. *Me.* I fought in the war, for the love of our ancestors. Only one of us to have come back from the thing." Her lips puckered again, and she stared into the middle distance grimly. "Does it mean anything to them? No. *A lady shouldn't don armor, shouldn't wield a spear.* Ridiculous. Women need to fight sometimes too, lad."

Jasen listened politely. He didn't think Shilara was sharing this out of any great sense of camaraderie, didn't think she was confiding in him. This was a woman venting, and on this rare occasion she had someone to vent to. Well, Jasen could oblige her today.

"Complacent," she murmured. "That's what they are." A sip of alcohol. It glugged in the bottle, barely upended each time she lifted it; it was close to full. Despite her tendency to drink through the day, Jasen was certain this was still her first—she made them last. Had to, with only a small stipend in the few hours of work she was granted each week. And she did like to talk about a person keeping his or her wits about them.

Another disdainful shake of the head. She opened her mouth as if to say more, but then closed it, words bitten off before they could come.

After a time, Jasen said, "I'm sorry."

Gressom looked at him with a frown and drawn eyebrows. "For what?"

"For what you said, about the captain of the guard looking to replace you."

"Why're you sorry? Not your fault, is it?"

"Err, no," he said quickly, heart beating sharply—another telling-off coming to him, from the village outcast this time—

"Well, don't be sorry for the actions of others," Shilara said, turning back to look toward Terreas's center. "Pointless. You can't apologize for someone else. Your words are meaningless, and theirs are unsaid.

Nothing is achieved."

Jasen chewed his lip. Was that true? Perhaps ... but he could still *feel* regretful, couldn't he?

He was fairly sure he could.

Shilara drank again, twice in the silence that filled the air between them. The tang of alcohol wafted on a momentary light breeze. Jasen decided that he was glad he hadn't taken up Shilara's offer. The stuff smelled bitter.

"Why'd you come?" she asked. Not demanding, not even really curious, by her tone; just a question now her complaints were out of the way. "Been a while since I've seen you."

"Sorry. I've been ... busy."

"Uh huh." Her voice held no malice, but still Jasen felt a twinge of guilt. Then she said, "Lot of hubbub in the village this morning."

"A little," Jasen said.

"What for?"

"Me."

"You?" Shilara affixed him with a beady eye again. "What did you do?"

It came tumbling out: "I crossed the boundary this morning. Only for thirty seconds! One of the boys from the village was out there, in the rye, and there was a scourge stalking him—and he's just eight, far too short to see over the crop, so he'd have just wandered and wandered—so I leapt over and grabbed him, and ran back—and that's it." He paused for a breath, and one breath became two, three, four ... before Shilara spoke again.

"Scourge are dangerous, Jasen," she said in a low, almost conspiratorial, voice.

"I know," he griped. "I've heard it plenty today, and I've heard it plenty every day before this one too. Scourge are a menace. They stalk the land they've claimed, lying in wait for a hapless fool to step out in front of their jaws." He squeezed his fist tight and knuckled his thigh sullenly. "I've heard the warnings. I'm not stupid. I wish everyone would stop treating me like I am."

A pause. Shilara watched him; Jasen felt her eyes on his cheek. He didn't rise to meet them, just dug his knuckles deeper into flesh—another red mark to add to those left by his father's fingers during the assembly meeting.

"You're no fool," she said. "Brave, I'd call you, risking life and limb like that."

Jasen's heart skipped.

"Really?" He daren't believe it.

"You say the boy was being stalked by one of the beasts?"

"We—that's Alixa and me—could see it moving through the rye. And then after I had Tery and was bringing him back, it burst out." He tried, and failed, to tamp down a shudder at the thought of it loping after them in great bounds, only the rye tangling about its legs keeping it from devouring Jasen and Tery both. If he tried, he could still pick up the scent of rot, like the faintest whisper on the breeze.

"You got away," Shilara observed.

"Barely."

"What was it like?" She leaned in, and now Jasen did look up, meeting her gaze. Only this gaze was mad. Her eyes seemed to bulge as she lit on him, wide and manic. "How did you feel?"

Jasen hesitated, coughed a strangled word. "I—you fought in the war, didn't you? When they first invaded?"

"So?"

"So you've seen them? Once?"

"Once," she agreed, and shifted back just a fraction. Some of that mad light faded—and then it was back, and she reached for him, clutched his forearm with a grip that was unnatural in strength for a woman. "I want to know how *you* felt. Up close to it, face to face … what did you feel in that moment?"

It came back to him, and for an awful moment he was not in Shilara's disorderly yard, but instead in the field of rye, fleeing with all the power he could push through his legs, as fast as he could, Tery gripped fiercely hard.

"Afraid," he said. "Terrified. I thought my life would end."

Shilara nodded, tiny movements of the head. "Yes." She reclined, but never once took that penetrating gaze off of him. "That's the nature of the scourge. And the rest of the village are right, on this: the world out there is overrun."

"I know," Jasen said.

"The scourge scent a man. They have no mercy, no decency. And they will persist in hunting their prey until they have him …"

"Or until he crosses onto this side of the boundary," Jasen quietly finished.

He swiveled on the hard seat, peering to look at the boundary. Miles out, and farther down this very gentle slope, he could pick out the thin line not by the wall itself—it was too low and distant for his eyes to train upon—but the transition immediately afterward to the untamed expanse of rye.

Rumors circled in the village. Jasen had heard tell for years that it was Shilara who had discovered the boundary, learned that this was the line the scourge would not cross. He had never believed it; why would the village shun someone like that? But perhaps they thought her a conjurer of strange magics, like Baraghosa, as well as a stubborn old woman who refused to take her rightful place in society and put down the weapons she surrounded herself with, and in their fear they had cast her out.

That begat more questions, and now Jasen had tired of them.

He rose. "It's been nice talking to you, Ms. Gressom."

"Shilara. I say it always."

"Yes, uhm, Shilara." He hesitated, and finished awkwardly, "I hope you have a pleasant day."

"Course I will," she said, and Jasen was plainly aware she would not—how did one fill so many empty days for so many empty years?—but there was again no annoyance in her voice.

He ambled back toward the path, stepping over the remains of a battered target.

"Jasen."

He glanced over his shoulder.

Shilara was frowning at him, a thin line pressed between her eyebrows.

"Yes?" he asked.

A long silence, and he wondered if maybe she *was* drunk, if the alcohol finally had taken her mind … and then she said flatly, "Tread carefully."

That was all. And so Jasen nodded, said, "I will," and turned away.

He felt her eyes on him until he was out of sight.

Not just her eyes followed him, but her frown. It wasn't the sort she'd worn when bemoaning Foggarty and the guard detail's desire to remove her from the sole job she had, nor was it the grimace she'd worn as she'd called the village complacent. This was a different sort, one Jasen didn't think he'd seen ever, and the ghost of it stuck in his brain like a stain.

5

The afternoon continued to pass listlessly. Jasen roved from place to place without intent, stopping and sitting down once in a while on a bench, upon the steps leading into a public building, or just an alley where he might lurk, unnoticed. A few villagers stopped and spoke to him, but not many, and those who did spoke shortly. Likely they had heard about today's excursion beyond the boundary. Perhaps they were conflicted. Perhaps simply disdainful.

Mr. Hughes filled the hole that eventually formed in Jasen's stomach. Jasen liked to visit the bakery early in the day, when the scent of pastries and the rich, heavy loaves hung over the entire street like a glorious fog. Today, he only realized his growing hunger when afternoon was crawling toward evening. The shelves were almost empty by then, and Jasen's favorite—a swirled pastry infused with a marmalade of crushed berries—was nowhere among the leftovers. He opted instead for a slightly flat-looking slice of fruit bread (dry, it turned out), paid with one of the coins his father gave him once a week, and made off before Mr. Hughes could ask about the outburst he'd witnessed earlier between Jasen and Alixa.

Three times, he looped around by the Weltan place. Each time, Alixa was nowhere to be seen. So he returned home; but his father did not return at his usual time, nor long after, so when the sky through the windows had started to dull as the sun sank, Jasen extracted himself from the empty house and pointed himself toward Alixa's one final time, just in case.

She was perched on the rock again when he arrived.

"Good evening, cousin," Jasen greeted.

She jerked around with a start. "Jasen! Don't scare me like that." And she clutched her heart, as if to keep the thing from bursting out of her chest.

"Sorry. Um … room for another?"

She fixed him with a probing sort of look, half a scowl; not very happy to cede space on the boulder to him, after the way the day had gone. But she relented, her pout not diminishing in the slightest, saying, "Yes, you may join me," as she scooched over.

Jasen lowered himself onto the soft carpet of moss. Normally he'd throw himself down casually at Alixa's elbow, but now he was slow and careful in his movements.

Alixa did not make conversation. And this quiet between them was not particularly companionable.

Jasen forced himself to say something, anything that might lighten the mood …

"So how were your family? You know, about today."

… and instantly failed.

Alixa pursed her lips. "Not pleased." That was all she said.

"Do you want to talk about it?"

Out of the corner of his eye, Jasen saw her frown deepen and thought she might turn on him and tell him to make off after all, and maybe never come back. But then she opened, the way a daidai fruit's flesh gave way at just an inch of pressure, relinquishing the sour stone at its core.

"It was *awful*, positively *awful*. Aunt Sidyera lectured me all afternoon—because she'd heard, somehow, even in that little room of hers she hardly ever leaves. I didn't even *start* weaving until mid-afternoon, because she just kept on and on and *on*." She squinted at Jasen, a glimmer of envy in her face. "You're lucky she didn't see *you* when we parted earlier, because I cannot *imagine* the talking-to you'd get."

Jasen could. It would be over-dramatic, incredibly repetitious, and likely Sidyera wouldn't pause for breath until her entire rant had been issued five times over. A nightmare, to be sure. He shot a nervous glance over his shoulder, just in case Sidyera was able to somehow detect his presence and drag her creaky old frame out here to tell him exactly what she thought, even if it took till dawn.

Possibly best to avoid the Weltan place for some time, after all.

"She's gone to bed," Alixa said, reading his face. "Though I've half a mind to go back and wake her up."

"Please don't," Jasen begged.

"Well, I ought to. Not like *I* crossed the boundary."

"I'm sorry."

Alixa huffed. Folding her arms, she went on, "And then my mother and father came home."

Again she ceased, and after waiting a moment for her to say more, Jasen asked, "And …?" He did not wish to ask—but perhaps this was his penance. Alixa could repeat her encounters, and he could add another layer of guilt to the mound piling up. Presently it came to his shoulders, but after Alixa's recounting it would bury him right to his crown, and he'd drown in it and it all would be over.

"My mother was disappointed," Alixa said, "*obviously*. It was clear on her face in the assembly meeting."

Jasen could see it plainly in his mind's eye. Aunt Margaut's face was an expressive one, better at the negative than positive, which Alixa had inherited. Hurt would be plainly wrought upon her features.

Another stab of guilt. Coming up to his chin now.

"She didn't *say* a lot," Alixa continued. "Only that I ought to reconsider who I spend my time with in the future."

Less a stab, more a punch in the gut.

Jasen almost blurted, "Really?" But he kept it in. He *should* feel terrible. He'd done a bad thing, crossing the boundary. Everyone knew it, everyone had said so, and so he should believe it.

A small voice began, *But Tery …*

He silenced it but frowned to himself, his gaze lost somewhere far beyond the mountains ahead of them.

"My father said more," Alixa said. Glancing at Jasen, she added flatly, "I shan't repeat it; it would be improper."

Jasen loosed a low sigh. His uncle Davyd was a loud man, quite the opposite of Aunt Margaut. In the days when she was around, Jasen's mother had told him that his uncle was boisterous in his youth, a rule-breaker. Margaut had tempered him, and two and a half decades of that tempering influence had made him an echo of her—just a much more outspoken one. Jasen hadn't enjoyed drawing the man's ire in his own hijinks, and he disliked even more that Alixa had endured his anger tonight. All words, of course—but as Jasen grew older, he'd started to think that maybe words were worse than fists. Bruises healed. The wounds torn by words didn't; they just festered, turning into scars that split apart, raw and bleeding just like the day they were opened.

"I'm sorry," Jasen said lamely.

It wasn't good enough. He knew it, and it was perfectly clear from Alixa's response: "Yes, well." She brushed at her hair, smoothing it into place across her shoulders. "What did Uncle Adem say?"

"Little," Jasen answered.

"He wasn't pleased, of course." Not a question.

"Of course not." When had anyone been today? Only the Malori parents seemed to occupy that camp, and Jasen had barely seen them; they'd been summoned, come in a red-eyed rush, swept up their boy, and instantly burst into tears. Doubtful there'd be an appreciative word out of them for a week.

Then again, after Hanrey got his time with them and spent a good hour putting them in their place, they might be too subdued to say a word at all.

"As expected," Alixa said, a hint of satisfaction beneath her annoyance.

Silence fell over them.

Jasen watched the mountains. Just above, but probably many miles beyond, a single opening had appeared in the cloud. The gash revealed a diagonal portion of sky turning pink: twilight was coming. Temperature had dropped again, and a frail mist had begun to cling to the mountains' base. Scourge certainly roamed it, and Jasen wondered idly what had happened to the one he and Tery had almost been eaten by. He'd watched it slink into the rye, of course—but where had it gone then?

If he said it aloud, Alixa would ask, "Who cares?" And Jasen shouldn't. Yet he couldn't keep himself from wondering at it.

What would his mother say, he wondered, if she were here? Would *she* be pleased that he had done a brave thing? Concerned for his wellbeing, of course. But happy? Pleased he'd done something beyond these walls? That he'd saved a life?

He reached into the neck of his tunic to finger …

Her amulet. It was gone.

He leapt up, fingers gripping for a thing that was no longer there.

"What?" Alixa demanded.

"My mother's amulet!" he said. He lifted the tunic's neck forward to peer down, one hand groping. "I've lost it."

The fresh scowl Alixa had started to don vanished. A look of worry replaced it. "Are you certain?"

"It's not here," Jasen said. His voice was rising. He patted and patted his neck, as if somehow it might reappear … and then, just in case it had fallen free, he tugged the entire tunic over his head. Alixa averted her gaze as he shook it, turned it inside out, patted himself again—

"It's not here!" he cried.

Had it dropped right into his trousers? He clutched at the belt—

"Jasen!" Alixa hissed and swiveled as far away as she could. Just for good measure, she slapped a hand to her eyes.

He yanked them off, frittered through, clad in nothing but his undergarments. Every second his groping grew more panicked. His heart beat faster, harder in his chest, and tears threatened … and still there was nothing. No lump to indicate the polished stone, tucked into a fold; no ridge hinting at the chain.

The amulet was gone.

"No," he moaned. "No, no, no …"

"Have you put your clothes back on yet?" Alixa asked.

"I can't find it!"

She fired a very daring glance over her shoulder, then immediately jerked back around and slammed her hand over her face again. "You can't just stand there like this—"

"How have I lost it?" he cried. "It was right here this morning!" And again he groped around his neck, hoping, praying that somehow he had made a mistake, that the thing had been there the entire time, hadn't gone anywhere at all …

He had not. The amulet, one of the only heirlooms he had, and the only thing he could carry with him each and every day—it was gone.

Tears threatened. "No …"

"Jasen," Alixa muttered. She twisted just incrementally, as far as she was willing to go. "It'll be okay," she said softly. "We can find it again. We'll just retrace your steps today. You said you had it this morning?"

"Yes," he said. "Before you went back in to get your roughing boots."

"Did you have it after that?"

He racked his brains. Long gone were the days when it felt new and he'd been aware of the cool stone against his chest at every turn. He fingered it throughout the day though, always had, to check it was there and to think of her. The action was automatic, and if he'd done it once today he must've done it a hundred times …

Only he could not recall reaching for it a single time other than the lone touch this morning. The onslaught of guilt, and the sudden wave of unhappiness and being without a place had overtaken him. In his preoccupation, he hadn't reached out for the amulet again until now.

Which meant he'd had almost a full day to have lost the thing.

"No," he said. "I don't know. Out here is the last time I know I had it."

"Okay," said Alixa. "Well, let's retrace your steps. Just … just put your clothes back on, and we'll go now, before it gets too dark. Okay?"

"Okay," Jasen echoed breathily. "Okay."

This was good. This was something. A plan. He must've dropped it—things did not just vanish into the ether. At some point, the chain must have come loose, and it had slipped out—maybe between two cobbles, or someplace he'd loitered while killing time this afternoon. Heck, someone might've laid eyes on it and taken it in to the assembly, where he might reclaim it.

He awkwardly fumbled back into his clothes, running hands along them one last time, just in case. Then he brushed through the grass at the boulder's base in case it had landed there—no sign of it—and then raked fingers through the moss on the stone itself. It was not long enough to conceal it, and he knew that it was futile, but that did not stop him from trying.

"Are you decent?" Alixa asked.

"Dressed, yes," Jasen said. "But by your standards, I doubt I am ever *decent*."

She still turned his way slowly, glancing at him through a very slitted eye. Only when comfortable that he no longer showed an excess of skin did she hop onto her feet.

"Let's go searching. Where have you been today?"

Just about everywhere, was the answer, and Jasen said as much.

"Well, why don't we backtrack from here?"

Jasen nodded—and then shook his head. "No. Maybe we should go back out to the wall."

Alixa froze. "Jasen …"

"Not over it," he said quickly. "But that's the last time I had it, on the way. What if I knocked the clasp when I touched it, and that's how I lost it? I'd have dropped it out there somewhere."

"You could've easily lost it in Terreas …"

"The lamps will be lit. If we scour Terreas now, it'll be too dark to check the route we took out here when we're done."

"But if we find it we won't need—"

"*Please?*" Jasen said. His voice had been rising again, his whole body seeming to grow itchy. He wanted nothing more than to be off—and Alixa was dawdling, trying to lay out a plan, when all he wanted was to rove, eyes raking for the thing.

"Jasen," she moaned.

"I want to find it tonight." And after a pause, he croaked, "It's my mother's."

Alixa relented at that, though she looked none too happy about it. "Ohh … we shouldn't be doing this."

But Jasen was already off, and however conflicted she might feel, she had little choice but to follow.

He retraced his steps to where he last remembered having it—or at least to approximately where he had been. Tracking up and down the dirt path, he scoured the grasses to either side of the exposed strip of earth. He ran a foot across them, moving those long strips of green this way and that … but there was no sign of it.

"It's not here," he said, and turned away from Terreas, out toward the grassy reaches leading down to the boundary.

"Are you sure we shouldn't just check the village first?" Alixa called from behind. "You were here all day; you had much longer to drop it."

"Path first," Jasen said without looking up from his search.

Alixa made a pained noise. "Fine. I'll search this side, you search that; we'll be quicker this way." She gravitated toward the right edge of the path, walking on the grass itself, and swept through clumps with a foot the way Jasen was. Probably squinting, as she tended to, but Jasen didn't look.

"You know what it looks like, don't you?"

"Yes. I've seen you wear it."

"It's a smooth black stone," he said anyway, "with pale spots across it. Kind of teardrop-shaped. The chain is silver."

"Mm-hm."

They trekked out, searching. Jasen's heart was pumping at one and a half times the usual speed, the kind of drumbeat it made when he set into a jog.

Once in a while he thought he saw it. Alixa must have had moments like that too, because she would stop forward progress and stoop down, running her hands through the grass instead. Those sent particularly hard spikes through him, little pulses of adrenaline that caught his breath. But it always turned out to be just a stone, or a clod of earth that was nestled far enough down to obscure its true color and shape.

Terreas fell away. Overhead, unnoticed, the gash in the cloud closed.

The mists at the base of the mountains thickened.

Twilight had well and truly fallen by the time they reached the wall. Everything had taken on a muted color. The grass was turning a kind of grey, and though the dark of Jasen's amulet would still stand out, his pace had slowed. Alixa's too; she'd fallen some twenty feet behind.

Jasen looked out into the rye. It whickered in a light breeze.

No scent of rot in the air just now.

"It's not here," Alixa said quietly from behind. "We should turn around."

Jasen frowned to himself.

"Jasen?"

Out in the rye? When he'd gone to save Tery?

A wave of nausea displaced the fear. Surely not. After everything today, it couldn't be out there. It couldn't.

And then the memory slapped him in the face as though he'd run headlong into it: tension around his neck as he barreled toward Tery. He'd been sure it was a particularly vicious stalk gripping him—but then it had snapped, and Jasen had felt free, almost unnaturally so.

"It's out there," he whispered.

Alixa began wearily, "Jasen …"

"It's out there," he repeated. "I know it. I felt the chain snap."

"Why didn't you say—?"

"I didn't remember. Didn't know." But he did now. The chain had definitely broken as he hurtled toward Tery—which meant his mother's amulet was somewhere out there—where the scourge lurked.

"Baraghosa comes soon," Alixa began, a desperate note in her voice. "If you ask, maybe he'll—"

"Where did I cross?" Jasen asked. Baraghosa be damned; he wouldn't ask that skeletal remnant for help if he'd fallen himself beyond the wall and a scourge were galloping toward him.

"Jasen, you can't—not again—"

"It's my mother's amulet," he pleaded, turning to her. The panic was back again, in his voice and in his eyes, boring into Alixa's. "It's all I have. I need to get it."

"But the scourge—!"

"I know how far in I was when it snapped." Not entirely true, because it had been so hard to tell as he waded—hadn't he almost crashed head over heels when he ran into Tery?—but he had a decent idea at the least. "And the scourge, they must sleep. They can't be stalking now."

"You can't be serious." Alixa's voice sounded thick with worry, a croak like she might be sick right here in front of him.

"I have to get it. I need to." And he began to track along the wall, trying to calculate how far along they'd gone before he vaulted it this morning. Not too far, certainly; it hadn't taken long to catch Tery's cries—

Or to see that dark shape stalking him in the rye.

Jasen swallowed. That didn't matter. Whether scourge were here or not, his mother's amulet was more important.

"I can't do this," Alixa whispered. Her breathing was hard, quick. "I can't."

"You don't have to," said Jasen.

"Mother and Father, they'll know. The assembly—"

"No one will know. Look how dark it is. No one will see us."

"They must wonder where we are. Maybe someone saw—"

"Then turn back," Jasen said. "Go home. I can do this alone."

Alixa looked torn. Her mouth worked up and down, and for long seconds no words came. Then she croaked, "I can't."

"Where did I cross, Alixa?"

She scrutinized. Her lips were downturned, and she looked like she might cry as she pointed and said, "Just there. I recognize the broken spot."

Less than a dozen steps away, Jasen spied it too: a broken stretch where a miniature trench some eight or nine inches long split the stone. He didn't recall noticing it this morning—but then he'd been tracking Tery on the way to it, hadn't he, and keeping watch over the lingering scourge on the way back to Terreas, not paying attention to the wall itself.

He moved to it. Resting a hand on the wall, he looked out.

A gentle breeze shifted the rye. Still no scent of decay, the rancid musk the scourge carried with them, which surely meant he was in the clear.

He placed a hand on the boundary. Inhaled.

"Jasen."

He looked to Alixa.

"Be careful." She was pale in the gloomy light, but there lingered no trace of argument on her face.

He nodded. Swallowed hard past the lump in his throat.

And then tossed himself over.

This time was harder. It should not have been: the amulet was his most prized, treasured possession. He could not—*would not*—lose it. Yet now, with time to think, and so many voices in his head all decrying this very thing, the wall felt larger somehow—and the world beyond it far more terrifying.

He stepped into the rye. Turned back for a second to check that Alixa had stayed put—she had, clutching her hands in front of her and pressing nails hard into her palms, her expression a mask of outright terror—and then the stalks swallowed him.

He pushed through, resisting the urge to look for the amulet before he needed to. Doing so would only waste time, and the quicker he was done here, the better.

He strode, trying to count paces. How many had he gone before he felt that sharp tug? A dozen, perhaps? But he'd been running then, and the steps would've been longer, carried him farther into the field.

He pushed, heart hammering. Stalks clutched at him from all sides. Great clumps of them were bent, snapped in the middle, destined for death, the grain scattering the earth before it was ripe to reseed it. These were the places where the scourge had come down hard in its frenetic chase. Half of Jasen was filled with relief that he was indeed on the right track. The other half couldn't help feeling dread. Its smell still resided here, faint, but sour.

He felt sick.

Deeper he pressed … and then he slowed. This must be about the spot.

He began to scour, sifting through with his hands. The grain was so long, though, so tall and dense. He had to stoop, grimacing as he used hands to part it. The earth was nigh impossible to see, and so he raked his hands over it, clawing frantically, finding only dirt, loose clods he turned into fine powder. Then he pushed forward again, flattening the rye down underfoot carelessly, the way he'd never dare to in the grain fields back inside the boundary.

It was somewhere here. He was certain of it.

An image sprung up from nowhere: the scourge catching it on a clawed toe, and the chain clinging. It would bound off, taking the amulet untold miles from here, and Jasen would never, ever see it again.

A cry warbled from his throat.

"Jasen?" Alixa called from someplace behind … or maybe that was just the movement of the rye against the wind, because though he listened for her voice again, it did not come.

He edged forward, groping, still finding only earth …

Something skittered by his fingers.

He retracted them.

Only a mouse, he told himself. And if a mouse were content to be here, in the realm of the scourge, he could be too.

Though I don't think mice draw their attention quite so well as I would, he thought.

He pressed on.

Had he missed it? His fingers raked and raked, but how did he know he'd been thorough? He might've missed a spot, a few inches square and no more … but that might be where the amulet lay right now, missed and forgotten.

The breeze whispered again. Rye swayed overhead.

Jasen gritted his teeth.

Come on.

Raked. Edged forward. Raked again. Edged forward. Raked.

Come on!

He shoved a particularly clumped cluster of rye down, stamping hard on the stalks with his foot as he worked over the top—

And his finger touched metal.

He gasped, snatched it, heart skipping—

It came up in his hand. The chain had not snapped, but somehow the clasp had come loose, because it lay open—but the stone was intact, hadn't been crushed by the scourge as it rampaged after them, as he now acknowledged he had feared.

Relief flooded him.

Another cry warbled from his throat, loud and without shame.

Now Alixa did cry: "Jasen?"

"I've got it!" he said back. He sounded hoarse all of a sudden, as though he'd spent the day shouting at the top of his lungs. "I've found it."

"Then come back over!" Alixa said.

For a moment, Jasen couldn't bring himself to stand. The sheer happiness that had overflowed him, after such intense fear, robbed him of his ability to stand. His legs felt like ooze.

"Jasen?" Alixa called again.

"Coming."

He lifted the amulet, about to place it around his neck, then thought better of it. He'd wait until he was out of the rye, lest another nasty stalk grab at him again and tear it free. Then he'd never, ever cross this boundary—because this world outside the bound *was* dangerous, cruel.

He shoved the amulet in his pocket, keeping one hand over it. Rising to his feet, he swiveled, head just cresting the rye as he turned to find the wall, and Alixa—

Somewhere behind, the rye rustled.

Not the wind—but something in it.

Jasen's heart skipped. The bottom fell out of his stomach.

The vile, bitter smell of rot met his nose.

Scourge.

6

"Jasen?" Alixa called again. Renewed panic filled her voice.

"Stay back," Jasen called in a heavy whisper. "And be quiet!"

"Jasen, you need to—"

Run, I know! he did not say.

He turned away from the rustling, directing toward the wall again. Putting on a burst of speed, he set into his third sprint of the day—

A growl filled the air. Something heavy moved—

"*Jasen!!*" Alixa screamed.

It had risen—

Now the ground vibrated, as it leapt—

Jasen twisted back.

His breath caught in his throat.

In the twilight, the thing was even more frightening. A streak of awful grey, the color of diseased flesh, only the eyes were distinct—and they were just as black as Jasen remembered, perhaps blacker, empty pits he would get lost in—

Then he tripped, and the world went sideways.

"*Jasen!*" Alixa cried.

He shoved back to his feet. Pain raced up his arm—one hand in his pocket, he hadn't been able to break his fall other than to twist, the way a cat did as it fell through the air.

He grunted.

All these precious seconds …

Pushing off again, he broke into a desperate sprint. He groped through the rye, pushing stalks aside, slipping through them far too slowly—and that damned *burning* in his arm, like he'd been stung by an oversized wasp, right in the elbow, its black venom spreading in each direction like fire—

The wall loomed—yet still the scourge flew, Jasen could feel every vibration as it landed hard behind him. Did it find itself tangled, like the other? He dared not look to check; would focus only on Alixa's eyes, panicked whites, as she screamed words he didn't register but which surely meant only one thing: that the scourge was drawing closer—and this time Jasen was out of luck—

A particularly fierce cluster of stalks refused to yield, pushing back, jabbing at his skin like barbs.

He pushed with all his might—

The scourge roared, right behind him. A blast of hot, rancid air kissed the back of Jasen's neck, and he felt every hair there wilt, like grass exposed to a noxious fog—

"*JASEN!*" Alixa screamed.

He tripped and spilled over.

The fall sent him tumbling into the very short span of grass between rye and the boundary around Terreas.

It also turned the world upside-down. He twisted in a desperate bid to save his arm. But that only put him more off-kilter, and where he might've kept his footing and been able to turn the stumble into an awkward vault over the boundary, back to safety, he instead went over. The boundary's stonework approached his face much too hard and fast—

He slammed his head.

Stars erupted with a fresh burst of pain, radiating out from his temple.

Jasen's head swum in a daze. Dimly, he was aware that he had impacted the ground—but that had been long seconds ago, hadn't it?

Another wave of airborne rot washed over him, parting the fog.

He blinked up at the sky—it was night; why was it night? Hadn't it been blue?—and then every sense returned in one fell swoop—just in time to see the scourge part the last of the rye mere inches from where he lay sprawled.

The sight of it sucked the breath from Jasen's lungs. Flesh hanging, the wolf-like thing loomed like a spectral nightmare. A thin scattering of stars had filled the sky where the clouds had finally seen fit to part, but the scourge's ghoulish body, too long and terribly proportioned, blocked them out.

Its mouth was a yawning maw, huffing like an overheated dog … and above it were those terrible eyes. Black, empty chasms, darker than the truest night, they stared down at Jasen. He could fall into their depths and perish.

It leaned forward.

Every hair, including those that had fallen flaccid and dead to his skin, rose. It was an animal's response, a last desperate bid to puff himself up and scare off this imposing threat—and that was all Jasen was: an animal. No better than these creatures that forsook their land, he was simply another creature in a chain, with no purpose greater, no meaning.

And now, Jasen was prey.

He wished he could run. But his whole body was frozen, his brain too; the gears spinning in it had come to a grinding halt.

The scourge pressed closer.

A hot breath caressed Jasen's cheeks. It stank to high heaven, enough that a man might vomit until his stomach gave only spasms and tiny sprays of bile. Yet still Jasen couldn't move. Could only stare into those eyes, coming closer, closer …

Its nose touched him on the forehead.

A dog's might be wet. This was dry, lank, cold.

It sniffed.

Working out what I'll taste like, Jasen thought.

Another sniff. Deeper, this one.

From somewhere very, very far away, a tremulous voice whispered, "J-Jasen …"

He didn't see; his eyes were shut tight, lest he stare into that cavern of a mouth, the last thing he would ever see. But he knew why Alixa spoke; he felt it, felt the vibrations of earth, coming nearer, and heard the way the rye parted, left and right.

More of them. They'd come to feast.

"J-Jasen …"

He wished he could tell her to go. To flee, so she need never watch.

No words would come. Only shallow breaths, leaving in shudders.

New noses pressed him, right to his skin. One, on the left, buried itself in the fold where his jaw transitioned to neck. There was something hot and sticky on it—the blood of a fresh kill, Jasen thought. He did not cringe; merely flinched just a fraction, before another found his chin.

They breathed.

Jasen did not.

Every inhalation was long. Each exhale rasped out.

Then they receded, noses leaving him one by one.

Jasen waited, his eyes pressed tight together. To look would be madness; to take a last glance into their jaws now they had scented him, deemed him worth tearing apart.

Alixa, he willed. *Go. Please.*

The scourge shuffled …

The rye shifted.

The vibrations of their feet began to … move away?

They were leaving him?

Jasen shook. He cracked on eye, just a fraction …

The scourge had turned their backs on him. They slunk into the rye. Only their backs remained, long and lumpy, the vertebrae of their spines protruding like misshapen welts.

And then they were in the crop, and going.

Jasen stared.

But … why?

He had no time to think, for as the scourge vanished into the field, Alixa's hand came down on the boundary behind him. "Jasen," she wheezed. "Come over."

The first time he tried to speak, his vocal cords would not work.

The second time, he said, "I can't."

"Please," Alixa begged. Now that his ears were attuning back to her from the scourge, he could hear the sound of tears in her voice, a warble threatening from her throat. She was close to falling apart.

So was he.

"Please come over," she whispered.

"I can't."

"You're not trying!"

No. But the adrenaline had left him, turned him into ooze. He didn't have the strength to move, couldn't, probably ever.

"Just wait," he whispered. Now the words were coming harder too; the adrenaline flooding out of him just as quickly as it had flooded in was letting the fear take over. His throat stuck, the way it did when he felt himself about to cry, but tried desperately to hold it together. A tremor had set off in his hands, buried in the grass to either side of where he'd fallen.

His skin was cold. So cold.

"Jasen," Alixa breathed. "*Please.*"

He closed his eyes. Rested his head against the boundary.

He should move. He should. He needed to. Those scourge had gone, but they weren't far away. They might change their mind. They might turn on their heels, lumber back over here. So Jasen needed to *move*, ancestors curse him, haul himself back over the boundary. He had his mother's pendant, and he'd been lucky enough to escape twice with his life. *So force yourself out of this fog, why don't you, and get back to Terreas instead of continuing to tempt fate?*

No use. The muscles wouldn't go.

Damn, but it was *cold.*

Alixa let out a pained noise. "Ohh, Jasen … Move! Move, damn you!"

"I can't."

"*Move!*"

He shook, hard.

Something sharp was pressing against his back

"Argh!" Alixa cried.

She gripped the boundary wall behind him, and with a cry like none other he'd heard from her, she leapt over the top—

Her dress caught. The pained battle cry in her throat turned to a note of panic.

She slammed hard into the earth at Jasen's side.

"Alixa," he breathed. A fresh burst of panic swept over him, unlocking him. He twisted, one hand grappling for her.

Lifting her head, Alixa turned frightened eyes to him. They were so wide, dominated by so much white—

A scourge roar rent the air.

One charged—no, two.

"Alixa!" Jasen breathed.

She stumbled up, and he grabbed for her shoulder, fighting to pull her to her feet too even as he barely managed to unfold his own from under him. They didn't want to go, didn't seem to know which should be where, for as soon as one was settled he staggered on the other.

Scourge leapt out of the rye, not more than twenty feet hence, a pair of them.

Alixa shrieked—

"Up!" Jasen wheezed. "Back—over—"

But her dress was stuck, tangled against a hard shard sticking out of the wall. The material pulled taut, and try as she might, she could not free it, could not rise properly, could not even twist to pry at it with desperate, nimble fingers—

The scourge leapt, one after another—

They didn't have time. The scourge were too close, decimating the distance too quickly. One more leap—

Jasen grabbed Alixa's shoulder to just shove her back over, drawing every last vestige of strength he had left in him.

The scourge roared, leapt again—the rye crumpled beneath their feet—

No time!

And then, from nowhere, burst a third. It darted out of the rye from the west, bounding in a great diagonal leap—

Jasen slammed his eyes shut, knowing this was over, that the three of them would tear him and Alixa apart in mere moments.

The sound of a violent impact shuddered Jasen's eardrum almost to bursting. But the scourge hadn't slammed into him or Alixa. They'd collided with—

One beast roared; another yelped.

A thud as a body slammed to earth.

Jasen cracked an eye.

The third scourge had intercepted the others. Now it reared in front of Jasen and Alixa, its back to them, and swung its claws at the two that had turned this way when Alixa fell. One of them staggered up from its side, where it had cratered a deep depression in the rye. The other snarled, batting out—

The scourge between loosed a roar of its own, and drove its claws across the other's face. It fell back, keening—and the third struck again, bearing down on it from above, the bony fingers of its paw splayed so its claws covered the widest possible swath. Its victim screeched—and it was struck again, and again, knocked down—

Alixa had clutched Jasen's wrist without him even realizing. "What's happening?" she cried—but that too was a wail, like the scourge's agonized cries, and her shriek was so high and wild that Jasen was sure all of Terreas would hear it; perhaps it could even be heard in all of Luukessia.

The first scourge had regained its footing. It crept a wide berth, blank eyes on Alixa and Jasen—

Before it could take more than a step, their savior leapt for its throat.

It screamed, kicking free—

And still its eyes stuck on the two children, never leaving. It was as if its one sole purpose was to get to them, and though something stood in its way, the creature barely knew about it. It only wished to pass, and it would do so at any cost.

It loosed itself from the third scourge's teeth, leaping backward. Then it came in again, even wider this time, staring as it put on a mad rush of speed—

The third scourge leapt at it. Catching it from below, it flung the attacker backward. Then it reared onto its back legs, paws risen to the sky, claws extended on those bony, protruding knuckles enshrouded in the dead, lank skin of the dead—

It swiped down—and the scourge below it shrieked, a *skree* of death, as its stomach split and its innards spilled out. In the frail light of the minute scattering of stars, the gore was pitch dark.

Alixa gasped and averted her eyes with a whimper.

The remaining scourge hesitated. It moved, like one would make a feint in a game of kick-about that Terreas's children played … but the awful sound of its companion being torn asunder triggered whatever fight or flight instinct resided in its brain. After one last, longing look at Jasen and Alixa, it loosed a low growl and then turned away, loping into the rye.

Their savior waited, back still to them, watching.

When it deemed the beast was a safe distance away, it pivoted—

Jasen's heart froze in his chest.

It was going to eat him and Alixa. That was the only reason it had come to fight the others off. This scourge was starving, willing to take down its brethren so it might secure a meal for itself. And in their dalliance, Jasen and Alixa had guaranteed their own deaths.

But the creature did not press in. It regarded them for a long, long time—perhaps only seconds, but in its black gaze those seconds drew out the way the Mr. Hughes stretched dough with a roller—and then, finally, it too loped away.

Not far, though. Just into the rye, perhaps twenty feet along the field's edge, and there it waited, attention once more trained on Jasen and Alixa.

She still averted her eyes. Her face was clasped in her hands. Sobs racked her body, her shoulders heaving up and down.

"It's..." Jasen began, and then lost his voice. He tried again. "It's okay. We're safe."

Alixa only cried harder.

He couldn't blame her. How many seconds ago was it that he had been close to falling apart himself? No more than thirty, surely. Yet it felt as if hours had passed between stepping out here to find his mother's pendant—three minutes ago, wasn't it?—and then running, and those foul creatures' noses upon him …

Now his fear had fled, replaced with utter bewilderment.

"Alixa," he prompted, tugging at her shoulder. "We need to cross."

She didn't move, at least not far, and then Jasen remembered why: her dress had gotten stuck. Keeping one hand on her shoulder, to reassure that he was there, he reached behind and unhooked the fabric. It felt torn, a small hole made where frayed ends now entwined each other; she'd have some explaining to do, followed by repairs overseen by Aunt Sidyera and her endless tongue.

But she was alive. They both were.

Thanks to …

Jasen eyed it briefly. Still, it watched.

"Alixa," he prompted again. "Come. I've freed you. Let's go back."

He thought she was going to be as stuck as he had been. Yet she moved, clambering awkwardly over the wall. She braced herself with only one hand; the other she kept around her mouth, hardly muting the sobs coming from her.

When she was over, Jasen followed. It was difficult, though he had crossed it with such ease earlier. His legs felt bruised somehow. And when he placed an arm down to grip, a stab of pain went through him, and the ache remained. This arm would hurt for weeks, probably.

He ran fingers across his forehead. The ache from smashing into the wall remained there. The centerpoint of it was hot and already starting to rise. Looked like he'd have some explaining to do as well.

Alixa fell against the wall on the other side. Jasen dropped down beside her.

She cried, hard. He thought to sling an arm over her shoulder … but this had been his doing, again, and he did not think she would appreciate it. So he did not touch her, just sat a few inches away, waiting for her sobs and tears to run out.

When they had, she closed her eyes and leaned her head against the boundary.

"What just happened?" she whispered after another long time.

It was a good question—and one Jasen had no answer to.

But he knew someone who might.

7

It took much goading to convince Alixa to accompany Jasen to Shilara's run-down little place on Terreas's edge. The encounter with the scourge seemed to have sapped much of her fight, though, because she agreed to be led, hemming and hawing as they drew closer.

Not that Jasen wished more anxiety upon his cousin, but he couldn't deny that he was glad to be able to push her more easily into this. It was a rare frame of mind that Alixa would be in to willingly visit Shilara, and presently he needed her. She had witnessed the altercation too, after all.

Though the village itself still saw some activity at this time, and indeed well past it, mostly focused on the tavern, many villagers retired when full dark fell. Shilara was among them, affording them the rare sight of her house without her perched in front of it, a flask in hand. Amber light gave her away behind curtains that were not pulled perfectly together, so she was still awake. If not, Jasen was ready to rouse her.

He hammered a fist on the door.

Alixa dawdled at the path. She'd not ventured but one step farther, and instantly retracted her foot upon doing so, as if the overgrown grasses might part and pull her under.

Jasen turned back to her now. "Come over here, Alixa."

She refused with a single shake of the head.

"Shilara will think it rude if you don't."

She opened her mouth to retort—but stuck between two improprieties, she found herself stuck. After a moment's hesitation, she moaned and shuffled to Jasen's back.

"Why does she not have any flagstones?" she muttered.

Jasen didn't respond, for at that moment the door opened.

Shilara frowned at them from the entryway. Lit from behind by the firelight leaking around the corner, she was, for just a moment, reminiscent of the scourge bearing down on them all over again.

The spike of fear was gone as fast as it had come.

"Jasen," she said. "Visiting twice in one day? To what do I owe this?"

Jasen could feel Alixa's glare on his back—or the glare she wished to give. In sight of Shilara, she'd be careful to adhere to the rules of polite society.

"We need to speak to you," Jasen said quickly, then, remembering his manners, added, "Please."

His tone must have convinced her of the seriousness of the matter, because Shilara nodded and said, "All right. In, the both of you." She stepped aside, waving Jasen and Alixa through the door and toward the sitting room with a fist. No flask in it, but she did hold the tip of a spear between her thumb and forefinger, and an onyx stone for sharpening it between the next two.

Jasen glanced at Alixa. Her face was expressionless, or as expressionless as could be expected after their encounter with the scourge. Yet Jasen felt the ire behind it, at him for having come here, herself for coming along, and for Shilara, for … just being herself, he supposed.

There was also a modicum of pain—for she was being invited into this outcast's presence. Alixa would be tarred by association.

He flashed eyes at her—*Please!*—and then went inside. No need to check she would follow; the tenets of politeness said that she absolutely would, and oh how she would despise him for it the moment they were free from Shilara's presence.

The house was about what Jasen expected: pokey, cluttered, untidy. It wouldn't be fair to say that Shilara never cleaned, but to claim she cleaned with any kind of regularity would be untrue. A faint coating of dust had affixed to most of the surfaces, and the smell of it was noticeable in the air. It wasn't enough to make him cough, but a few hours in this place and he was sure a tickle would settle in the back of his throat.

The small entryway gave over to a sitting room on the left. A fire burned in the hearth, stacked high, as though Shilara expected to be up much of the night and wished for its light to last her close to dawn. The mantel was cluttered with trinkets, and though Jasen did not do more than casually rake his gaze across them, he saw they were souvenirs of war: a set of daggers, four chipped arrowheads leaning against the wall, a sword's brass pommel, end shattered where once it had connected to the rest of the weapon.

She had one painting: a boat on water. The colors were murky, as if a thick blanket of fog had descended upon the scene.

Jasen hesitated, gaze lingering.

"I had to take up a hobby eventually," Shilara said, pointing at it. "Can't drink and practice strikes all day. Sit, boy, sit."

He obliged, dropping onto the wooden foot stool he'd sat upon earlier. An uncomfortable twinge took immediate root around his backside again; *Remember me?*

Alixa had stepped in the room, but no farther. Jasen glanced at her ruefully; she'd crossed the boundary with less reservation. Here she just looked as though she were about to pass her very bones from beneath her skin.

"Go on," Shilara told her, indicating a second armchair. It was ratty-looking, stained by dark liquid on the arms, where the threadbare fabric was close to splitting.

"Yes, well, thank you," Alixa mumbled. She planted herself primly upon it, right at its edge.

Her eyes dropped to the floor. A rug filled the space between seats. On it were two mugs and a plate covered in something blue gone dry; paint, possibly, or just the juice of some long-since eaten berries. The rug had once been an animal of some kind, its coat thick and grey. Its head remained, looking into the fire with empty sockets for eyes. At the sight of it, Alixa's lips gave a very faint downward tug.

"Unlike you to visit twice in a day," Shilara repeated. She lowered herself into her seat, watching Jasen intently. "Let alone at this time of night."

"Sorry."

Shilara waved him off. "Why've you come?"

"I went out again," Jasen said. "Past the boundary."

Shilara's frown deepened. "Why?"

"I … lost something out there earlier today. I needed to find it."

"And did you?"

"Yes." He'd stowed the pendant around his neck on the hurried walk back to Terreas. From now on, he planned on taking stock of the thing more. A *lot* more.

"Well, I'm pleased to hear that." Shilara's hands began to move again. Not particularly paying attention to what she was doing, she began to run the sharpening stone across the edge of the spear's tip.

Alixa's mouth gave another downward quirk. Her hands were clasped between her knees; now she gripped them just a fraction tighter, turning the knuckles yellow.

"We ran into scourge out there," Jasen said.

"'We'?" Shilara's penetrating gaze shifted to Alixa. "You ventured out too?"

Alixa's lips pursed. "I crossed," she said, the words low and scraping, as though they were being used to grind the moss off her favorite stone.

If Shilara was bothered by Alixa's curtness, she did not show it. Instead, she immediately demanded, "Why?"

Alixa sniffed. "My cousin was in danger."

"And you believed you could help him?"

Alixa puffed up. "There were no scourge when I crossed over. My cousin—"

"His name is Jasen, child; use it."

"—was struggling to stand. I believed I could help him."

Shilara nodded at that. "I'm not scorning you. But you should know, both of you, that a man or woman cannot stand between the scourge and another human. They will be torn apart. It's folly to even try."

"I didn't," Alixa replied snippily. "I stood next to him."

Jasen glanced between them nervously. Shilara was one for saying what she thought, which was surely almost as offensive to Alixa as any of the woman's other faults. He trusted Alixa to continue her bare minimum of courtesy, right to the end of this visit. What he wasn't sure about, however, was how much of a hole she'd burn in him after it was done.

Trying not to imagine her recriminations already, he said to Shilara, "Three scourge set upon me out there."

"Jasen." She pressed her lips into a flat line. "I warned you of them just this afternoon."

"I know," he said hastily.

"You shouldn't venture out. The scourge are dangerous."

"I know."

"You might have outrun them twice now, but—"

"Shilara, I didn't outrun them," Jasen said over the top of her.

She stopped.

"I fell," Jasen continued. "Out by the boundary. And three of them came up to me, out of the rye. They pressed their noses to me and scented me. But—it wasn't like you said earlier. Remember? You said that if they scent a man, they won't stop until he's dead. But these three, they scented me, and then they just … they just … they *turned around*," he said desperately. "All three. They backed away, and returned to the rye."

"Hogwash," Shilara said.

"It's true," said Jasen. "It happened. Didn't it?"

Alixa's face was flat. Yet she did confirm the story with a single incline of the head, and a short, "Yes."

"You saw this?" Shilara asked her.

"Yes."

"Exactly as he tells it?"

Now it was Alixa's turn to thin her lips into a perilous line. "Yes." Her knuckles were close to white now.

"I don't believe it," said Shilara.

"It *happened*," said Jasen.

"I'm not disputing you, lad," she said, waving his words away. "Not with her confirmation."

"*She* has a name," Alixa said, both muted and saccharine all at once.

"Alixa Weltan. I know who you are."

"Well, perhaps you might use my name when speaking of me."

Please, don't fight, Jasen willed. Before the sparks could turn to full fires, he cut in again. "There's more, Shilara."

Her penetrating stare bored deeper. "Go on."

"After Alixa climbed over the wall to help, two of the scourge came for us again. We couldn't get away in time—but then a third came."

Jasen took a deep breath. This was going to be the hardest part of all to say, the part that he didn't think Shilara would believe in a thousand centuries.

"That last scourge … it saved us, Shilara. It leapt ahead of the other two, and fought them off. It—it even killed one of them, right there in front of us."

"You're lying," Shilara said flatly.

"I'm not," said Jasen—and something in his tone must have given her pause, because her eyebrows twitched in strange comprehension. The frown she wore became a desolate look of confusion. And the blade and stone she ran together in her hands ceased, the grating noises giving way to pure silence.

"This one scourge fought two others off," Jasen said. "And when we were safe, it looked at us, turned around, and retreated too."

"Jasen isn't lying," Alixa confirmed.

Shilara peered from cousin to cousin, eyebrows drawn low. "It can't be," she muttered. "There's no such thing as a good scourge."

"This one was."

"You must be mistaken," said Shilara, and Jasen felt his stomach drop.

"We're not mistaken!" Alixa cried. "I saw it, just as Jasen did!"

"There is no such thing as a good scourge," Shilara repeated. "As close as they get is when they're dead—and even then they're no good. They stink to high heaven."

"Well, I don't know what to say," Jasen said lamely. "This one protected us. Even when it slunk off, it kept watch, like a sentry."

Shilara shook her head. The pad of fat around her neck quivered. "I don't believe it."

"Well, you ought to," said Alixa stiffly. "See the welt on Jasen's head? He received it when he fell in the chase." She said nothing of the hole torn in her dress, but then Jasen didn't expect her to. Holes were terribly improper—although given the way she'd considered the chair before sitting upon it, Alixa knew full well that Shilara was perfectly familiar with them.

Shilara rose, setting her spearhead and stone aside. She crossed to Jasen in two short steps—the room was barely more than four or five across, furniture removed—and clutched his chin. Her fingers were hot, and strong. She tilted his head toward the fire, letting the light from it properly illuminate the growing red lump across his forehead.

"The scourge didn't do this," she said. "They'd have split your skull in two."

"I never said they did," Alixa snapped.

"I fell over and banged my head on the boundary," Jasen said. "And I think I bruised my arm too."

"Hmm." Shilara let go. She took a step back and then looked Jasen up and down, assessing. "Hmm." She turned to Alixa—

Alixa's stranglehold around her own knuckles grew tighter still. In a moment her fingers would snap off entirely, Jasen was sure.

"You've dirt on you," Shilara observed.

Alixa spluttered, casting panicked eyes over herself. Sure enough, she found a smear of it upon her knees, and she reached out to brush it off, then ceased with hands three inches shy, for brushing it off meant dirtying Shilara's floor. Agitated, she finally settled for gripping the dirty spot in a tight fist and wrapping her other hand around the first to fully hide it.

Shilara lowered into her seat once more. This time, she did not reclaim her spear tip.

"You're certain this happened? Both of you?"

"Yes," Jasen said.

A beady eye turned to Alixa. "And you?"

"Certain," she said, sounding somewhat strangled and tightening her hold on her clothes.

"You've not been drinking? Eating peculiar fruit? Smoking odd leaves?"

Each of these earned an indignant splutter from Alixa. "*No!*"

"None of that," said Jasen.

Shilara mulled this over … then leaned back in her chair, befuddlement apparent once more.

"How can this be?" she wondered aloud. "I've seen them, up close, and never once have they—"

"Up close?" Jasen said, leaning forward, eyes lit with more than a reflection of the dancing flames in the hearth. "You mean when you fought them in the war?"

"More recently than that," she said distractedly, waving a dismissive hand. "I've run up against scourge many times, even this year, and never have I seen—"

"*This year?*"

Shilara stopped dead. She came back to the room as if from a faraway place.

"I shouldn't have said that," she began.

Jasen was practically at the edge of his seat, a half-inch from falling off. He leaned as far as he could go—as far as the bruises covering his body would allow. "When did you fight them this year? Was there an attack on Terreas? Did they try to cross the boundary?"

Alixa's voice came high now, a squeak. "An attack?"

"No," Shilara said—and then bit her lip. A slightly mad look had come across her, eyes a mite wider than usual.

Jasen's excitement flared. So that meant—

"You've crossed the boundary," he breathed.

"Ohh," Alixa moaned faintly.

"I …" Shilara began, and stopped. "The boundary …" she said, trying again, but that sentence also died an early death.

"You *have*," Jasen said—and for all the fear at his two crossings, for all the terror that those terrible beasts had struck into his heart as they stared him down, his excitement overflowed with renewed vigor. This woman had *crossed*. She'd been *beyond*—and she could tell him—

But before any of the thousands of questions being to formulate could take shape, a ruckus went up outside, creeping through a crack in the window where a pane must have shifted.

Alixa twisted upon the edge of her chair to peer through the gap between the curtains. "What's—?"

Shilara had risen, was leading the way to the front door already. Jasen followed, and he grabbed Alixa by the hand as he passed, tugging her onto her feet.

The front door was thrown open, and they spilled out to louder

cries—

And Jasen realized with sudden dread exactly what was happening in Terreas.

Baraghosa was here.

8

Though he came only once a year, Baraghosa's visits were the same each time—and they always were seared in Jasen's mind … last year's most of all.

So when he, Alixa, and Shilara left her house, he knew exactly where the villagers would congregate to herald his arrival. And after bidding Gressom a brief farewell—she would not venture into the throng, of course—Jasen found his feet carrying him inexorably to a destination he very much did not wish to visit.

Baraghosa always went to the assembly hall first. And thus so did Terreas's villagers crowd around it, drawn out by shouts, some meant to rouse the village, others to intimidate the strange merchant. So by the time the man reached Terreas's heart, a vast group of people had collected.

Jasen and Alixa arrived in the packed street. Torches were lit in the assembly hall still, and the chimney coughed out a frail plume of smoke, no doubt tainted with the odor of the unpleasantly scented candles. It was not typical for the assembly to work this late into the night; only pressing matters kept them past nightfall.

Baraghosa, of course, was a very pressing matter.

Still more people were arriving even as Jasen and Alixa added their bodies to the throng. A young-ish couple, maybe thirty, stopped by Alixa. The woman, a matronly sort whose hair she smoothed back into place, said, "Has he arrived yet?"

"Not yet," Alixa answered.

The woman nodded. "You both ought to get nearer the front."

Neither Jasen nor Alixa replied.

He felt sick. So, so sick.

An image of Pityr flashed through his mind, boyish face laughing happily.

Chatter filled the night, the cacophony rising to the skies, now almost entirely devoid of cloud. Stars twinkled. Jasen envied them, for not one knew what was about to unfold—and if they did, they were so many eons away that not a single spark among them would surely care.

Jasen waited.

Alixa gripped his wrist. He reached up as far as he could with his fingers, to touch one to her knuckle.

And then the chatter grew more violent. Louder cries filled the air, a cacophony, and there were curses among them, coming from mothers, fathers, sisters, and brothers. They began near the front, but the back of the crowd reacted in an instant, joining their voices as one against Baraghosa.

Or not as one. For this had gone on for many years, and the village was not united in their derision. The broken families wept—but the untouched among them, those Jasen could not help but view as callous, cruel, and detached—these people railed against the shouts of the others. The woman to Alixa's right was among them, folding her arms and yelling, "He's doing us a service!" The sidelong glance she fired the teenagers served as extra punctuation.

And as the nauseating dread reached its crescendo in Jasen's midsection, he saw Baraghosa come.

The man was preceded by lights. Like two great fireflies against the sky, white orbs heralded him, dancing above the rooftops. Not much brighter than the moon when it was full, they might be pretty if one did not know who or what they presaged. Knowing the truth, Jasen only felt nauseated at the sight of his strange magic.

The crowd shuffled.

As one, they could pummel Baraghosa, tear him limb from limb the way the scourge had threatened to do to Jasen and Alixa this night. But the magic he wielded was slippery, dangerous, unknown—if indeed it was magic at all, although it must be, for him to slink through the land of the scourge unassailed year after year—and so the villagers receded, parting like the mountains to let sharp blasts of air between them.

Jasen couldn't see him. Didn't wish to. Yet he knew him well enough.

"Monster!" some shouted.

Roars of approval went up from around the person who'd cried out. Scattered disdain, including another yell from the woman at Alixa's side, filled the night in retaliation.

The woman at Alixa's side tired of waiting. Grabbing Jasen and

Alixa around the neck—Alixa yelped, while Jasen shouted—she grunted, "Get to the *front!*" And she marched them forward, parting the crowd, her fingers tight like vices.

The crowd split. Jasen tried to jerk free. Yet there was little strength left in him, and though the woman drew angry calls—"You're a monster too!" Jasen heard before that voice was lost behind—none made a move to stop her.

Then they were at the front, and the woman released them both with a shove.

Alixa landed on her knees. Jasen stumbled, then twisted after the woman, one hand slapped to his neck.

She was already retreating to her place in the crowd, disappearing in their number, not looking back.

Jasen gripped Alixa by the arm, pulling her up—

And then he had no choice but to look ahead, to see—

The crowd had moved back from the assembly hall entirely, although Baraghosa had come through a junction farther down the street and hadn't yet reached the hall's entrance. Everyone knew where he was going, with whom he planned to meet, and none would stand in his way.

He slunk past, preceded by those peculiar white lights …

Jasen's gaze fell to him, unwilling, yet drawn like moths to a flame.

Clad in deep purple clothes fitted tightly to a spindly frame, Baraghosa reminded Jasen of a spider. His hair was dark, like his eyes, and swept to one side. Though plain-faced, there was something disconcerting about him, the expressionless way he regarded every person he laid eyes on. It was a look of purest detachment, almost boredom … yet there was more beneath it. His face was a mask, but beneath this veneer was calculation, even joy. Though his lips barely moved from the flat line they so often appropriated, as if drawn on that way, every time a villager cringed away from him they seemed to move just a fraction in the faintest, most ghostly facsimile of a smile. And he would edge deliberately closer to that person, turning that cringe into a frightful trembling.

It was the closest Jasen had ever seen Baraghosa to smiling, and it made him feel more ill than he had ever felt.

Thin and almost unnaturally tall, Baraghosa could've taken great long steps, crossing the distance to the assembly hall's door in a fraction of the time. Yet he drew it out

He enjoys this, Jasen thought—and he hated him all the more furiously for it.

Baraghosa passed. His eyes swept disinterestedly across the crowd.

They passed over Alixa, who turned away, her hand on Jasen's wrist becoming a claw. Then they fell to Jasen—and though it was only an instant before he moved on, Jasen felt as if he'd fallen into some great abyss.

He's one of them, he thought. *Scourge made human. They share the same eyes.*

Then Baraghosa was beyond them, and Jasen released a breath that brought no satisfaction to his tight chest and frenzied heart.

"Vile man," whispered Mrs. Tomlins at Jasen's left.

"You're sick!" someone else shouted farther that direction.

Another: "At least bring your seed into our village if you're going to defile it with your presence, sorcerer!"

Baraghosa did not turn. But he said, "Not until a deal is struck."

Was that what Jasen hated most about him? His voice? Perhaps. It was emotionless, not remarkable in any way other than being slightly too high-pitched. Yet it sent a chill down Jasen's spine, Alixa's too, perhaps most of the village—and he never had to raise it. Even over the villager's shouts, he could speak as though he were talking in a silent room, and he would be heard.

Jasen hated it.

At last, Baraghosa slunk to the assembly hall door. He stopped upon the step leading in, lifted one spindly arm, and gently *rat-a-tat-tatted* against the wood. Even that was audible above the noise of the crowd, as if amplified somehow.

The door creaked open.

Adem stood inside, face terse. Beside him was Hanrey Smithson, looking almost comically small and fat beside Jasen's father. Hanrey's cheeks were crimson, and Jasen wondered if perhaps he had shouted himself that color, or found himself at the end of a flask of grain alcohol to get through this night. Possibly both.

Neither Adem nor Hanrey greeted Baraghosa; Adem simply said, shortly, "Come in." And he stepped aside.

Baraghosa entered.

The white lights drifted above the assembly hall. They'd stay, dancing in lazy circles until Baraghosa departed.

A handful of villagers piled in after him, and against his better judgment, Jasen again found his feet moving of their own accord, taking him forward.

Alixa was possessed too. Though she choked out a strangled-sounding cough, she followed in Jasen's wake, clutching him the whole time.

They stepped through, and for the second time in a day, Jasen was assaulted by the odor of those candles. Most had been full and tall in the sconces when he'd stood in here earlier. Now, only small pools of wax with inch-long wicks remained of them. Soon the flames would snuff themselves out in the pools they'd melted beneath them, and someone—Eounice, probably—would set new candles in their places.

The tables filled by the assembly remained at the far end of the hall. Eounice remained in her place, and if she was standing politely at Baraghosa's arrival (though Jasen doubted it), he could not tell. Matron of the Assembly Griega Marks helmed her seat in the center, her headpiece positioned perfectly. Neither looked pleased to see Baraghosa.

Aunt Margaut sat to the left of where Hanrey would shortly take up his seat. And the empty seat beside Eounice would be filled by Adem.

The two councilmen led Baraghosa to the same spot where Jasen had stood just this morning.

Behind, as many villagers filled the assembly hall as could.

Another wave of nausea spread over Jasen. Too many were teenagers, his age or less, and they were crowded right to the front by the mob, pushed in like herd animals.

For all the shouting on the street, here silence reigned.

Adem and Hanrey took their seats.

The moment their backsides had touched wood, Baraghosa extended an arm to all of them. "Good evening, Terreas assembly." And he bowed, almost unnaturally low, as though he were a puppet on strings. "May I say," he finished, rising, "what a pleasure it is to meet with you once more."

"Terreas greets you too, Baraghosa," said Griega, voice metered. "How do we find you?"

"Most well," he answered. "Most well, indeed. How do I find *you*, Assembly Matron?"

"Equally well," Griega answered.

"Wonderful. And your assembly?" Baraghosa's head turned, and Jasen could see him as though he stood before him, raking those coal eyes across the remainder of the gathered council in turn. "How has life treated you all since last I visited?"

They answered, in turn, and Jasen listened. He hated this part. It was so *proper*, so *polite* and *nice* and *friendly*—and this man deserved none of those things. That the assembly engaged in this dance with him disgusted Jasen, made his stomach clench.

Aunt Margaut was last to answer. Hers was the thinnest statement of all, curt like Eounice's: "I'm fine, Baraghosa."

"So lovely to hear it," he said. There was a faint lilt to his voice,

barely audible—this was polite Baraghosa, charming Baraghosa, the Baraghosa who seemed to be perfectly friendly, and not the demon all of Terreas knew him to be.

"I've thought of you often this past year," he went on. "Many a night, I've spent hoping that the rains are kind, that the sun blesses you, that your fields are fruitful with a grander harvest than ever you have before laid eyes—"

Eounice slammed her walking stick to the floor. The sound was louder than it had any right to be, and stilled Baraghosa's words.

"Oh, let's dispense with this flowery nonsense, why don't we?" she grumbled. "We all know why we're gathered here. Let's just get to it, yes?"

Baraghosa rubbed his palms together. They whickered, dry.

"Yes, let's move past these formalities," he agreed.

Griega nodded. "Please proceed, Baraghosa."

He did not tarry. "How much seed do you require for the season ahead?"

Eyes went to Margaut. She sighed, lacing her fingers, the same way Alixa so often did. Drumming them idly against her knuckles, she said, "We will come about as far short as we did last year. Four of our fields will stand empty once they've been picked, and our winter squash will go perhaps far enough to leave the same gap when the hail arrives."

"The same as last year," Baraghosa repeated. He drew the words out, and Jasen pictured his face as he savored the feel of each of them on a tongue that was leathery, just as haunted by drought as his hands. "You're sure?"

"Perhaps more," Margaut amended, looking as though it caused her great pain to do so.

"Yes, I anticipated as much. Your village seems to have grown in number this year—so wonderful amidst all this blight, truly. It fills me with great happiness to know …" Eounice had lifted her stick to slam it down again, and so Baraghosa's words petered out. When she'd lowered it again, he said, "How much more do you think, Mrs. Weltan?"

Aunt Margaut bit her lip. Heaved a sigh, and reached a hand to her temple. "Another two fields' worth, for both seasons."

"Six fields' worth of seed for summer, and six for autumn," Baraghosa mused. Head cocked, he touched a hand to his chin. "Twelve fields in all …"

The assembly hall was silent, tense.

"Difficult," Baraghosa said at last.

Jasen gritted his teeth. It wasn't. It never was. Baraghosa always had enough seed, *always*. The assembly could ask for one hundred fields' worth of seed, and Baraghosa would produce it. This was just him getting his kicks, same as ever.

"You must have enough," someone behind Jasen said, almost begged. There was the sound of an elbow being driven into their hip, and he spoke no more.

Baraghosa tapped the side of his chin with a long finger—his fifth, the smallest, Jasen saw, yet still it was unnatural in its inches.

"Twelve fields' worth of seed," he mused again.

Long, long quiet …

Eounice broke it by growling, "Enough of this, Baraghosa."

Jasen pictured the corners of his lips flickering up, just for an instant. "Twelve fields' worth of seed it is."

"You can provide it?" Hanrey demanded.

"I can. Of course, there is the matter of my price; one of—"

"We know your price," Adem cut in stiffly.

Baraghosa nodded. "But of course you do."

And he turned … and those dark little eyes, impossible to peer into, swept over the crowd, raking slowly from left to right. Not for one second did he consider any adult—for adults were worthless to Baraghosa.

He wanted a child, one of these teenagers or ten-year-olds, or even that boy of six—though perhaps not, as his gaze moved past him without pausing.

Jasen saw it every year, and never did it ease the agonized squirming in his stomach.

It always went the same. Baraghosa would single a child out with a too-long finger, selecting them for Terreas's part in this trade. The child's parents would scream, cry. The assembly, much of the village in fact, would push, would remind them that without this devil's deal they would go hungry, that their fields would not produce enough to feed Terreas's growing numbers, would remind those parents that they had not complained the just last year, or the year before, or the year before …

And so, tear-stricken, they would be beaten down. Their child would be wrested away from them to accompany Baraghosa away, out of Terreas …

And never be seen again.

Like Pityr.

Past face after face he went, only his head moving as he tracked—

Over Alixa—

She clutched Jasen's wrist tighter still, hard enough to dig crescents into his skin as she closed her eyes, breath caught—

Then Baraghosa looked at him.

The moment seemed to draw out forever—

It *did* draw out. For Baraghosa did not look away. His perusal ceased, those onyx depths fixated on him as the scourge had stared so single-mindedly not two hours ago.

Jasen's heart skipped.

Baraghosa lifted a hand.

A spindly finger pointed right to Jasen.

"I choose him."

9

What usually happened was this: Baraghosa made his choice. The boy or girl chosen would typically have been accompanied by their parents, or grandparents, or other guardian, and upon Baraghosa's choosing, they would fall apart. The mother would clutch her son or daughter close, falling into a muddle of tears. The father would stand in their way, forbidding Baraghosa from taking the child, offering up threats or bribes alternatively. Frequently, one parent or the other, sometimes both, would offer themselves up. Several years, Jasen had even see adults fall to their feet at Baraghosa's knees, like peasants swearing fealty to a king like the stories of old.

Yet their cries would be met with deaf ears, from Baraghosa and the assembly both … and ultimately the child would be taken, the family's cries lasting long into the night.

Tonight there was a stunned silence—or perhaps that was only how Jasen saw it. His whole world had become stilled amber in that one moment, and he could only stare in horror, Baraghosa's pointed finger and those three damning words ricocheting in his head like a stone rattled in a tin.

I choose him.

This was it.

He was this year's sacrifice.

Adem thrust to his feet, and his voice, steady, echoed in the hall:

"No."

Voices from the crowd rumbled. Eounice silenced them with a slam of her stick.

Baraghosa turned, only halfway, so he was still pointing at Jasen, his pencil-thin body side on to the boy. An eyebrow drifted up his forehead. "No?"

"I refuse you," Adem growled. "This is my heir."

"Sit down," Hanrey grunted.

"No."

"You *agreed*!"

"Before it was my boy this scoundrel decided to take!" Adem thundered. Heat rose in his face, and rage contorted his face into an expression Jasen had never seen before.

Adem whirled, jabbing a finger at Hanrey. "This swine is not taking my child from me!"

"And what say you we do instead?" Hanrey barked. "Let our newborns starve?"

Adem's words came from between gritted teeth. "*Not my boy.*"

"You ruddy hypocrite," said Hanrey. "This vote was three to two in favor of making the year's trade. You said yourself, *Rabinn*—" he said it like the name was dirt, even less "—that this is for the good of Terreas. You have agreed, year after year after year. And now the deal hits your house—involves *your son*—you turn your back on us all!" This last sentence was roared.

"Quiet yourselves!" Eounice shouted.

"I will not let that *ghoul* take my son!" Adem boomed.

Hanrey was on his feet now too. "You selfish bloody—"

Margaut grabbed him before he could stride beyond the table.

"You watch your tongue when you speak to me, old man!" Adem snapped back.

"Watch my tongue?"

"Hanrey, sit," Margaut pleaded—

"*Watch my tongue?* Your mother should've given you a ruddy smack on the backside and taught you some respect, instead of lying on her back like some—"

"Enough!"

The last cry was Griega's. She had risen, and though her face had barely changed from its usual severe moue, fire danced in her eyes. And like Baraghosa, though she had not raised her voice even as high Hanrey and Adem had, it cut through the rest of the sound in the room, and brought it to silence.

Hanrey scowled. Adem scowled back, his nostrils flared and eyebrows pressing a heavy line in between them.

"There will be no further disrespect in the assembly hall," Griega said, looking from Hanrey to Adem in turn. "I will not allow it. You may disagree, but do so with dignity, especially in front of our guest."

"He's no guest," Adem spat. "Just a crackpot peddling lies."

Baraghosa had barely shifted, just watched the tirade unfold with that lone eyebrow still quirked. Only now that the assembly's attention had returned to him did he turn entirely their way, retracting that digit pointed at Jasen and lacing his fingers together in front of his midriff.

"You do realize, of course," he said, "that without paying my price, I cannot provide you with seed."

"Your price can go—"

"Adem," Eounice muttered.

"And if I cannot provide you with seed, it is very much as Mr. Smithson says. You will not be able to feed your newborns, and some of you will, most assuredly, die." He bobbed his head, looking back at Jasen, driving a wedge of ice into his chest. "In the scheme of things, is this one life worth giving up for so many others?"

"Yes," Hanrey said immediately.

"No," Adem said at the same time. "Not my boy."

"Your boy over the rest of them?" Hanrey said.

"Yes."

"Hypocrite," the old man growled. "You're a fool."

"I refuse to lose my son—"

"You know loss already!" Hanrey cried. "What's another when you're versed in it?"

Margaut and Eounice together shouted together: "HANREY!"

"You wish for every family in this village to know pain like that?" Hanrey demanded. "You wish for them to hurt, all of them, because you refuse? You wish for them to watch their wives and children die?" He thrust a stubby finger at Jasen. "He is the price. Do the right thing and let him go, the way any other *noble* villager among us would—the way many have."

Alixa clawed his wrist tight. She was crying, Jasen realized; he felt her shoulder heaving against him. "No," she whispered, although it came as more of a croak. "Please …"

"Smithson is correct," said Baraghosa. "Your people will starve. As a member of the assembly, surely you must see the *necessity* of—"

"Shove your 'necessity' up your backside," Adem said. "You're not taking him."

"No?"

One word, hard and menacing: "No."

"Hmm. Well then. And the rest of you back this decision?"

Eounice and Margaut exchanged glances, the latter looking far more nervous than her elder.

"We voted against agreeing to your deal," said Margaut. A nervous quiver shook her voice.

"I see." No disdain there, no displeasure. "I trust I know where your vote lays, Mr. Smithson. And you, Assembly Matron?"

Griega said nothing.

Baraghosa inclined his head. "But of course. In favor—as you would be. It is for the good of the village, after all." Glancing back to Eounice and Margaut, he said, "Would you consider changing your mind? It would be of great benefit to your people, after all." When Eounice did not say anything, he pivoted to Margaut. "Mrs. Weltan? Might you say yes?"

She shook her head, averting her gaze. Her lip trembled.

"You're sure? I understand you have four children, Mrs. Weltan. Why, one of them is here in this very crowd tonight, is she not? Your youngest?" He turned, and though his gaze raked past Jasen and Alixa, her nails dug into him again, and her breath caught haggardly in her throat. "It would be a shame for you to watch any of them wither," Baraghosa told Margaut, abyssal eyes on her downturned face once more.

"I grow my own food," she said softly. "My children shan't go hungry."

"Ah, but do you know what hungry people do? They grow desperate. The rules of civilized society soon cease to apply. And though your garden is plentiful now, you must see what will happen once Terreas's fields are empty, and stomachs are still not full?"

"Don't you dare threaten my sister-in-law," Adem started.

"I'm not threatening anyone," said Baraghosa, "simply telling the truth. Hungry people will take. They will take from you, Mrs. Weltan. They will take it all."

Aunt Margaut's fingers tightened. Like Alixa's in Shilara's sitting room a half-hour ago, her knuckles had gone entirely white.

Baraghosa waited … but she said nothing.

"I see," he finally ceded. To Adem: "You will not bend?"

"Never."

"Hmm."

A backward look at Jasen, whose blood ran cold.

Alixa gasped, nails pressing deeper—

Baraghosa turned back to the assembly, and said four words and four words only:

"You will regret this."

And with that, he departed, leaving a room full of silent, disbelieving villagers—and the knowledge that, this year, for the first time in a long, long time, Terreas would not have enough food to feed its people.

10

The moment the door closed, fury broke out.

"An outrage!" one man cried.

"Hypocrisy!" shouted another.

"You've sent our boys and girls off all these years!" shrieked one woman, old and grey and clutching her shawl like it would dart from her shoulders and out the window, never to be seen again. "Yet you balk at your own! *Shame on you!*"

A chorus went up at that, all just slightly out of sync: "For shame!"

"Shame!"

"*SHAME!!*"

Hanrey was loudest of all. Without Baraghosa's presence to soften him—as if it ever had—he threw himself to his feet, shoving the table clear in one great shunting movement.

"Of all the despicable—" he started.

"Don't you start again," Eounice shouted at him. She shoved her chair back, rising too—

Someone grappled him by the shoulder, pivoted him round. He stared into the face of an angry man lined with wrinkles, and a scar across his lip that ran down like an orange stripe.

"You're a *coward*, boy," he wheezed into his face.

"Get off him!" Alixa cried, wrestling Jasen free.

"Should've gone with him while you had the chance!"

"Shameful child," parroted another.

Jasen turned on his heel. The voices came from every direction, all fighting to be heard. And so many were directed at him, or his father, calling them fools, simpering children, shirkers of responsibility, betrayers of the village—

The woman who'd grabbed Jasen and Alixa by the necks and shoved them up to the front was standing at the back of the crowd.

Jasen caught sight of her face in the corner, by the door—one of the last to enter, apparently, and the last Baraghosa would've passed on his exit. An expression of purest disgust darkened her face. At the sight of Jasen catching eyes, she opened her mouth and spat a string of curses at him, black enough that they probably reached the ears of his ancestors back to the beginning of his line.

Hanrey was fighting to get at Adem, blocked by Eounice on one side and gripped by Margaut, who he shook off every time her hands found his shoulders. Adem, to his credit, was fighting just as hard to get at the old man. Held back by two strong farmers called forth from the crowd by Margaut, he made no headway.

"You're a traitor to our people!" Hanrey roared.

"And you're a callous, uncaring old man."

"I've shown more care for this village today than you have in your entire tenure as assemblyman!"

"You're spewing *dung*, you ornery old badger."

Griega said, "Enough of this."

Hanrey ignored her, just craned his squat neck around to look past Eounice and stare up into Adem's face—probably willing him close enough to head butt. "You're a hypocrite and a traitor. You've killed our people."

"You're an old fool," Adem spat.

"And you should've died with your poxed wife!"

That did it. Something in Adem snapped. His face changed, twisting with purest rage. He shoved at Eounice—

"Don't you push me, either of you!" she shouted.

"You say that to my face, you old bastard," Adem said.

"You heard the first time."

"SAY IT TO MY FACE!"

"*That is enough!*" Griega said.

Her voice was no more raised than Jasen had ever heard it, yet still she cut through the bickering, although not as totally as before. Though the crowd fell into silence, and Hanrey and Adem both quieted, neither ceased their stare-down.

"You're a waste of skin," Adem told him, "not even good as the leathery husk you've resembled these past twenty years."

"And you—"

"Don't, Hanrey," Margaut warned—and so did Griega, standing and raising a hand to still him.

"Cease," she said.

Hanrey bristled. Beneath his beard, his lips twitched, as if he was daring himself to say more. Yet he stayed silent, scowling furiously, letting his glare do all the talking for him.

"There will be no more of this," said Griega, addressing both the assembly and the gathered villagers. "The disregard for our fellow villagers this night is appalling, and I will not stand for it, not in this assembly hall, nor anywhere this side of the boundary. If you wish to squabble, take leave of us and cross it. Defile scourge land with your words, but not this place. Do you hear?"

Hanrey opened his mouth—

"Shut it," Margaut warned, voice hard. "You've dispensed enough hateful words for one night."

"I did not mean that—"

"Be quiet, you old goat," Eounice told him. "And take your bloody seat again, instead of standing around like an idiot. That goes for you too."

Adem obliged, though he looked none too pleased to be doing so, and he only deigned to sit once Hanrey had parked his backside once more.

Eounice lowered herself into her chair, and Margaut took up her seat too, though not before dragging it sideways, as far from Hanrey as it would go without sending her beyond the edge of the table's side.

"Now," said Griega, taking her seat last, "we will resume discussing matters with *civility*, if you please."

"He's ruined us," Hanrey said, low grumble of worry leaking out.

"Baraghosa is not taking my son," Adem replied.

"How many others have you sent away all these years?"

From the crowd, a woman's voice Jasen half-recognized called, "You let him make off with my Rufus four years ago."

"My neighbor lost her Polly," said another, older, although Jasen did not know it or the name—someone before his time, perhaps, or at the very least when he was too early for these visits to scar his mind the way they'd come to. "You oversaw that, Assemblyman Rabinn."

"Hypocrite," Hanrey grumbled.

"*Be civil*," Griega said. Hanrey just huffed, folded his arms and turned away.

"I'm just worried about our children," said a heavyset woman. She was young, Jasen knew as he recognized her as having been one of the older children at school when he started, although the fat cocooning her made her appear much older. A swaddled newborn lay in her arms, oblivious to the chaos around it. "I'm afraid for them."

The grumbling discontent resumed.

"You ought to be ashamed of yourself," Hanrey barked at Adem—

"You ought to learn to shut your damned mouth."

Eounice cried, "Adem! Hanrey!"

"Sold us out for a no good, disrespectful boy—"

"Don't you dare talk about my son like that—"

"—whose lack of manners plainly comes from a man who hasn't the first clue of how to be a good father."

Adem was on his feet again—

"*GIVE HIM TO BARAGHOSA!*" yelled someone from the crowd—

It was beginning again. Voices fought for volume, growing louder by the second. They came from every direction, disorientating, dizzying—

He should be pleased he'd escaped Baraghosa's wrath—but this? The alternative?

The newborn in the fat woman's arms shifted, began to cry.

The child might, Jasen thought, be one of those to die.

His stomach twisted.

Eounice was shouting over the noise now. Jasen caught, "—was your child? Would any of you be stood here demanding that they be let go? *No!* You'd—" And then Hanrey was shoving the table, and Adem had grabbed the old woman's stick, was raising it as he shoved past, and Griega stepped out, her eyes burning—

Alixa was a terrified statue at Jasen's elbow. "What's happening?" she cried.

All this damned noise, this chaos—those awful candles, scents so cloying, making it so hard to breathe in this room, over-full, the air hot, hot—and all those children, who'd evaded Baraghosa, but who now might not be fed, who might not see the next summer, the spring, perhaps even the winter, all because of him—

"*I'll go with him!*"

The words had tumbled out before Jasen knew he would say them, before he could catch them.

There was a pause. Like Griega and Baraghosa before him, Jasen had cast the room into sudden quiet.

The blaze in Adem's eyes turned to fear as he found his son's gaze.

"I'll go with him," Jasen repeated.

Alixa stared.

The *room* stared.

"Son," Adem began. The shock had stolen much of his voice, so what came out was a muted, strangled sort of noise.

"I'll do it," Jasen said, quick, before his father could try to convince him otherwise—before he *himself* could try to do the same. His decision was made, had been made in a moment. And if he thought, for even a second, that it was not the right thing to do, he would never go—and these people, in this room, would die.

"I'll go with Baraghosa for the seed."

"Someone needs to get him," said someone in the crowd.

Another, more shrill: "*Someone get Baraghosa back!*"

The door was thrust open, and someone leapt out, shouting. More than one person, by the sound of it. Jasen dared not look; he couldn't bring himself to watch them, happy and hopeful, knowing that it meant he had chosen to go with Baraghosa, out beyond the boundary—to die so they would not have to.

"Jasen—" Adem began again.

"It's decided," said Hanrey sharply. "The boy has made his decision."

"You're not serious," Alixa whispered, tugging at his wrist. She'd clutched it all this time, as though it might keep him from going—and still she held firm, both of them knowing she couldn't keep him here no matter how tightly she held, no matter how hard she dug her fingernails into his skin, the way she pressed them into her own palms.

"You're not doing this," she whispered.

He looked her in the eye—and she knew; he could see it there, plain as day. So he said nothing.

Her lips trembled. "Jasen."

The assembly were discussing—what, Jasen wasn't sure. Same as the crowd behind him. Their voices all blurred indistinctly. He could pick out no words, and nor did he want to. He could focus only on one thing: that this was the right thing to do. He had been chosen. It was his duty not to let the village down.

Be like Pityr, he told himself as his gaze fell through the floor, burrowing a long way into the earth. *Go willingly, as he did.*

Go and embrace it.

A fragmentary voice piped: *You always did want to see beyond the boundary.*

He had, true. Although not like this.

Not like this.

As the noise of the room droned around him, Jasen thought of his fate. He tried to summon anything more than numbness. An echo of the terror that had clutched his bones when coming face to face with the scourge today would be something. A twinge of sadness? Hope to see his mother again?

None of these came. He was only numb to it all.

When the door burst open again, he came back to his senses. Eounice was narrating again, by the sound of it, talking about choices, but she ceased as someone spilled in from the outside.

Jasen looked over his shoulder, his expression flat.

No Baraghosa.

It was a villager—Daniel Carmichael, who'd probably escaped Baraghosa's clutches no more than five or six years ago himself. He was a reedy man without much strength, who busied himself most days with penning poems he read once a month at the tavern, to a cursory applause.

"He's not out here!" he cried.

"What do you mean, not out there?" Hanrey demanded.

"His lights have gone!" Daniel gasped for breath, sucking lungfuls in two great gulps. Sweat clung to his brow as though he'd run the paths etched around the mountains' sides and come back without pausing. "We can't see him. He's already gone."

Murmuring broke out.

Alixa echoed it. "How?" She frowned at Jasen, shimmering eyes below knitted eyebrows. "It takes longer than this to leave the village. The walk to the boundary alone takes …"

Jasen shrugged, a dull lift of the shoulders. "He possesses strange magic." A few times, Adem had mused that perhaps Baraghosa came from the west, from a land across the sea, whose name they'd only heard whispered—Arkaria. Jasen had thought one day he might see it.

Over the course of the last fourteen hours, though, his every aspiration had been taken from him, then stamped into the ground and turned to dust.

"Then he shan't go," said Adem firmly.

That started Hanrey off again. "You've no fiber, Rabinn! Your boy has more of it than you!"

"We have settled this," Adem snarled, thumping a fist on the table—and no doubt imagining what it might be like send it into Hanrey's red face. "The council decision is three to two against Baraghosa's deal. Jasen is not going. We've settled it in the way of our people."

"You blasted—"

"The boy *wants* to go," shouted the neck-grabber from before. "Maybe that should be our new way from now on!"

There was a nervous, low tide of agreement through the crowd, and more than Jasen would've expected.

But then, of course there would. These gathered families had been spared destruction for another year. Now an out had presented itself, they had no reason not to agree to Jasen's departure.

If he had wished to back out, he need only look to see dozens more in this room had made the same decision—the right decision. Go with Baraghosa in exchange for seed. Save Terreas.

The tides of a brewing fight were rising again.

Jasen decided to head them off. Stepping forward to gather the assembly's attention, he said, "I'll go look for him."

Hanrey: "Will you?"

"Yes." Jasen swallowed. There was a lump in his throat, one which refused to be dislodged, dry and papery, like Baraghosa's palm. "I'll find him, and I'll tell him I'll go." Another painful swallow. "And he'll bring the seed."

If there was any relief in the room—and surely there was—Jasen didn't feel it. He only felt his father's eyes burning a hole in his face. Yet he wouldn't meet them, couldn't, and looked only to the other assemblymen and women in turn.

He had seen his father heartbroken once before. He did not wish to see him so again.

"You have our blessing," said Griega, inclining her head. "Go, child. See to it that you find Baraghosa before he has traveled far."

"I will."

He turned to leave—

Alixa still held him.

He paused, looking into her red-rimmed eyes. "You stay here. I can find him alone."

Her mouth opened, closed, a runner of thick saliva between her lips from her crying. Then she shook her head, violently, sending her hair down onto this side of her shoulders. For now, she did not right it.

"I'm coming with you," she said.

He understood. Not with Baraghosa—but to help find him. It would be their last jaunt together.

They ventured out into the night. Jasen did not look at the gathered villagers in the assembly hall as he passed, and least of all the woman who'd manhandled him and Alixa to the front of the crowd. He was doing this for a good greater than him, and one look at her, victorious and unaffected, could be enough to overturn this choice, shifting him to spite.

People were still collected on the streets outside, though the crowd was smaller than when Jasen had last been out here. They clustered, some engaged in low conversation, others simply tense, watching the assembly hall or casting eyes over the night as they waited.

"Are you the boy Baraghosa chose?" one asked as Jasen slipped out.

He did not answer, though another did: "Yes, that's him—the Rabinn boy."

"You're too late," the first called to Jasen's receding back. "He's already gone. No sign of him."

"No food for my daughter now!" Mrs. Aber shrieked from down the way. She was stricken, as though she'd been crying an hour already, and Jasen turned back to catch a sight of her anguished face, mouth turned down at the corners as far as it would go.

Alixa tightened her hold on Jasen's wrist, pulling him back around. "Ignore them."

Were it so easy.

They turned down a side street which was empty, and down another, pulling away from Terreas's village center. Jasen wanted to take advantage of the incline, angling themselves so that they had a clear view of the night, not one blocked by rooftops and chimneys, only a handful of which now sighed thin trails of smoke into the heavens. He needed to get out to where he could see the walk down to the boundary, for there he would locate Baraghosa, he was certain: his lights would dance as he made his slow, deliberate walk to the wall separating this last haven in Luukessia from the rest of the ruined isle.

Yet the buildings grew sparser, and still Jasen saw no sign of Baraghosa's lights.

"Where is he?" he muttered.

Alixa squeezed him. "We'll find him."

Out they went, and the village became sparser. Instead of houses run up side by side, gaps were open between them. Through these valleys, Jasen spied the decline leading to the boundary, and then way out past it, though he could not pick out the wall itself against the darkness beneath the frail starlight.

There were no lights.

And he realized, at last, as the last of the houses gave way to nothing but night, that Daniel Carmichael had been right.

"Baraghosa's gone," he whispered.

And with him, so too had gone Terreas's last hope.

11

All at once, Jasen was tired. It came as no surprise: the day had been long, far more eventful than normal, and he had run for his life twice now. Short distances, to be sure, but when adrenaline evaporated it left a cavern of exhaustion behind. Add to that the evening's encounter with Baraghosa, and how *that* had ended up, it was no wonder his muscles sighed, and his legs wanted to give out.

"We should get back," Alixa said quietly.

Jasen shook his head. "I need to sit."

"Here?"

He nodded.

Under usual circumstances, Alixa would likely not have obliged. The moss-covered rock by the vineyard was as close as she ever got to letting herself, or anyone in her presence, plant themselves on anything that was not a proper chair. Dirt clung, after all, and that was not civilized.

Jasen wondered idly why she bothered. The way the assembly hall had degenerated, it was patently obvious that civility was as scarce as the seed in Terreas. Possibly the village had held some once. If it did, most of it had gone the way the rest of Luukessia's peoples had, nothing but a memory.

He sunk onto the grass. Alixa lowered herself beside him. She'd not let go of his arm all this time. Now, as she crouched, it was as if she remembered that she'd latched onto it. Carefully she unwound her fingers and let go.

"Oh, Jasen," she sighed. "I'm sorry."

He followed her gaze.

Rings of impressions encircled his wrist from her nails. In the darkness, with only dull light from Terreas leaking from behind, they had no color but dull grey. Jasen knew, though, that they would be

blazing red, possibly for days.

If he lived that long.

Baraghosa is gone, he reminded himself. He had a full life ahead of him still.

Though, would it feel like one?

He sighed. He slipped his fingers past the collar of his tunic and wrapped them around his mother's pendant. The stone was cool.

In spite of it all, it brought the faintest sense of comfort to him.

They sat in quiet for a long time—or Jasen sat, anyway; Alixa crouched, shifting from time to time on her knees as the ache no doubt settled in.

After she shuffled for maybe the twentieth time, a voice from behind said, "Plant your backside down, girl. You've already torn a hole in your dress and muddied your knees. What will a little more hurt?"

Jasen and Alixa turned.

Shilara was watching them from a short distance away around the rear of a storage shed. Tucked beneath the wooden eave, in the day she might've been taking advantage of its shadow.

"How long have you been out here?" Jasen asked.

"Long enough." Shilara stepped out. She raised her hand—and in it was her ceramic bottle. She pressed it to her lips and tipped it up. Very high up, this time, unlike this afternoon when it had been mostly full.

This afternoon. Ancestors, how was this all part of the same day?

Shilara meandered to them and landed heavily on her backside to Jasen's left.

"Care for a drink?" she offered, and extended the flask.

He opened his mouth to say no—and then thought, why not? He'd relegated himself to dying out in the Luukessian wilds, torn apart by scourge to save the people of his village. If he ever deserved a nip of alcohol, it was this very moment. After all, if Baraghosa reappeared and Jasen made off with him, when would he get the chance otherwise?

He took the flask.

Alixa, to the other side of him, spluttered, "Jasen!"

"Let him be," Shilara said, waving a dismissive hand. "He's had a long day."

He tipped it up, up—this thing really was on the verge of emptiness—and then fluid touched his tongue. Not grain alcohol, like he'd expected; this had a stronger kick to it, a fire that made him want to cough. He *did* cough, in fact, taking the bottle away and brandishing it at Shilara before he could hack a lungful into it.

She chuckled. "I remember my first taste of whiskey. Reacted much the same as you did." And she drained the last of her bottle, tilting her head back so the base of her skull was parallel with the earth. Just for good measure, she patted the bottom of the bottle. Couldn't waste even a single drop. "Liquid gold," Jasen's grandfather had called it.

She deposited the bottle by her hip. Leaning back and bracing on her hands, she looked to the stars. "So what happened? The snake show his slimy face again?"

"He did," Jasen confirmed with a sigh.

"Whose family is he shattering this year?"

"Mine."

Her head turned so fast Jasen thought he heard her neck crack. Sharp eyes bored into him; Jasen felt that penetrating stare even without turning to her.

"Jasen," she said, her voice hard. "That's not true."

"It's true," he said softly. "Baraghosa picked me."

"The boy's lying," Shilara said to Alixa. "He must be."

Alixa shook her head. "He was chosen." She sniffed—as close as she was willing to come to crying in present company.

"Ancestors," Shilara muttered. She fell back, as if in shock. Apparently unable to find words, she repeated it again, accusing the night sky in a gentle sigh of resignation: "Ancestors above."

Jasen murmured, "You can say that again."

Their trio was quiet for a time … and then Shilara twisted suddenly toward him and demanded, "But you're still here; you haven't gone. Did the assembly vote down the deal?"

"My father changed his mind. Three to two, Baraghosa was rejected. Hanrey Smithson wasn't pleased."

"Hanrey Smithson can choke on a clove, bitter old coot that he is. Who was the other? Not Eounice? She is still part of the assembly, is she not?"

"Still there," Jasen confirmed. "Griega was the second yes vote. My father would've been the third, but …"

"Griega, yes, of course—but then she would, wouldn't she; looking out for the village, although if you ask me—no, not my place." Shilara waved away her unfinished thought. "Your father—well, I'd be very much surprised if he had agreed, and that's putting it very politely. Shocked it's taken this long, to be honest. The slippery eel was bound to pick the child of someone on the assembly sooner or later. Your mother ought to be thankful it never happened to any of you nippers," she finished, leaning past Jasen to address Alixa.

Alixa chewed her lip. "Yes, well," she said, "it wouldn't have mattered. The vote always goes three to two."

"Adem Rabinn would've changed his mind in an instant had you or your brothers been selected one year," Shilara told her. "No shadow of a doubt about it."

"Hmm." Alixa sounded unconvinced and lapsed into silence.

The night air breathed softly through. Jasen had heard village elders reminisce about warmer temperatures in lower Luukessia, back in the days before the land was overrun, but the mountains bordering the village were a blessing as much as they were a curse. The valley between them, which condensed the air into a thick mist the scourge could stalk through, also kept the nights from being unbearable. What might've otherwise been a hot lick of air that left the body sticky with sweat was instead a cool kiss of a breeze.

No scent of rot came. Buried by the smell of dust in Shilara's home, then the pungent stench of those awful candles in the assembly hall, the lingering scent of it that had taken root in Jasen's lungs seemed to have finally been expunged. Or maybe that was time. After all, it had been how long since he was out in that field last, gone stock still in confusion as one scourge fought two of its brethren to save him and Alixa? A lifetime, it felt like.

"I don't understand how we come so short each year," Alixa finally said. "Terreas does not double in size each spring. How do the crop-growers fail to produce enough seed to build a surplus?"

"Your mother tends to the fields," said Shilara. "And you've several plots around your home. Did she never tell you?"

"I don't dare ask." Then, after a stilted silence, another small concession: "I'm destined for weaving, not tending."

"Our staples come from grains. Those foods are produced with the seeds themselves. It's difficult to build up a surplus when you're using the crop's new blood to feed the village. Then," Shilara added with a heave, "there is the matter of the south fields. The mountain claims a little more of them each year."

"My mother doesn't speak of it."

"Most people don't talk of things that bring fear to their hearts."

Quiet again. It was not exactly amiable, but between Shilara and Alixa's mutual softening toward each other—other stressors distracted from the improperness of talking to an outcast—it was at least a little more comfortable.

"So why're you out here?" Shilara asked. "I'd have thought your families would be keen to have you home by now."

"I said I'd look for Baraghosa," Jasen admitted. "I told the assembly I'd go with him."

Her steely gaze was on him again. If the sharpness of it had been at all diminished by the drink, Jasen could not tell.

"You volunteered," she said with disbelief, "to go with him?"

"Yes."

"There's nothing out there for you, Jasen," Shilara said. "You could do better than to die in the wilds with a slimy conman, taking advantage of our people. Just because you want adventure—"

"I didn't volunteer so I might seek adventure," Jasen answered quietly. "I volunteered because it's the only way to ensure the village does not starve. But Baraghosa is gone, so …" The sentence ended with a shrug. Easier that than voice the truth that kept turning over and over in his mind—

That Terreas's people would die because of him.

"Then you should count your lucky stars," said Shilara. "There's nothing out there for you. Nothing out there for most anyone. Now think no more of it."

A stony note had entered her voice. The conversation was over, and if it was not clear by her tone, it was apparent a moment later when she collected the ceramic flask from beside her and rose.

"Goodnight," she bade and turned her back on them.

A chill breeze kicked up between them, and on it was carried a lingering note of the last of Shilara's alcohol, breathed from the scant drops left on the lip of her flask. It was almost sweet in the night like this, none of the burn in it …

Whiskey.

Shilara had whiskey.

"Wait," Jasen commanded, up on his feet in a moment, the thought still incomplete in his mind. Why had he caught on that?

Shilara stopped. She looked back, frowning. "Sorry?"

"I said—" He strode to her, crossing the distance awkwardly, which was partly down to the long grass underfoot, and maybe down to the fact that the small amount of liquid he'd partaken of was unfamiliar to him, strong, able to send him just a touch wobbly. He stumbled on the last of the distance, and Shilara stuck her arm out. He grabbed it to steady himself, then eased off lest Alixa huff.

"I said," he repeated, and this short exertion on the last embers burning in him was enough to make it sound breathy, "to wait. I … Shilara, you said that, in your flask—it's whiskey."

"Aye, it is," she said slowly. "Or rather was. Running out of the stuff now."

"Jasen, what are you ..." Alixa started from behind, then trailed off into silence.

"We don't make a lot of whiskey," Jasen said, "here in Terreas. And everything that we do make, it's tightly managed. And yet you …"

"Well, I got some," Shilara said—but she said it a little too quickly. And although the night had muted the world's color into a sea of grey, Jasen was sure that her cheeks would've bloomed with a deep red.

"From the village?" Alixa asked.

"Of course n—" And then she clapped a hand over her mouth, eyebrows arcing up with the same shock that lifted Jasen's almost to his hairline.

"You've been out," he said. "You've passed the boundary." There was a note in his voice of—awe? Surely not, after everything that had happened to him today?

"Keep it bloody well down, would you?" Shilara whispered fiercely. Her eyes darted about, and though the liquor had dulled some of her senses at this late hour, the whiskey especially having eroded her good sense ("*What little she had anyway,*" Jasen could imagine Alixa saying huffily), he thought now that as she probed the darkness for passers-by or hidden watchers, she would be at her peak. The slightest little movement, and she would be on it.

She was still talking: "… anyone knowing my business …"

But Jasen barely took it in. Because there were a thousand other questions suddenly taking shape in his mind, and it was everything he could do not to blurt them in an incomprehensible mess.

"There are people out there," he said suddenly.

Shilara stopped short, favored him with a sharp glare. "There's no one here. Not that it would bloody well matter; whole of Terreas can probably hear you, the way you're shouting."

"There are people beyond the boundary," he whispered breathily.

Alixa made a queasy noise.

"Where are they?" Jasen asked. A new question bubbled up after it, granting no time to stop and answer. "What's out there? How do you leave?"

Shilara's muted look silenced him.

"You leave," she said flatly, "by crossing the boundary."

"But what about the scourge?"

That question came from Alixa. It took both Jasen and Shilara by surprise. They twisted to look at her. Her eyes went wide, as if she'd only just realized she'd said anything, and echoed Shilara by clapping both hands to her mouth, stifling anything else.

"What about them?" Shilara demanded. "Go on, girl. Speak."

Gently, Alixa lowered her fingers. Eyes averted, she mumbled, "How do you keep them from murdering you? They … they try to kill people." A hesitation. "Except Jasen. He's … immune, or something."

Another query hit Jasen, and he whirled, eyes all whites. "Do you have one of the scourge to fight for you? Was it the one that came and fought for us?"

"No, I bloody well don't," Shilara said hotly. If she said "bloody" one more time, Jasen thought Alixa's heart would give in. It had hardly fared very well today as it was. "And would you both stop with that? Scourge do not fight for anyone. They're mindless beasts, dumb as rocks, each of them, but they don't fight for anything other than a meal. Only reason the poxy things share is because their brains have to focus so hard on chewing that their vision gives out. Wouldn't know if one or a hundred scourge were lined up and sharing the same corpse." She tutted, a click that came low in her throat rather than from her tongue on the roof of her mouth. "Mindless things."

"The one that fought to save us had a mind," Jasen said.

She pursed her lips at that, and gave the only answer she could: a terse, "Hmph."

"So where is it you go?" Alixa asked quietly.

"Yeah," said Jasen. "There must be other people, right? If they're brewing whiskey? Are they far? Are they—?"

"*Enough,*" said Shilara. The word was not particularly loud, nor especially hard, but she said it with a force that stilled Jasen's vocal cords. The silence that followed seemed even louder.

"That's it with the questioning," she said. "Both of you." She wagged her finger, which was hooked through one of the loops alongside the neck of the ceramic flask. The subtle waft of whiskey floated in the air again, sweeter than it had any right to be. "My business is my business. As for what's beyond—it does not concern you, nor should it interest you. You've had a lucky escape tonight—yes, *lucky*—and you'd do well not to question it or pursue that snake so he might take you out into the wilds."

"But the seed—" Alixa started, voice a high squeak.

"It'll be fine," said Shilara gruffly. "It's about time this village figured its situation out. Chew up these fields, for crying out loud." She swept an arm over the expanse of grass that led down to the boundary, invisible in the night. Everything was out there. Only the mountains could be picked out, and then simply because they blotted out a jagged portion of the sky. "Plant seed in them. Adjust our staples. Find efficiencies."

"How's that any good this year?"

Shilara huffed through her nose. "It will be fine. And if you're thinking of leaving—both of you; yes, I can see it in your face, girl, though you'll deny it—"

"My name is Alixa," she grumbled quietly.

"—then put it from your minds. You've been saved from a cruel death today. Do not be fools and seek to embrace it."

"But the seed—"

"*It will be fine.* It has before, and it will again."

And without another word, Shilara turned and stalked off, leaving Jasen and Alixa alone and quiet in the chill grip of a summer night.

12

"It's not going to be okay."

These were the words Adem spoke to Jasen three nights later, in a house that felt even more unwelcoming than ever. His voice was quiet, but the words filled Jasen with dread.

A fire burned in the hearth. It was futile, really; the cold that seemed to inhabit the room, all the rooms in this house, was not displaceable

For the past few days, Jasen and his father had barely seen each other. Except for the night when Baraghosa left, they'd barely crossed paths with each other. Intentionally? Perhaps. Jasen had wished to avoid him. When he'd returned home that night—the next morning, really, because it certainly must have been long past midnight when his weary legs brought him back to the stoop of his home—Adem had exchanged scant words with him.

"Did you find Baraghosa?" he'd asked.

"No," said Jasen.

A jerk of a nod. Then: "Good."

Little more was said. They bade goodnight, and momentarily Jasen thought that his father would reach out and embrace him. Maybe not the full-on kind like his mother used bestow upon him, but perhaps a one-armed clutch. Yet he hesitated at the last moment, and both retired to their rooms. Jasen didn't sleep. In the room next door, he wondered how his father fared.

Since the night Baraghosa left, Jasen had kept busy. He did not do so in the village itself, for he quickly learned that he attracted attention there. It wasn't the sort of attention that Shilara garnered on her rare trips through the village. She was regarded with a kind of fear, people stared at her, but kept their words low and muttered as though afraid she would hear, and drag them out to be outcast with her.

To Jasen, however, they spoke openly. The scorn drenched every curse word they directed at him. They talked as if he were the lowliest of insects, dwelling in dirt not remotely deep enough. Others, those who weren't angry, cried. On that first day—that was how Jasen thought of it already, the first day after Baraghosa had gone, after Jasen had failed to find him, thus sentencing Terreas to starvation—he had seen two parents with young children catch sight of him and burst into tears. The first was alone, and a handful of onlookers rushed to console her, biting off snide remarks at Jasen. The second was with her husband, and he turned her away, clutching their babe close between them.

After that, Jasen had directed himself to the outskirts of the village. Although he considered stopping by Shilara's, he opted not to; she'd never before lost her temper with him the way she had on the night of Baraghosa's visit, and though it hadn't been a very violent outburst, there was no denying the tone or the way she had broken off their conversation. She might not hold a grudge the way the townsfolk did, but Jasen did not wish to know for sure.

Instead he loitered at Terreas's outer bounds, killing time as best he could, which was not very well when Alixa wasn't around. Jasen didn't think her absence was any more frequent than usual—Sidyera demanded long hours at weaving, after all, and stretched them yet longer with her rambling. But he felt the times without her acutely. And strange as it might be, he had come to look at those scarlet crescents dug in his wrist with a kind of affection—a reminder, he supposed, that at least someone here still wanted him.

When he was home, it wasn't usually until late, but Adem wasn't there. He often arrived after Jasen had climbed into bed, eyes closed, willing sleep to come. The first night, Jasen had stepped out to say hello. Adem's words were short though, and Jasen had gone back to bed, wishing he could bring himself to say something more.

Was his father avoiding him, the way Jasen had long tried to steer clear of his home until the latest possible moment? Perhaps.

Perhaps he was simply engaged with assembly business.

Tonight, though … tonight they found each other, in a house filled with sad quiet.

Jasen picked at the material under his backside. It felt dusty, though he knew it wasn't. Smearing his fingers together, he tried to dislodge the tacky feeling, but gave up.

It wasn't going to be okay. That was what his father had said.

"Father …" Jasen began, but what could he follow it with?

Adem leaned forward. A low sigh came from him, as if the act of bending forced it out rather than any conscious use of his muscles.

He gripped his temples. Skin bunched into rises around his fingers.

A piece of wood popped in the fireplace.

"We're in trouble," Adem said into the vacuum that followed.

He sounded so resigned.

Jasen bit his lip. "Are you sure there's not …"

Adem shook his head. "No." He sighed again. "We've inventoried the seed, tried our best to see where and how we can make it stretch, but … it's just not possible."

"What about the fields between the village and the boundary?" Jasen asked, recycling Shilara's words from the other night as if they were an original thought. "That's all grassland. Can't it be turned into …" He trailed off as Adem gently shook his head. The motion was tiny, the barest shift from side to side in his hands, but it killed the words coming from Jasen's throat.

"Why?" he finally asked.

"Sightlines," Adem said wearily. "If the scourge ever cross the boundary, we need to be able to see so that we might mount a defense."

Jasen wanted to ask, *What defense?* If they flooded into Terreas in droves, no amount of armed guards could fight them off. One on one, maybe, with a lucky sword strike to the neck. But against an invading army of the monsters?

No chance.

Unless maybe *he* stood at their fore.

What had Alixa called him?

Immune. That was it.

Jasen Rabinn, human shield. That was something he could do.

It might, just maybe, make up for him failing to leave with Baraghosa.

"The farmers and the guards have talked it over at length," said Adem softly. "We grow crops out there, we endanger ourselves yet further." Sliding his head down farther, he rested the heels of his palms against his temples. "Besides, even if we turned every inch of available earth into farmland, it doesn't help us this year. And Baraghosa only assists for the year ahead, not beyond."

And so died that slim chance that Terreas might scrape through, even if it did mean this year they would struggle.

Jasen once again stopped himself from fiddling with the fabric of his seat cushion. He turned fingers to his breeches instead, pulling at them where a line of stitches ran down each side. He kept finding stray ones, and he wondered if they'd been loose for some time, or if perhaps the rye's assault as he stumbled through its clutches had been what dislodged them.

Better not fiddle. This would only damage them worse, cause them to need mending sooner. If Sidyera were here and could see him, she would lecture him for a half-hour on the importance of taking care of his clothing.

"Even Margaut is having second thoughts," Adem said, his voice barely audible.

Jasen's stomach dropped, leaving a hollow behind. Margaut was one of the stauncher voices opposing Baraghosa's deal with Terreas. That she had come to reconsider, even in the short time that had followed, spoke to how dire the village's situation was without the year's annual trade.

He licked his bottom lip, then the top. "Maybe—" he began. His voice came out very quiet, and croaky, as though he had not used it in quite some time, and his vocal cords had half-forgotten how to produce sound.

"Maybe," he said again, and the word was clearer now, although he spoke in the same subdued tone as his father, and it only felt loud in the smothering quiet that wished to settle between them, "I should try to follow Baraghosa. Beyond—"

"No," Adem said.

"—the village—"

"I said no."

"He can't have gone far," Jasen said. How quickly could Baraghosa and his strange lights entirely disappear from sight?

Perhaps he simply snuffed them out, Jasen thought, so as to leave undetected. He was a magician, was he not? Magicians could do that.

But if he were a magician, surely he could evaporate himself entirely, disappearing from Terreas and conjuring himself into being some place a hundred miles away. Maybe on the continent to the west, if the scourge did not roam there too. Or even if they did. Jasen supposed it did not exactly matter; the man could slip through them with ease.

Was he immune too?

"You're not going," said Adem. He spoke with finality. He'd lifted his head now, and his eyes were on Jasen, hard. Anger seemed to fill them, fury the like of which Jasen so rarely saw, yet which was coming out time and again this week. "I won't have you going with that … that sorcerer."

"But what about the seed?"

A pause. Then: "We'll have to find a way."

"How?" Jasen asked.

This pause was longer.

When Adem broke the silence, the hardness had trickled out of his voice. "I don't know." Now, there was only desperation in it, a solitary note.

He'd have heard talk of it these past few days. That would have been all the assembly had been dealing with. Meeting with the farmers, evaluating the seed stores, going over census data, making calculations … all of this would have occupied almost every waking hour for Adem and the rest of the assembly since Baraghosa's departure.

That he did not have an answer now, even the barest ghost of one, after so long assessing their options, confirmed Shilara's immediate view of their situation the night Baraghosa had left. It was difficult to extend their grain supply beyond their current fields without impacting food availability, creating the same problem they were ultimately hoping to mitigate. The gradual loss of their fields to the slow, syrupy stream of dark basalt from the mountain, which ate away at more of their arable land year after year, only made matters worse.

And the population's growth … Jasen thought back to when he was young. Terreas had not grown a great deal in the ten or eleven or twelve years he could remember, at least when he thought over the streets, the places where new houses had been built. Matter of fact, the number of houses in Terreas had hardly changed. Shilara's, after all, was right on the outside where new homes were constructed—yet it was an old place, certainly older than her, and it looked it.

From the skies, Terreas might not have increased its size at all.

Yet when he thought back to when he was a boy of four or five, he recalled fewer children of his age. Now, everywhere he turned he seemed to spy mothers and fathers with young babies. A family with a boy or girl of his age might then have three children all under five, and a growing stomach that indicated another on the way. Homes were rapidly filling, and though those outer reaches of Terreas had only been added to slowly throughout Jasen's life, in another ten or twenty years he thought he'd see a runaway expansion, chewing up the grassy space between village and boundary.

At least, that would happen if these kids would survive to adulthood. With Baraghosa's deal nixed, half their futures hung in the balance.

A dark cloud of guilt settled over Jasen's shoulders.

Damn it. Why had the man left so quickly?

Adem must've caught the distraught look on his son's face, for he said, "Solutions will come from those of us in charge. For you, it does not bear thinking of—finding an answer to our seed conundrum, *or* trying to locate Baraghosa, wherever he now treads. Understand?"

Jasen did, although he felt no better for it. He wished to do something. And he *could have* done something, if he'd found Baraghosa. Short-term, it would have prevented the tense conversations the assembly had been conducting, as well as dispelling the stormcloud that had settled over Terreas. Longer-term …

Children won't die, he told himself.

One life in exchange for many.

It had seemed so terribly unfair, last year more than ever, after Pityr was taken. But now …

"Do not trouble yourself to think of it," Adem said softly, tugging Jasen from his thoughts. The corners of his lips rose in a smile—but it was so awfully weak, and the shadows thrown by the dying fire in the hearth turned it into a grimace. "Go to bed."

"Yes, Father," Jasen agreed—because what else could he do?

He pushed onto his feet and walked stiffly past his father's armchair to the doorway. Partly he hoped Adem would catch his wrist as he went by, the way Alixa did. That he would press his son tightly to his chest, and in that embrace the pain would disappear, running out of his legs the way water was drawn to the earth to pool and vanish into the dirt. Yet Adem did not, did not even say, "Goodnight," and so Jasen left without words of his own either, and after shutting his door and stripping down to his under-things, he clambered into bed and stared at the ceiling.

How he wished he'd been able to say something, anything. That it would be okay, that everything would work out.

Empty words. That was all they would be. Emptier, from Jasen; he was a child, had none of the expertise his father held, had been privy to precisely zero of the conversations that more educated people had shared these long three days. How could anything he said be more than a polite banality?

Still, that did not stop him from wishing he could do something, anything at all.

He turned it all over for a long time, and it all came back to one thing: finding Baraghosa. Yet he was gone, could be anywhere in the world right now—and the world outside was filled with scourge.

Alixa's description for him came back: *immune*. That was what he was. He could walk through them unharmed, like Baraghosa, and find him, offer himself up for the trade.

That simple fact returned: Baraghosa could be anywhere by now.

Jasen could walk Luukessia's wilds for his whole lifetime, and never, ever come close to finding him.

Nothing. There was nothing he could do—for Terreas … or for his father, whose pained face, clutched tight in his hands, Jasen saw in his mind for long hours after his ruminating had come to its end.

13

When Jasen tried to model, in his head, what the aftermath of Baraghosa's departure would look like, he had only one thing to draw on: the death of his mother.

Those first days had been awful, so bad he was convinced his heart had been ripped out, leaving a wound that would never heal. He'd cried with more than his body had to give, racking sobs that left his eyes red as blood, agonized his lungs and stomach as he heaved, over and over, then finally left him an exhausted heap.

Eventually, that had subsided. The pain hadn't gone, though Jasen was ashamed to admit that in the years since it had eased, much as he wished to be broken forever out of loyalty for the woman he'd loved so dearly.

Maybe it would be the same for Terreas too; that the tension that had started so high would diminish as time went on.

He knew every time he considered it, though, that there was no way it would work that way. Maybe to begin with; after all, Baraghosa's seed was useful for the following winter and summer, meaning there was no change to Terreas's fortune immediately after the failed trade. So perhaps in these months, some of the village's disquiet would ease off. However, come planting season as the summer's harvest was taken and the fields replenished for autumn, the shortfall would be apparent—and then return to the forefront of the village's collective mind over and over for the next year, as families found themselves without enough to share among themselves. Parents would give up meals for their children, wasting away to nothing themselves … but those children would not be well fed either, even as their guardians sacrificed their small rations, and they would die.

Anguish would strike again, and again, and again.

And anger would come hot off the back of it, fiery rage that would tear Terreas apart.

But it turned out that even Jasen's modest hope that the Terreas's anxiety would diminish, at least until the issues became more pressing, was misplaced. Over the next two weeks, the tension only mounted. It was like an axe hung over the village, bladed end polished and sharp, ready to drop at a moment's notice—and over Jasen's neck it hung closest of all, filling his stomach with a black, crawling sense of dread. The dread was always there, coiling when he woke and slithering into the night, lurking in the shadows of his dreams.

Today was the worst morning yet.

Jasen and Alixa ambled through the village's outskirts together. She'd taken to sticking by his side, close enough that she might reach out and grab him by the wrist if she needed. A month ago, Jasen would have told her to step away, to give him some space. Now he was glad for her presence. She clung to him for the same reason he was happy for her to cling: to feel less alone.

Out here, the villagers were fewer. But around they were, meandering to and fro, heading to fields for their work, or taking care of chores in and around their homes.

Near every one spied Jasen, and each affixed him with a deathly glare.

This morning, Milton Haynes, a man who was not much past a boy, was out on the stoop of his house. He sucked on an empty pipe and his brow was furrowed as he looked down at a small, leatherbound pocketbook he held in his left hand. His right raked through dark hair, making it stick up in odd tufts.

When he caught sight of Jasen and Alixa, he rose with a start.

"Poxy little blighter," he sneered. "Traitorous little rat."

He looked like he was readying for a fight; his body was tensed, ready to spring. One wrong word, and Jasen was sure he would leap to the path and sock him across the face. Yet he only bobbed there, on his toes, his beady eyes pinned on Jasen and his cousin.

Alixa held her breath. On Jasen's left, she was blocked from Milton. Even so, he felt her hand hover very close to his wrist.

Jasen glanced at Milton and then trained his eyes to the ground.

Keep walking, he told himself. *One step after another till you're past.*

"You're a bleedin' waste of skin," Milton called from behind him. "And a coward!"

The door slammed, hard enough to probably rattle not just the hinges but the entire house, and Haynes was gone.

Alixa loosed a low breath.

"It's okay," said Jasen. "It's okay."

She did not reply.

This had been the way the last fortnight had gone: people shouted abuse at him, and Jasen kept his mouth shut. Why bother to point out that he'd gone after Baraghosa himself, attempting to override the assembly? There would only be a new complaint then: that he had a poor eye, hadn't been quick enough, hadn't tried hard enough. Hell, he'd been accused of purposefully sabotaging the village by offering to find Baraghosa, and then fleeing to a dark alley and whiling away the time until the sorcerer had left.

"I ruddy well saw you, you backstabbing little cretin, and I'll let everyone I see know it for every day till I die!" one particularly animated old woman had screeched into his face. Some eight inches shorter than he was, she'd more than made up for her diminutive stature with a barbed tongue. That she'd followed him, screeching, for almost fifteen minutes had made her even harder to ignore.

There had been a change since those first few days, though. The shouted insults were diminishing. At first, Jasen hadn't really noticed; the slight decline day by day was difficult to appreciate when he was still being chastised at every turn. But at some point it became obvious: most of the people who saw him did not shout, not anymore.

Instead they clustered together, whispering, keeping a close eye on him until he passed. They turned their backs to him to obscure their words, looking back over their shoulders with steely gazes, as if daring Jasen to approach them.

This, Jasen thought, was worse.

When someone was hurling curses at you, you knew exactly how they felt.

Now, they might be talking about anything.

"Something is going to happen," he'd said to Alixa on the mossy rock by her family's vineyard two nights ago. The sky had been streaked with orange and purple, the mountains forming jagged grey shapes in front of it. Little clouds had puffed in the air that night, but the nearest mountain coughed a steady plume of dark smog into the approaching night.

"Don't say that," Alixa had muttered back. "You don't know it will."

"It will," Jasen said softly. "I'm certain of it."

"Like what?"

He shook his head. "I don't know. Just ... something."

Did the adults know better? He wondered late at night, when he felt most powerless—and most afraid to sleep. Could they forecast what might be about to occur?

He longed to ask his father. Assembly hours were long though, growing ever longer since Baraghosa's visit, and Adem's struggle was wrought upon his face every time Jasen saw him. Better to wonder to himself than add more weight to his father's shoulders. They sagged as it was.

Alixa looked back toward Milton's house. She shuddered, and inched closer to Jasen's hip. "I never liked him," she said.

"That's not very proper of you to say," Jasen replied.

"No." She sniffed. "But it's true. Always sitting there on his step with that book. He thinks he's intellectual." Rolling her eyes, she added, "Pityr always said—" And then she cut herself off, falling into silence.

Jasen didn't need her to finish. He'd spent just as much time with Pityr as Alixa had; more, really, just by virtue of being a year older than she was. Pityr's departure with Baraghosa had served to imprint many of his words in Jasen's mind, where they'd surely stay forever.

Milton Haynes, Pityr had said, thought himself better than the rest of the village. He was too intelligent for work in the fields, too smart for menial tasks such as patrolling the boundary, grinding grain, or mending clothes. He was simply better.

And sitting on the step with that book in hand was a grand show of it, a reminder.

Pityr hadn't mocked him, nor had Jasen. Haynes was just another member of his village, another "character," as some of the elders liked to put it.

Today, Jasen despised him for it. And though he would never admit it to himself, he added Milton's name to a mental list he'd been keeping—those citizens of Terreas he would be happy to let starve. Not that he would, if he had a say—though maybe Baraghosa's magic . . .

No. He swept the thought away before it was allowed to bloom. Spite was not a positive quality, and these people were hurt and upset and afraid for their lives. They oughtn't be punished for that.

Still, the smallest kernel of it remained in the back of Jasen's mind.

Abel and Maude Stanhoe rounded the bend toward them. Jasen didn't know them very well; he knew their names from his father's mentions, but little more. They were older, and kept to themselves, and were notable only in that they had a peculiar smell about them every time they passed, sort of musty.

They were looking behind themselves, walking quickly.

"Well, I never," Maude mumbled quietly. "Woman shouldn't—"

She turned and caught sight of Jasen and Alixa.

The harried expression upon her face intensified. Tugging at Abel's arm, she brought his attention forward so he could see too—and then, with a huff, they pressed close together and gave a very wide berth around Jasen and Alixa as they passed, trotting as quickly as their little, aging bodies could manage. Abel muttered something in Maude's ear on the way round—he had to lean up to do so, because he was at least two inches shorter—and she nodded. Never once did her eyes veer from Jasen's face.

Alixa cast a look over her shoulder. It was short, and her head snapped back around almost immediately.

"They're still looking," she whispered.

"I don't expect they can hear you."

Jasen twisted himself to look after the old couple.

"Jasen," Alixa hissed. "Don't!" Then: "Are they …?"

"Still looking, yes."

Alixa groaned.

"What's got into them?" Jasen wondered. "Who—?"

And then, swinging around to peer ahead again, he locked eyes with the person who had so offended Abel and Maude. Shilara Gressom was making her way around Terreas's edge, on the way back from the village center, it looked like: although she carried her usual flask of grain alcohol, she also carried with her a ceramic milk jug. Very large, it had been stoppered with a mismatched lid, and twine was wrapped from top to bottom of the jug to keep it in place. Shilara carried it loosely by the handle; it swung back and forth on two fingers like a pendulum.

"Morning," Jasen said as they met in the path. He tried to sound cheery. He was fairly certain he didn't manage.

"Hello," Shilara said, somewhat flatly.

"Getting milk?"

"Aye," she answered. "Where are you off to?"

Jasen shrugged. "We're just walking. Right, Alixa?"

Alixa nodded. She had a wary look about her, half an eye on Shilara. She'd tucked herself just behind Jasen, falling back only a couple of inches, but enough to put him between her and Shilara.

"Wouldn't recommend going into the village proper," Shilara said. "They're not a happy bunch."

"Oh," said Jasen.

"I've not seen it like this," Shilara went on, shaking her head, "not for a long time. Tension is the worst it's been since … well, days before and after the war, I reckon, when the scourge came. Way this is going, someone is going to get hurt. Maybe a lot of someones."

Jasen's stomach dropped.

"Oh," he said again weakly. What else was there to say?

Alixa took hold of his wrist, gave it a tug.

He turned to her.

"Maybe," she said—and though she bowed her head closer to Jasen, almost whispering, she had her eyes fixed firmly upon Shilara now— "maybe we should go somewhere to get seed." She took a deep, steadying breath. "Maybe that's what we should do."

Jasen hesitated. He glanced at Shilara. If she was aware of Alixa's gaze on her—and Jasen thought she was; it was hard to miss Alixa's dark eyes boring holes like they were—Shilara did not show it, for she had turned her head halfway toward the direction she had come.

Alixa continued: "If only there was someone—" She stopped for a breath, another great one that she drew into her chest, filling it before blowing it out in a single gust. When she spoke again, the quaver that had threatened was gone. "If only we knew someone who knew how to avoid the scourge … and also knew, say—" another pause to swallow; her throat shifted visibly, "—where we might find seed."

Now Shilara did turn her way.

Her expression was icy. "And who do you suppose would go and retrieve it?"

"I would," Alixa said. She caught Jasen off-guard; his head snapped around.

Apparently Alixa had taken herself by surprise too: her words came out a squeak. She clapped her hands to her mouth. Her eyebrows rose, and her eyes flew wide. She looked like she had out by the boundary.

"You would," Shilara repeated, half a question, entirely doubtful.

"Yes," Alixa said fiercely.

"Alixa," Jasen said. "You can't be serious."

She stayed utterly still. "I am."

"But …"

"But what?" she asked.

"It's … it's the *boundary*, Alixa," Jasen said. "You're terrified to go near it. And you should be," he added quickly, fully aware that he sounded exactly like Shilara and his father and mother, and Hanrey and Eounice and Griega, and every other person who had ever dispensed this piece of advice to him throughout his life, and which he had longed to ignore.

"Yes?" Alixa asked, her face blank now, as though listening to something that didn't involve life and death.

"Remember what happened when you climbed over to help me?" said Jasen. "Think about that. That's what it's all like out there."

Shilara remarked, "So you do listen."

"It's dangerous," Jasen finished to Alixa.

"Maybe it is," she said. "But *she* knows how to navigate out there, and to stave the beasts off." She thrust a finger at Shilara, over Jasen's shoulder.

"*She* has a name," Shilara snapped.

But Alixa's fury had been roused, and there was no stopping her from pouring out everything she'd held in these past two weeks.

"Someone has to do *something*," she said, voice high-pitched yet hard, like the sound of a hammer. "If no one does, Terreas is in danger. The people here will wither and die, and on the way they will tear themselves apart. That affects all of us. It affects our families. It affects our future."

Jasen began, "Alixa ..."

"Someone needs to go out there and find Baraghosa—or better yet, find seed another way, so we never have to deal with him again," she said, talking right over him. A tinge of pink had kissed each of her cheeks, darkening with every frantic sentence she spilled. "Whoever needs to go, they need to know what to do out there—where to go." She looked pointedly at Shilara. "They need to know how to survive the scourge." A look now to Jasen.

"I don't know how—"

"You have some kind of immunity to them," she said quickly.

Shilara scoffed.

"And even if he didn't, *you* know how to fight them," Alixa said. "You've done it before, you can do it again."And someone," she said, and here her throat warbled, "someone has to be *brave*."

"Well, that rules you out, chickenheart," Shilara said.

Jasen clenched his teeth.

But Alixa wasn't cut down. Instead, she took another steadying breath. Schooling her features into a look of sheer determination, she stood ramrod straight. She met Shilara's gaze head on. "Have you ever noticed that this boundary is drawn around us like a fence around a herd of goats?"

Shilara pulled back slightly. "Some of us don't take kindly to being compared to goats."

"I am going," Alixa said. "No matter how afraid I am, or any of us are, it is time someone in this village stands up, is brave, and does the right thing—and chooses not to be penned in here to die in fear like a goat. Otherwise we're all ruined. So I am going," she repeated. "I have decided."

Shilara's eyebrow drifted up. She did not say a word; just affixed Alixa with an assessing eye—or maybe this was simply the stare of a woman waiting for an opponent to crumble, to break under the force of her gaze alone, and to cede that Shilara was right.

Yet Alixa did not move.

Jasen gave her a troubled look. "Alixa …"

He wanted to ask how long she'd been thinking on this. When had she come to these decisions? What had that process looked like? When had she decided to bury her need to be proper and speak to this outcast? Why had she decided that it must be *her* to go, Alixa Weltan, fifteen years old, petite and prim, who could not bear to have a single strand of hair out of place? Why her, when it could be anyone else?

All of these questions bubbled up in the face of Jasen's doubt. But he had time to ask not one; for that moment, back from the way they'd come, they heard a scream—

Jasen jerked around to Shilara in alarm. "What's—"

Then more came, all from that same direction.

Shilara broke into a run, pushing past Jasen and Alixa. She thrust her flask into a pocket as she went, stowing it by her leg, and tugging out—was that a *knife* she had, blade concealed in a compartment sewed along her hip and the handle obscured beneath her smock?

"What do we do?" Alixa asked.

"Follow," said Jasen.

He broke into a run—

And then realized:

"*Fire.*"

In the confusion, he hadn't seen it, hadn't picked it out against the dark color of the distant mountain. Now, though, he saw a billow of smoke in the distance, growing thicker by the second.

Something was burning.

A second realization followed immediately on the heels of the first one:

His house was that way.

Jasen's run turned into a sprint. He touched a hand to the pendant at his neck to make sure it was still there—yes, accounted for—and then pumped his legs as fast as they'd go.

Alixa was pounding behind, not keeping pace—but right now that didn't matter; all that mattered was getting around this bend, following that cloud of smoke—

Closer, closer—

His heart raced.

He could hear it now, over the screams, hear flames as they ate at wood, at the thatch of a roof—

Don't be my roof, he sent up the prayer to his ancestors, to his mother. *Do not be my roof . . .*

"Get back!" someone cried—

"—might be inside—"

"I said to get back!"

Shilara hit the junction, forking right—in the direction of Jasen's house, where a building burned, because it certainly had to be a building, going by the size of the black cloud rising heavenward—

She stopped and turned, panicked eyes finding Jasen as he hurtled in her wake—

No, no, no . . . !

She reached out to grab him, but her hands were full, and Jasen dodged, going wide but feeling her fingers graze his skin anyway—

And there it was.

The bottom fell out of his stomach. His vocal cords constricted, cutting off the scream that he wanted to cleave the air with. His lungs tightened, and a black wave of adrenaline surged through him as flames tore through the only home he had ever known.

14

"Fire!" he yelled.

Damn it, why were people just standing there? Why weren't they doing anything?

As Jasen shouted it, the small gathering of onlookers jumped into motion. They sprinted away—to where? He wanted to scream at them to come back, to help him, because the sight of the fire had robbed him of his ability to move, to do anything—what *could* he do? How did he stop this?

Then he realized where they were headed: the well.

Water, Jasen thought. *I need water!*

Another thought hit him at the same moment, ignited by the crash of a beam in the roof crashing down beyond a smoky window—

What if my father is in there?

He made for the door—

Shilara grabbed him by the shoulder, whirled him round.

"What are you doing?" she demanded.

Alixa was behind, terror wrought upon her face.

"My father might be in there!" Jasen cried.

And my mother's things. All her memories. Everything we have of hers.

Panic washed over him, a new wave of it, different than the one he'd felt upon seeing the house. This was not the fear of losing a home—he would be able to rationalize that later, if he tried, because homes were only buildings you stayed in after all—but the terror that he could lose his father and the small collection of mementos he had that were tied to his mother.

He had almost lost this pendant once. He could not lose anything else. Not when it felt like he had so little as it was.

Even the memories he held dear were scant, seeming to become fewer as time went on. There was the story she read, a book with a stream and willow trees—those were the things Jasen remembered—those and her voice, dispensing the words slowly, as though they were sweet candied fruits. He remembered the sound of her sewing, fabric yielding to needles made of bone, as she mended clothes by the fire. She would hum, and Jasen could almost recall the tune she came back to again and again, lilting and slow.

Yet every time he looked over his small handful of recollections, he was certain he had lost track of something else, the way her flowery perfume had eventually faded to nothing from her few frocks, folded and waiting for a woman who would never come to wear them again yet he did not know what memories, precisely, he had lost ... *could not* know.

The pendant was tangible, real. He would not lose that.

That thought steeled him. He would stagger through the flames, enduring their heat—

He turned, stumbling for the house again—

"*Jasen!*" Shilara cried. She caught his arm and clamped down tight on it.

"Let me go!"

"You can't go in there!"

"My father—"

"He'll be out!"

"But what if—"

"If he's in there, it's too late."

The words were like a punch to the gut. The breath was stolen from Jasen's lungs, joining the cloying smog filling the skies. Vying for space with the silvery plume coughed from the cratered mountain, the black streak went up and up and up, a great tower of it, constructed bottom end first.

Too late.

Shilara clutched Jasen's shoulders. "Your father is no fool. He won't be in there."

Jasen began again: "But—"

He pictured the scenarios, a hundred of them all at once. His father had been exhausted lately by so much assembly business. What if he had taken early leave today, returned home for a nap? The smoke might grow strong enough to rouse him—but what had his mother warned him, when Jasen was young, telling him as she extinguished the flames in the hearth? The smell was not always enough to wake a person. And the thickness of it on the air would smother a person before their eyes could flicker open.

That might've happened to his father.

Or what if Adem had been home when the fire was lit? The fire might've started quick, embracing the timber fast, breathing into the thatch overhead. Adem might've panicked, rushing to check on Jasen, to confirm that his son was out of the house. Or he might've known already and instead gone to salvage some of Jasen's mother's things. He'd gather armfuls in a frantic panic—and in that time the flames' rapid spread could have impeded his exit. The roof might've caved in, trapping him—

Jasen swallowed. Tears burned in his eyes.

His father was dead. He was certain of it.

Shilara gripped him harder. "Listen to me, Jasen. You cannot go in there."

He opened his mouth, but

she spoke before he could. "We have to fight this blaze. That's all we can do."

Fight the blaze. Right. Yes. He needed to stop the fire before it could take more of his house, before it could turn it to ash.

He nodded shakily. Swallowed. "Right." His voice was breathy. Behind him, heat seared; he felt his skin warming, reddening even from here, barely a step up the path.

"Come. The well."

Jasen nodded again. Right. Water. That was what they needed. Water, and buckets—

Bucket. There was one in the kitchen, by the door leading out the back—

No, wait. Couldn't get it.

Had to rely on the buckets at the well.

Shilara pulled him into motion. "Quickly now!"

He obeyed. His legs didn't seem to want to do the work. But once they'd started, once he'd wrenched himself properly onto his new task, instead of fearing for his mother's things, his father's life—*stop it, damn it, or you'll freeze up again!*—he sped into action.

Alixa raced behind—and then Shilara was behind as Jasen broke into a sprint.

People had come from their homes. They stared in clusters.

"What are you standing there for?" Jasen shouted at no one in particular. "Help us!"

A few were galvanized into motion. Not all, though.

Not even most.

A few wells serviced Terreas, plus a creek. The creek was too far away to be of any use, snaking toward the opposite side of the village from the mountainside. The nearest well was close enough though, maybe three hundred feet of streets and turns away. Jasen raced for it, bumping into people who'd stopped, looking skyward with confusion at the plume of smoke building in the sky. From here, they'd not know whose house was aflame—so why wasn't anyone *moving*?

"What's happening?" someone called after Jasen as he hurtled past.

"Fire!"

A handful began moving, jogging after him. There were shouts of "Water!" Someone yelled, "I've a pair of buckets—" Another person looked alarmed and hurried his wife back into their house, slamming the door behind.

A few of the first runners were on their way back now, clutching a pail in each hand. They moved as quickly as they could; too fast and the water would slosh out, half of it wasted before arriving back at the flames tearing through the Rabinn home.

A heavyset man, approaching middle age, whom Jasen recognized but whose name he suddenly could not place, had taken up position by the well. He spun the handle as fast as it would go. As Jasen approached, the pail returned from below, dripping water. It was strung up on a rod, tied about the ends on a triangle of rope, itself tied to the single rope descending into the well.

"Hold your bucket," the man said to a woman waiting.

She stuck it out, and he tipped the well's pail, water filling hers.

"Go," he said, and she went, hurrying with just this one bucket.

"Here," the man shouted to Jasen. "Help me thread up another bucket, will you?"

Jasen snatched one up.

He fought with the knotted rope where the first bucket hung. It would not go at first, and Jasen realized why: his fingers were slick with sweat. Taking a panicky breath, he rubbed them down on his trousers, then tried again.

This time it unthreaded.

He slid a second pail onto the rod then retied it in place.

The rod was not quite wide enough for two buckets. They tilted, both pushing the other outward slightly, so neither would come up full. But it was as efficient as they were going to get until Terreas figured out a way to funnel water directly from the creek.

"Get yourself a couple," the man said. "I'll crank this." He was already turning the handle, fast as he would go. Color rose in his face, above the bristles of an untamed beard.

Buckets were stacked beside the well. Yet more lay scattered about the dirt, dropped unceremoniously. The assembly complained about the buckets from time to time, tried to appoint someone to be in charge of putting them away in their rightful place: some storehouse, no doubt even more inconveniently placed. Today, Jasen was as thankful as he had ever been for untidiness.

The two buckets on the rod hit the water below just as Shilara arrived.

The man began cranking the opposite way.

Alixa appeared too, and then a handful of men and one woman who'd obeyed the calls to action. One man's face was streaked with soot. He carried two buckets. Sweat oiled his forehead already.

"Jasen," Shilara began, reaching for his shoulder again—

"Pail," the man at the well said.

Jasen stuck one out just as the two sunk into the well came back into view. They weren't full, obviously, had lost a few more inches of water each than they probably could've carried—but it was still better than a single bucket at a time.

Jasen filled one then stuck out the next. That filled too, he rushed away, leaving Shilara and Alixa behind. Alixa was crying, by the look of it.

So too would Jasen be, if he let the tears come.

The jog back home was terribly slow. He wished he could run, but when he tried to move faster, the water sloshed inside buckets and he had no choice but to slow again with a strangled groan.

A crowd had formed about the house, but
only a handful of people were fighting the fire.

Jasen thrust between two people who were watching. They parted too slowly, and he barked, "Move!" at them. That sped the pair up, though he caught the dirty look they shot him.

The woman who'd taken a pail of water ahead of Jasen didn't seem to know where to throw it.

Jasen didn't either, truth be told. The flames were everywhere. They seared, scaldingly hot. Too close and his skin would blister.

How had he thought he could battle his way inside? The thatch was alight, and through the windows, black smoke billowed, giving way with random currents of air to reveal a molten glow.

Jasen froze. That glow was everywhere.

How had it gone up so damned quick?

That was a question to answer later. For now, he had to act.

"Here," he told the woman and led her toward one corner of the house. Best to start there, wasn't it? He flung one pail and then the other onto the wood, split open, flames licking the air through the gaps. They shrank back as the shower fell across them—but were back mere seconds later, as though he had done nothing at all.

He stared in horror for a moment—

This was futile.

No. It couldn't be.

Turning on his heel, he raced back, shoving through the idle men and women who had come to watch and do nothing at all.

The firefighters were few, and the delivery line they had going was not enough. Jasen knew this as he raced back to the well, passing two people, far too spread out from each other for their water to have much effect. He knew this as he waited in the growing queue by the well, as the overweight man cranked, sweat pouring down his face, and pails were filled, much too slowly, a pair at a time, before the buckets were lowered again to the water that was much too far away …

Shilara caught up.

"Jasen," she wheezed. "Are you—?"

He shook his head, didn't answer. Didn't want to think about it. If he did, for even a second …

His turn came much too late. He bobbed up and down on his feet, unable to keep still. He wanted to be running, damn it, back to his house, back with not just two pails of water but two hundred, two thousand—whatever number it took to extinguish every tiny spark alight in his home right this moment, he would carry them, every pail. He'd empty the damned creek, take ice from the top of the mountain if he had to, if only it meant he could drown those flames and take back his home before everything of value in it—every memory he held dear—was lost.

He hurtled back with two pails, three quarters full.

The smoke cloud had been smeared by a gentle wind now. Now it looked like a tower beginning to topple.

The crowd was larger.

Jasen shoved through—

"Son!"

He turned, almost tripping—

Adem was there. He'd come down the adjacent path almost at the same moment.

He hadn't been in there.

Jasen dropped his pails hard. One fell over, spilling its water across the path. Jasen didn't care, though; all he could do was surge for his father, meeting him in a run, slamming into the man's midriff and holding him tight, holding back tears that cut lines through the soot beginning to accumulate on his face.

"You're all right?" Adem asked. One arm around Jasen's back, he clutched him tight, his fingers tight in Jasen's hair. "Thank ancestors you weren't in there."

Jasen wanted to say, "Thank ancestors *you* weren't." But he was too choked up, couldn't say a thing.

His father pulled back, took Jasen's face in his hands. He looked him over, assessing, checking for damage.

"Are you all right?" he asked.

Jasen just nodded. Finding his voice, he said shakily, "Where were you?"

"Assembly meeting. Willard Rafferty summoned me." The neighbor opposite and across by one. Jasen felt a surge of gratitude to Willard Rafferty, as if by summoning his father, it had been he who'd secured Adem's absence from the flames in the first place. Or maybe it was for having the sense to call Adem here, and inadvertently let Jasen know that his father was alive? He was not sure. Everything was a muddle now.

The heat behind was not helping. His head hurt.

"What now?" he asked Adem.

Adem looked over his head. His expression was pained. "To the well. That's all we can do."

His father helped him up. Jasen collected the pail he'd left—only the fallen one, as someone else—maybe Shilara, as she was just departing through the crowd—had taken the full pail and emptied it over the burning building. Where, Jasen couldn't be sure; for all the work thus far, they'd not made a dent. If anything, the blaze was only getting worse.

He and Adem ran side by side to the well. There, they joined the queue. Alixa was there, and she sobbed, clutching Adem as he asked if she were okay. Shilara listened but did not interject, nor even turn from her place in line. After all, she was outcast; why would she meddle now an assemblyman was here?

They ran back and forth for twenty minutes, half an hour, more. Every trip brought more fatigue. The heat addled Jasen's senses yet further. The smoke made him cough, somehow more pungent every time he returned to the blaze to tip two pitiful buckets of water onto it, hardly drips compared to the fire. Soot clung to his skin, blotting his face, his hands. His clothes blackened.

Still, that vast cloud in the sky grew.

Still, the fire raged in the Rabinn home.

Jasen and Adem had raced back two pails full each, when—

A creaking sound rent the air. Groaning, louder and louder, the front of the house began to buckle—

"Whoa!"

Adem threw down his pail and grabbed Jasen by the shoulder, halting his forward momentum as—

The beam above the front door gave way in a shower of sparks. A fresh dark billow burst forth, adding to the streak overhead.

The roof collapsed. Only there—but new oxygen breathed into the space, and the glow brightened, embers suddenly bright as the sun in the thatch, in the timber of the roof, the walls—

"No," Jasen whispered.

Another firefighter came—

"Back!" Adem cried.

"But the house," Jasen began.

"We can't stop it, son," Adem said.

"But—then what—"

"We've no choice."

His words were like a fire upon Jasen's very skin, burning slow up from fingertip to his face, like it was under his skin, truth a blazing flame he didn't want to feel.

"We have to let it burn itself out."

No.

No, no, no.

But another beam cracked, and another part of the roof gave way, this one across the main room. Sparks belched skyward, carried on a thick plume of smog. A wave of heat came with it, and Jasen stumbled back as it slammed across his skin.

This was it. Their worst fears.

The house was lost.

For a long, long time, Jasen could only stare. His mouth hung open, and his heart thudded hard in his chest. Tears threatened, a sob desperate to ride his every breath. Perhaps the tears *did* come, but the heat stripped them away, turning water to vapor before they could mark fresh channels in the soot marring his cheeks.

His father stood by him, an arm around Jasen's shoulder.

"Come," he said after … how long? Jasen wasn't sure. More of the roof had gone down by then. Fresh patches were alight, parts of the thatch the flames somehow hadn't made their way to until now.

Jasen wouldn't go. Wouldn't. He would stay here, would watch, as everything he had ever known went up in smoke; as those last keepsakes of his mother's were turned to ash and cast into the sky, where they might scatter atop the mountain, or far down the hills of Luukessia. Maybe they'd be carried to the sea.

It didn't matter where they went. Nor did it matter how beautiful she might have found it. These memories were Jasen's, his father's.

They ought to stay here.

Someone had robbed him of them.

And who was to blame?

The arrayed crowd still watched, a mass of them. Barely any had lifted a finger to help. And now he looked at them, truly looked rather than brushing past and shoving through as he fought to save his home, he knew: some of them were *happy* this had happened.

They had watched the destruction of the Rabinn home, would continue to watch it, and thought to themselves: *This is deserved.*

15

"Something has to be done," Jasen murmured.

He sat with Shilara and Alixa. They'd left the house, still aflame. It would take hours before it was entirely burned out. Perhaps not until tomorrow, or even the day after.

His father had gone—somewhere. Jasen heard him say where, voice strained, face tight. Holding back tears? Perhaps. His father never shed them easily, always fought to keep them back.

Jasen had thought on this for long hours, sitting in quiet. Shilara and Alixa had tried to engage him. He had not replied, merely sitting on Shilara's stretch of overgrown lawn, quiet and staring distantly. They'd given up, mostly at Shilara's urging—"He needs some time. Don't try to force him,"—but now his decision was made. And so he broke his silence.

Alixa looked at him. She bit her lip. "What, Jasen?" she asked gently. "What did you say? You mumbled."

"Something has to be done," he repeated. He raised his eyes for the first time in—hours, maybe. Maybe days. "This can't go on. The people out there are scared. They're angry."

"You think they did this?" Alixa asked.

"Yes," said Jasen. He was sure of it, utterly sure. He'd not know who, maybe ever—but someone had set those fires, and not by accident.

Alixa closed her eyes. "Ohh …"

"What do you want to do?" Shilara said.

Jasen pursed his lips.

He thought of the crowd. He'd seen their faces over and over, fighting for dominance with the images of the destruction of his home. Most were indifferent, but a sprinkling of them were pleased this had happened.

Jasen hated each and every one of them.

And yet, at the same time, so awfully conflicting—he could understand. Not totally. But he knew *why* they felt that way. And perhaps, if it were him, he might feel the same too.

It was a peculiar thought, one of only a few Jasen had experienced in his life that felt particularly *adult*. He did not like it … but he felt, low in his gut, that it was true.

He should want to spite these people.

Yet they needed hope. They needed saving.

"Shilara," he said. "The village where you get your whiskey. Where is it?"

She hesitated.

"Please," he prompted.

"A place called Wayforth," she said. "And keep your voice down, would you?"

"Is it inhabited?"

Shilara shook her head. "No one left. Scourge cleared them out."

"So you just … find stores of it?" When Shilara nodded, Jasen continued, "Are there any other stores there, do you know?"

"I haven't picked over it …"

"But a granary? They'd have one, right?" Or have had, anyway. No one there to lay claim to it anymore.

Shilara nodded again, slow. "Aye. They would."

"Jasen," Alixa began.

"We need to go to Wayforth," said Jasen, "and come back with seed. Plenty of it. Enough to fill the fields here in Terreas. Enough to assuage everyone's fears."

"*We*, I assume," Shilara began, "includes me."

"You're the only one willing to cross the boundary," said Jasen. "And you know where you're going. I don't."

"'I'?" Alixa rounded on him. "If you're going somewhere, you're not going alone."

"Alixa—"

"No," she said, over the top of him. "I will not let you leave me here. If you're going, I'm going too."

"It'll be dangerous," Jasen warned.

"So?" Alixa said. "I'm brave!"

"I never said you weren't."

"I can do this."

"Take hold of your horses before they carry you away from your senses," Shilara said. She held up calloused hands to stifle the cousins. "*I* haven't said I'm going yet."

Jasen turned to her. "Will you?"

Shilara pursed her lips in quiet thought.

"Please?" Jasen asked. "Look, I know these people haven't been very pleasant to you—"

She stared at him stonily. "Downright horrible, most of them. You may have had your house burned today, but they've been working on me at a lower level of interest for *years*."

"—but they're afraid. You said yourself: you're worried about what happens next. Well, what happens after this? And the next thing? If Wayforth has seed, we might have a way to save Terreas."

"The seed might not be any good," said Shilara. "If it's improperly stored …"

"We have to trust they knew what they were doing. They survived for centuries before the scourge came, right?"

"Perhaps." Shilara's pursed lips tightened. She looked uncertain, thinking deeply.

"Please, Shilara," Jasen said. "We can fix this."

Silence.

Then, glancing between Alixa and Jasen: "Both of you are up for this?"

"Yes," said Jasen.

"Definitely," Alixa agreed.

"Then we ought to move swiftly," said Shilara. The uncertainty was gone from her features instantly. She bore the look now of a woman in command, a sober woman who knew exactly what she wanted and exactly how she wanted it done. "Tensions are high enough here as it is. If we move quickly, we can neuter them before worse damage takes place—or worse, someone is killed over it."

"Killed?" Alixa cried.

Shilara ignored her. "Wayforth is a few days' travel. The sooner we set off, the better."

"So now?" Jasen said, standing.

"No. Too visible. We'll be gone a while—and no one should know. Not your parents. Not your family," she said to Alixa. "Not your friends. No one knows about this."

Jasen nodded quickly.

"Tonight," said Shilara.

"That's when we leave?"

"We cannot delay," she confirmed. "Another week of this, and—well, it might be your place next," she said to Alixa. "Or the assembly hall."

"Tonight then," Jasen agreed. To Alixa: "You in?"

She'd seemed unsure, as though the spell of her professed bravery were wearing off—or maybe that was the worry on her face at the thought of her home being next. But at Jasen's question, she wiped her expression, replacing it with a determined, steely look. "I'm in."

"Tonight then," Shilara echoed. "Meet here. Can you do that?"

Jasen nodded, and saw Alixa do the same out of the corner of his eye.

"What will we need?" Alixa asked.

"Protection. You've daggers, yes?" At Alixa's nod, Shilara went on, "Clothes. Those on your back will likely do. Pack lightly. We won't be on foot—"

"Are we stealing a horse?" Alixa asked.

Shilara ignored her. "—but we ought to keep supplies to a minimum. Too much to carry, and he'll tire—"

"Who is he? One of the horses?"

"—and we need room for as much seed as we can carry."

Jasen nodded, listening raptly, as Shilara continued thinking aloud to herself.

Tonight, he thought.

Tonight he would leave Terreas, crossing the boundary once again, and willingly.

They'd face scourge, perhaps in untold numbers.

Might they die?

Jasen didn't know. He didn't care. Terreas needed help, badly—

And it was he, Alixa, and Shilara who would save it.

16

Jasen was numb.

He supposed Adem felt much the same.

The Weltans had invited them to stay. Not forever of course, though that was unsaid; this would not, could not be the arrangement forever. The Weltan house was large, but between Jasen's four cousins, his aunt and uncle, and of course Sidyera, who watched haughtily from the doorway to her room, where the curtains were forever drawn but who at least did not say anything—between everyone, adding two new bodies to this house was impossible.

Aunt Margaut had done her best to take care of them.

"Make yourselves comfortable, please," she said, ushering them into the living room. "Morrys, move for your uncle and cousin, would you?" She waved the youngest of the boys—though older still than Alixa by a year—out of the seat he'd been perched upon, watching his family with unrestrained interest.

He obeyed but went only as far as the hearth, where he stood and watched Jasen lower himself onto a seat with plush cushions, as if these people were wild beasts he'd never set eyes on before, rather than blood relatives.

Jasen's bottom touched the plush fabric, nicer than the seats at home—or that *had* been in his home, this morning—

A pang of sorrow went through him.

"We can't," said Adem. "The soot—"

Jasen leapt up, and swiveled to stare with horror where he'd touched down. True enough, a dark stain of soot marked where he'd been. The fabric was dyed a light pinkish sort of color, embroidered with orange, blue, purple and yellow flowers. All bright, in other words—and Jasen's imprinted backside was stark.

"It'll come out," Margaut said kindly. But her lips had thinned, and she did not smile as her gaze took in the sight of the cushion.

"I'm sorry," he said.

"Why don't you change?" Aunt Margaut said. She was still staring at the mark on her chair. Morrys, over her shoulder, had seen it too, and kept looking dramatically back and forth between the dirtied fabric and Jasen. Jasen doubted the boy's eyes could get any bigger.

"Jasen, you're about Morrys's size; he'll have something for you. Morrys, go help him find a change of clothes, please, will you? Adem, come with me. I'm sure Davyd will have something. He's a little broader than you, so it may be a little loose, but maybe I could pin back …"

They disappeared, leaving Jasen with Morrys.

Morrys stared.

"Um …" Jasen hesitated. "Do you want me to …"

Morrys jerked into motion, waving for Jasen to follow. He said not one word though, neither then as he led, or when he brought Jasen to his bedroom, which he shared with Stephan, nineteen and not home. Morrys didn't say anything as he found clothes for Jasen to wear, too; just looked through his drawers, and thrust out a change of trousers and tunic.

"I, err … I think I need to go wash up first," said Jasen. "I don't want to make your things dirty."

Morrys just nodded. He opened his mouth, breathing in as though he might say something, but did not.

Jasen extricated himself, promising he'd be back for the clothes shortly, and made his way outside. A pair of water barrels stood side by side ahead of a trough. The sun had been out enough lately to clear most of what normally filled it, leaving a greyish-white water line against the stone. Jasen pumped the water into the trough, then washed his hands, vigorously combing his fingers across to ease out the caked-in soot. It took an age; the water ran dark, very dark, for long minutes, and still his fingers weren't clean.

When he bowed his head under, he bit back a curse. The trough was halfway filled, and the neighbor's dog strolled up to drink out of it. Dogs didn't know better than to avoid murky water like this, and even if they did, he didn't wish to have to apologize to another of the Weltans as they pretended like it was all okay, faces strained at the sight of Jasen's dirty water.

He pumped one last time with wrinkled fingers, and muscled the trough around. Then he resumed cleaning himself, at least as best he could.

Finally, when his hair was sopping and stuck to his head, and water had run down his tunic and glued it to his back, he surveyed what he'd done. Dirty water muddied the ground beneath him, but only on the surface; the earth was hard, and after a week of baking in the sun and not a drop of rain, the water couldn't penetrate too deeply.

He shoved the trough over with much effort, emptying it entirely. Then he filled the bottom, sloshed it around with his fingers to clean off the black particulates, and emptied it again—easier this time, now it was lighter. Then he shoved it back into place, moving it one side after another. The exertion made him sweat—it really was a heavy thing, thick and all stone—but he was wet already, and about to change.

He dried off with his clothes, stripping down to his underclothes by the vineyard, and keeping a close eye about to make sure no one saw. His underclothes were damp at the top around the back, from where the water had run down his body, but no matter.

Creeping back into the house, he was fortunate to dodge most everyone—

Except Morrys, who he almost collided with as he re-entered his bedroom.

Morrys's eyes almost fell out of his head.

"Sorry," Jasen breathed, and snatched up the change of clothes from Morrys's dresser. "Just changing!" And off he dashed, slipping through the nearest door.

Adem's scavenged clothes were too big for him. Margaut did her best, but they still dwarfed his frame even after being pinned back.

Fortunately, Sidyera was there to proffer wisdom.

"Yes, too big, much too big," she mused, as if that were not remotely obvious to everyone. The spindly woman tugged at fabric, running fingers that seemed far too long across the folds. Her lips puckered, as if she'd eaten something almost unbearably sour—and though Jasen did not stand too near, he detected the same sort of odor he'd smelled on Abel and Maude this morning. Musty again—from being shut up too long. Did she step outside for more than a half-hour each day? If her time in the sun was half of that, Jasen would be surprised.

"I'd have to turn it in here," she droned, indicating places with rough touches. Adem bore them; Jasen was not sure he could have managed the same. "Lose some of the material here, I think—cut it out, I imagine, just down here … oh, but this will need refolding, Margaut, I can't take it in the way it is now. You've done your best, I know, but it's not quite perfect. See down here? I'd need to lift this fold, adjust it like so … then I can—"

"Ouch," Adem hissed, flinching.

"Stabbed you, did I?" Sidyera said, brandishing the offending pin. "Go on, Margaut, you do it."

"Davyd will be back in another couple of hours," said Margaut. "I'm sure he'd be happy to give you some things, just to help tide you over." She didn't sound it, and sure enough: "It would probably be best to visit the tailor, of course …"

"No need to visit the tailor, no need," said Sidyera. "I can do it all here. I've the tools. And Alixa might help. She is slow, but gaining precision, yes …"

"I'll take a visit to the tailor tomorrow," said Adem to Margaut. "Thank you for helping me in the interim."

Sidyera make a noise that suggested she was not well pleased. Nevertheless, she went on fussing, patting almost every inch of Adem. Jasen admired how he could ignore her like that, going on talking softly to Margaut … but this was perhaps one way in which he did *not* desire to be more like his father.

The evening's meal was an awkward affair. To start, there were not quite enough seats about the table, so two extra had to be fetched. They did not match the others, which seemed to cause Margaut and Davyd pain. Jasen's was also quite small. A seat from Morrys's room, Jasen recalled seeing it in his cousin's childhood. Painted bright blue, although now beginning to chip on hard edges, it was a good four inches shorter than the other chairs. Jasen took it at Alixa's side, squeezing in a gap where a person should not be positioned, and came up far below her even sitting as straight as he could.

Sidyera was opposite. She seemed to leer down at him, although she was not a great deal taller than Jasen.

"Terrible business," said Davyd. He shook his head. "Truly awful. So unfortunate."

These were the platitudes repeated again and again. Adem would get drawn in, and for a time they'd discuss what had been lost, whether the assembly might be able to help, if Adem's position would ease that process. Adem was weary though, and none of Jasen's cousins knew what to say (especially Morrys; Jasen hadn't heard even a word from him still). Sidyera, normally so disposed to lecture, appeared to have lost her voice … or, Jasen thought, she had been neutered: he'd caught Margaut having a quiet word with her in the kitchen, something that sounded much like a request to be gentle with Jasen and his father today. She'd obliged, though her puckered lips grew tighter by the hour, and the lines spreading farther across her cheeks. Jasen wasn't sure how long she could hold it. Until dawn, possibly—sleep would help with that. But another evening? Surely not.

So silence reigned, for a time … and then Margaut or Davyd would repeat that meaningless phrase yet again.

Did they think pointing out how terrible it was would take it away? Make it better somehow, that their lives had been lost to smoke and flame, dusted across Terreas as ash?

His mother had once described to him the purpose of a yawn, when he'd asked, inquisitive as four-year-olds often were. She said it was to signal other humans—because humans, like simpler creatures, were animals too, and had their own tics that went unnoticed, often understood, but communicated ever more strongly than words.

Perhaps these words from his aunt and uncle were the same sorts of signals? A sign that they felt it too, this pain that would come, but which was presently a numb buzz in Jasen's chest, not fully comprehended.

He felt, sitting there and pushing stewed carrots and beef about his plate, that perhaps he had stumbled on some greater truth of humanity, but could not sufficiently grasp even a fraction of it. And that part he had?

He hated it.

The evening drew on for much too long. The Weltans continued to offer company and more empty condolences. There were more silences then, and they grew both longer and more suffocating as the candles on the mantel burned down and the streaks of color in the sky vanished into black.

Finally, yet too soon, it was time to retire.

Margaut yawned. Davyd had gone to bed already. Margaut had stayed up, looking anxious. Her hands gripped each other, and she'd been watching her knuckles for the best part of half an hour. Every time she'd spoken, she lifted her head as if she'd been unceremoniously roused from a deep sleep, falling back into it when the short exchange had ended.

"I really should turn in," she said carefully.

"Oh, yes, of course," said Adem. He'd gone fairly still himself this past half-hour, staring into the nothingness just above his chest where he reclined, leaned back as far as he'd go. Now he sat forward, blinking in a daze. "It is late."

"Mm," Margaut murmured. "Are you … do you mind sleeping in here? I have blankets; I'll just go grab them for you." And off she went, a little too quickly.

When she came back it was with a pile of woolen blankets. The heap was large, and very colorful even in the fading light, but hard to deny that they did not appear comfortable: it was a sort of scratchy wool that Jasen associated with thick winter clothes, very warm but not especially pleasant against the skin.

"If you just use the sofa," Margaut said, passing them to Adem. "It's not the most comfortable place to sleep in the world, but for a night …"

"It's perfect," said Adem. "Thank you for your charity."

"Jasen, are you all right in here?" Margaut looked even more apologetic than she had a moment ago. "There's a blanket in there for you too. It's the red and orange one … it's a little smaller." She patted it, at the bottom of the pile in Adem's hands. "And there's one extra, so if you bundle that up … it's not a pillow as such, but …"

"It's just one night," Adem assured her in the kindliest voice he had.

Possibly not just one night, though, was it? Finding a new home might take some time. Then there was the matter of furnishing it, of rebuilding a wardrobe, assembling a new collection of possessions. Jasen didn't have much, but he wouldn't want to get by with nothing forever. A few books would be nice. Keepsakes, if he could find it in himself to want to keep anything ever again.

Nothing would replace his mother's things, of course. Those were gone, turned to ash, carried away on the breeze.

It might not be more than one night for Adem … but for Jasen, it would.

"Come, Alixa," said Margaut, guiding her up with a hand on the shoulder. "Say goodnight to your cousin and uncle."

"Goodnight," Alixa bade. Her eyes caught with Jasen's—and then she was departing. She did not look back. She seemed settled in silence; Jasen could not recall her speaking at all this night.

Adem went around the room, blowing out most of the last candles. Only one was left, an inch or so remaining of it. It didn't have the pungent smell that the assembly hall candles did. In fact, as far as Jasen could tell, it carried no scent whatsoever. If it did waft the subtlest fragrance, it would not for long; the flame was small, barely above the pool of wax beneath it. Before long it would snuff itself out.

Adem handed a blanket to Jasen—not the red and orange one, but patchwork, every color under the sun.

"It's bigger," he said. "You take it."

"Father—" Jasen started.

Adem waved him off. "This one is plenty big enough." He unfurled it, throwing it across his legs and chest. It was big enough, but only just; there was not much loose wool to tuck in around himself. Fortunate that it was summer, and he did not need much to stave off the chill.

He produced a pillow with one blanket and handed it across the space to Jasen, who took it and placed it down where his head would lay. Lowering himself onto it, he adjusted to get it as comfortable as possible. Which was not very, as it turned out—the fibers rubbed at his face.

Perhaps if he were to go completely prone …

Adem sunk down on the opposite chair.

For a time, they were quiet.

"It'll be all right, son," Adem finally said.

That was all. No more, no less. Much the same as their short talk a few days after Baraghosa had gone: he was broken, weight crushing him, and his reassurance was scant.

The words rattled in Jasen's mind for a long time.

It'll be all right.

It would.

Jasen would make sure of it.

17

The candle failed to snuff itself out. Perhaps Jasen had not given it long enough; it was hard to tell how long it had been. What felt like hours might have been minutes. He was sure of only two things: the candle's flickering flame was smaller than ever, the light it cast so dim he could pick out the landscape of this room only by grey edges; and that his father had fallen asleep some time ago, filling the air with soft snores.

How deeply would his father sleep? Jasen was not entirely sure. He'd not been an especially unruly child. He had had unruly *ideas*, certainly, of the world beyond Terreas. But he had kept quiet enough, not challenged his parents the way some wayward souls did about the village. So he had never tested the limits of his father's slumber.

Well, he had to move sometime.

And if Adem woke? Jasen could just say that he was going to the privy.

Nonetheless, he was slow at rising from the seat. Every tiny sound he made seemed far too loud in his ears. And though they were easily muted by his father's gently rumbling breaths, he was convinced that one wrong move, one creak as his bare foot touched the wood floor and it gently shifted to take his weight, and his father would wake up.

And that would be the end of all his planning.

Adem did *not* wake up, though Jasen did hold his breath.

He hesitated at the threshold from the room and turned back.

His father was an indistinct shape on the couch. Only his left leg was decipherable in the darkness, where the too-small cover had slipped away from him.

"I'll be back soon," Jasen whispered.

He would. He had to keep that in the forefront of his mind, or he wouldn't leave. This trip was not like Baraghosa's; he would return, he and Alixa and Shilara. He was not leaving tonight to walk to his death, as he'd expected, but to come back a savior and put Terreas right at least.

He sneaked through the house till he found Alixa's bedroom. The door was ajar, and he gently tapped it with his knuckle. Then, pushing it gently open, he stuck his head through the gap.

"Are you awake?" he whispered.

"Yes," came the response.

Alixa was up in a moment. More catlike that him, she seemed not to make a sound as she padded about the room.

She'd slept in her clothes too. Mostly ready, she scurried about grabbing some last things while Jasen lingered—

"Come in here," Alixa whispered, "before someone sees you."

"What if someone comes in to check on you?"

"Well, then you hide, don't you?" Alixa slid open the drawer of her bedside table, retrieving the small knives she practiced self-defense with. They were sheathed in leather pouches, and she clipped them to a belt she had slung on around trousers; the world outside was no place for a dress, after all.

"It doesn't matter anyway; I'm done," she said, pausing before crossing to him to squat at the side of her bed, reach under, and retrieve a knapsack. "Come on." She handed it to Jasen, let him slip it over his shoulder; then she slipped past and out of the door, down the corridor much more quickly than seemed possible for her quietness.

Outside, the night air was cool.

Alixa gently eased the door closed behind Jasen. It had a latch. If he touched it, no doubt it would whine, waking up the whole Weltan household. Alixa slipped it silently home though, and stepped away.

"Come on," she said, taking the lead.

Jasen followed.

Soft lights lit small slivers of the village here and there. But mostly Terreas was quiet. The moon was nearing full, and it illuminated the village with a frail white glow.

A passerby would pick out Jasen and Alixa with ease, if there were any at this hour …

Good thing they were heading toward the outskirts.

Shilara's house loomed. The curtains were pulled as they were when Jasen and Alixa had last visited: not perfectly. Amber light leaked through the partition. The dust on the panes turned it cloudy.

They quickstepped down the garden. Jasen felt particularly naked and glanced over his shoulder to sweep a look across this little slice of

Terreas. There was no one watching that he could see—and why would there be? Still, it didn't stop the crawling at the back of his neck.

Alixa tapped on the front door.

Shilara's movements inside were noisy in the night's quiet.

She opened the door a few inches, leaning around to peer out.

"You're here," she said.

"I said we would be," Alixa retorted, a touch defensive.

"Mm," was all Shilara replied. She held up a finger—*One moment*—and disappeared, closing the door behind her. Some rustling … and then it was opened, and in one swift motion Shilara was out in the moonlight with them, the door shut with a dull clunk.

She had about her a satchel, slung low around her waist—and on the other side, sheathed at her hip—

"Is that a sword?" Jasen whispered.

"Of a sort," she said with disinterest. "I'd call it more of a dagger, personally."

Alixa cast it a look Jasen could not miss even in the dull light of the moon. Her lips were tight, and her eyes slitted. She averted her eyes without saying anything.

"Where are we going?" Jasen asked.

"Stables," said Shilara, already setting off.

"What about your fireplace?" Alixa asked, throwing a pointed finger up at the misted window. Orange light still crept through the gap between curtains.

"It'll burn itself out."

"Or burn another house down!"

"I leave it going all the time. It won't. Now would you bloody hurry up? We've not got all night. I'd like to set off before dawn."

Alixa breathed a *humph*. She argued no more—though she did take a few glances back at Shilara's home as she and Jasen rejoined the path and followed along behind her. When Alixa looked over her shoulder the last time, to see that the building was out of sight, she stifled a soft groan.

Jasen patted her wrist and lifted a low smile. He doubted it was reassuring.

Shilara stood not much taller than Jasen. He had never seen her determined before, at least not until today, hurtling toward the blaze that swallowed his home. Now, he saw how quickly she moved when she was. Marching far faster than she ought to be able to, she easily outpaced Jasen, and even more so Alixa, without seeming to expend any effort whatsoever.

"What are your supplies?" Shilara asked over her shoulder.

"Waterskins," said Alixa, "some changes of clothes. Hard cheese, salt pork." Sniffily, she added, "Cutlery."

"You bring any plates along too?"

Whatever Alixa's response must have been too impolite to say, even in current company in the dead of night, when they were leaving the village, perhaps to face death head on; she worked hard on clamping her jaw tight. A muscle in it twitched from the effort.

"Have we missed anything?" Jasen asked.

"Plenty," said Shilara. "Some of it obvious, much of it not. Don't you worry, though. I'll have us covered. Not like you've done this before."

"No," he agreed.

That didn't seem to placate Alixa. Her expression was still tight.

The stables were toward the north side of Terreas. Adjoining a field presently knee-high with leafy plants, it housed a grand total of six horses: four stallions, plus two mares kept in reserve.

Jasen had rarely come this way before Pityr left, and his visits were still infrequent. Alixa liked to look at the beasts though, and he'd followed her now and again. A cursory fence was built around the halved field the horses shared, and Alixa wondered if the horses could communicate; the mares were separate from the rest, to avoid unwanted foals, but they and the stallions tended to cluster when they weren't grazing or being ridden, all in a group by the fence between their paddocks.

The fields were empty, and the stables quiet.

Shilara let Jasen and Alixa in by the door, holding it with an arm.

"Hurry it up," she said. "And quiet; if they're startled, this becomes tenfold more difficult."

"I know," said Alixa shortly.

The stables stunk of straw and manure and the faint ammonia of urine. The horses must be about due a mucking out; probably tomorrow, by the looks of the straw that had spilled from the horses' enclosed sections into the corridor forming the building's spine. It was wadded in clumps.

Shilara led the way down the aisle.

"Which are we taking?" Jasen asked.

Beside him, Alixa craned her head to peer. The horse on the left was asleep lying down.

"Milo," said Shilara. "The village won't miss him."

"Do the stablemasters know we're borrowing one?" said Alixa.

"Oh, aye," said Shilara. "I came up here earlier today and told them so myself. 'I'll be needing to borrow a horse to take a pair of youngsters out of Terreas,' I said." She shook her head. "'Do they know we're borrowing a horse?' What a ridiculous question to ask."

Alixa's tight expression grew tighter, but she did not reply.

Milo was stabled in the farthest pen on the left. Black and white, he'd parked himself against the back wall, lying down but awake. He turned his head as Shilara, Jasen, and Alixa came into view, and regarded them with round brown eyes.

Shilara clicked her tongue on the roof of her mouth twice in quick succession. Jasen had heard the stablemasters doing the same as they corralled the horses in the adjoining fields. A command, or perhaps just a noise that the beasts found particularly interesting; whichever the case, it did the job. Milo clambered to his feet and clopped to the gate.

"Evening, lad," said Shilara. She ran a hand from his nose, up his head and down one cheek. "You're coming for a ride."

"Are we getting on him?" Alixa asked. There was a note of excitement in her voice, displacing the irritation a moment before.

"Course not." Shilara opened the gate outward and gestured for Milo to come—another little command the stablemasters had taught him to follow. He obliged, hooves clicking against the stone as he passed the uneven threshold where the straw underfoot suddenly thinned to a thin dusting, most wadded in urine-soaked clumps. "Three of us on the back of one horse? Milo might not mind, but we'd not have the most comfortable time, crammed in together." A shake of the head. "Engage your brain before you ask questions, girl."

Alixa's dark frown returned. She glanced away and folded her arms.

Saddles and bridles hung from the wall. Shilara took a set while Milo patiently waited. Then she geared him up—Alixa did her best not to look too interested, although Jasen caught her stealing glances, frowning all the while—and quietly led Milo, plus Jasen and Alixa, outside by the way they'd come.

"Where to now?" Jasen whispered as they passed the closed door. "The boundary?"

Shilara shook her head. "Back home," she said. "The long way."

"We aren't setting off?"

"I still have things to get. I've a wagon."

A wagon? Shilara would've had to have made off with that too. Not *stolen* it exactly; Terreas had a collection of wagons that could be borrowed as needed. They were few in number though, needed for little more than transporting harvest. Jasen hoped the village wouldn't miss one, but suspected they might.

It's not for long, he told himself. *Only till we're back. That won't be an age.*

The path Shilara took them on was even longer than Jasen expected. It wove around the edge of Terreas itself, right out onto the outermost pathway, cut alongside the fields and then open green. They passed the fields at the base of the nearest mountain, the one that breathed a plume of grey smoke skyward each day. Rock had flowed down its side from a cleft high up. Now and again it glowed orange, and everyone knew what it signaled: another spill of molten stone was coming to take away yet more of their land. It didn't take much each time—but those small amounts of lost land added up. At the current pace, in twenty, perhaps thirty years, Jasen could see it beginning to devour the closest houses too.

Back at Shilara's, she led Milo and Jasen and Alixa around to the back. The wagon was parked there, as close to the house as it would go. She'd managed to scavenge branches from a sapling somewhere and slung them over it. Fairly redundant; when Jasen asked, she said she'd taken the thing after dusk fell, wheeling it with her hands, which he found impressive, though she waved him off and said it was easy enough with your hands, rope, and time.

"Clear that off," Shilara instructed Jasen and Alixa, pointing to the rudimentary camouflage. "Front end first, so I can hook Milo up."

They stepped forward to obey—

Alixa gagged.

Jasen stopped in his footsteps. He'd detected it after she had: the stink of meat and blood. And not good meat, either. This was just something dead, and though the night had cooled, the dead creature had not expired this night. It had been killed a day, two days prior—and the heat had started to dial up its scent. From a distance, it wasn't obvious, cool night air breathed through the mountains wafting it away. But up close, it caught in the back of Jasen's throat.

"What is that?" Alixa choked out. She retched.

"The discarded remains of two pigs and a cow," said Shilara. "The wagon's covered in it; horse will be too. There are buckets in the back for us."

Alixa had gone entirely still.

"For us?" Jasen asked.

Shilara explained, "Scourge aren't carrion-eaters. We'll attract flies by the swarm, but scourge? If we catch their attention, it'll be visually, or by happening across one. Smell won't draw them in." She fiddled with Milo's bridle, realigning it to attach to the wagon. "Go on, help me out. We haven't got all night."

Jasen stepped toward the wagon.

He saw it now: under the thin, patchy layer of branches acting as camouflage, the wagon itself looked wet, and not very uniformly—a bloody coating, complete with, in places, thin strings of fat that had become glued to the wood.

He levered up a branch—

His knuckles grazed a damp plank. It was cold and tacky. A thread of liquid clung, thinning and drooping as he brought his hand away, until it snapped.

Ugh.

"Give him a hand, girl," said Shilara. "Can't have your cousin do everything."

Alixa still hadn't moved. She seemed not to dare to even look at the wagon—

"Go on," Shilara prompted.

At that, Alixa looked around. She met Jasen's eyes—and in them was fear—before finding the wagon at his side.

A pained sort of noise warbled in her throat.

"It's only a bit of blood," said Shilara—but though she had the tone that Jasen had heard adults putting on around children when they knew better, there was a touch of glee in there too. "It won't hurt you."

Alixa looked as though she thought it very well *could* hurt her—

"Night's ticking away," Shilara said. "What happened to being brave?"

That got Alixa moving. She was stiff though, and she gagged again as she came to the wagon's edge.

"It's okay—" Jasen started to reassure her.

"Oh, ancestors," she moaned, loosing the first branch with the lightest touch, clutching a leaf between a thumb and forefinger. She flicked it to one side very slightly, letting it drop as soon as was physically possible.

She reached for the next—

The wagon jolted, and her fingers brushed wood.

She yanked them back, staring horrorstruck at the darkness marring her fingertips.

Shilara clamped down a grin from Milo's side. "Whoops. Thought he was getting flighty. Seems calm now, though. Carry on."

Alixa began a soft murmur to herself. Jasen could not pick it out, but when he glanced sidelong at her face, she looked petrified. Every movement she made to clear away the branches was incredibly delicate and hesitant, as if she was assessing the cleanest possible points to touch.

But it would be futile. Shilara's words rung in Jasen's mind, as they surely did in Alixa's: there were buckets in the back for them.

Shilara had affixed the horse at the same time as the wagon was cleared of its camouflage.

"Good work," she said. "Now hop in the back and grab those buckets, would you?"

Alixa looked queasy.

"I'll do it," Jasen told her.

He hefted himself over the side—a particularly ungainly way of clambering aboard a wagon, but it got the job done.

There were supplies stowed in the back, mostly in sacks, so Jasen could not pick out what they were. Changes of clothes, probably; something they could lay across the wagon's raised sides and stow themselves away for the night should a downpour start too? There would be sacks for the seed Shilara planned to take. Waterskins—that was probably the fattest sack, leaning oddly against one side.

At the front were what he sought: two buckets. And they were awful. Packed to the brimming with inedible organs and trimmings, they were a mass of slick darkness. As Jasen took the handle of one, sleeping flies were jolted to life, and flitted into the night en masse. The second yielded another miniature swarm.

He climbed down via the front, sitting to do so, then brought the buckets round.

By the wagon's side, he waited.

"Go on then," Shilara said impatiently. "Get to it."

"What are we doing?" Jasen asked. He was certain he knew the answer—the wagon itself was a reasonable template of what was expected of them—but he wished to hear Shilara's instructions. For if he were wrong, he would only know from her mouth … and oh, how he wished to be wrong.

"Cover yourselves in it," said Shilara.

Jasen looked down. He felt a sudden touch of faintness.

Alixa, at his side, gagged.

"Oh, bloody hell." Shilara stepped to him, and took one bucket. Dropping it at her feet—the contents made an unpleasant wet noise—she reached in, picked up some discarded lump of flesh, and began to smear it across her face. She shut her eyes and pressed her lips firmly together to prevent any creeping into her mouth.

"Well, go on," she said as she moved on to her neck and opened her eyes to see Jasen and Alixa had not moved.

He cast a glance at his cousin.

If she had been horrified before, this was another level of disgust entirely.

"Sorry," said Jasen.

He reached into the remaining bucket, slowly …

It was cold and greasy upon his fingertips. A shudder ran up his arm, breaking him out in gooseflesh. The blood seemed to be partially congealed—or maybe it was just the cool night making it seem thicker. It coated his fingers like a thick oil, his palm …

The thing he removed looked like a liver. It probably wasn't—the butcher used those—but Jasen didn't know what it might've been.

Not that it mattered. He had one task now: covering himself.

Looking apologetically again at Alixa, he shut his eyes tight, pressing his lips as hard together as he could, and began to rub it over his face.

The smell was wretched. An iron tang so close to his nostrils it delved into his lungs. He coughed, almost gagging—how could Shilara be so unfazed by this?—but pushed on, telling himself, *My face is the worst part. It'll be easier after this.*

Alixa still hadn't moved when Jasen dared to open his eyes.

"Chop chop, girl," Shilara barked.

Alixa tried to speak. No sound came from her mouth.

"Get your words out. Come on."

"I can't," Alixa said. She sounded strangled.

"If you don't do it, you won't be crossing to Wayforth," Shilara said.

Alixa let out a low noise, pale in the bare moonlight. "But …"

"I mean it," said Shilara. She reached into the bucket and lifted a fresh handful of viscera. "Now get to it."

Alixa watched in horror as Shilara rubbed the bloody organs across her face again, darkening the color to a murky pitch as a new coat of blood was laid on top of the old. She scrubbed them from her forehead down, and the organs brushed lips pressed tight—

Alixa gagged, turning away. She brought up nothing—but it sounded as though it was a very, very close thing.

Shilara smirked. "You'd never make a butcher, would you?"

"Butchers don't rub innards across their faces," Alixa said.

"You're gagging and you haven't even started yet," said Shilara. "Not much bravery here at all."

Jasen bit his tongue. Shilara and Alixa could be as bad as each other, and standing here now, as Shilara lorded it over the girl's discomfort, he did not believe this would be the last of it.

But Alixa was brought into jerky, disgusted motion. With pained eyes darting to Jasen, she reached for the bucket—

She gagged again.

"It's okay," said Jasen. "The face is the worst of it. I promise."

Alixa didn't reply. A trembling hand dropped into the bucket . . .

Her fingers made contact with the bucket's contents. She made a high-pitched noise that came from her throat—her lips seemed afraid to move now, as if an organ might launch itself down her gullet if she parted them—and retracted her hand—but she pushed on, sinking it lower, lower . . .

Again, Jasen didn't recognize what was lifted clear. A gelatinous blob of some kind.

Maybe if Alixa could pretend it *was* a gelatinous blob, and not the interior of some gutted animal, she would fare better.

She lifted it to her face, very slowly. She stared at it in her hand, drawing closer, her eyes getting wider and wider . . .

Then they clamped shut as it was just inches shy.

It remained there.

Her lips were locked tight. A moment later, she gripped her nostrils with the fingers of her free hand, locking them closed.

She made a sound again, a high-pitched noise between a sob and a squeal, and pressed the organ to her cheek—

And promptly vomited, bringing up a fountain of bile.

Her retching went on for a long time, punctuated only by Shilara's muffled laughing fit.

Eventually, Alixa's vomiting petered out. She continued to retch, dry sounds that produced no fluid. But the sheer act of emptying herself of the meager contents of her stomach seemed to exhaust her both physically and mentally, for with Jasen's help she applied a covering of animal blood. It was a slow task, and every punctuating gag made Jasen flinch back, in case she somehow found a new source of liquid and sprayed him with it. She did not—and, looking beaten down, she was finally coated in blood and stank to high heaven.

"There," said Shilara. "That wasn't so bad, was it?"

Alixa gave her a weary look and said nothing.

"Mount up, you two," Shilara instructed, climbing aboard. "You'll ride behind me. Go on, now. We've spent long enough dallying as it is."

Jasen boarded and Alixa followed, taking care not to place themselves near their supplies.

Sitting was unpleasant. Blood had turned their clothes damp, and sitting pressed them against Jasen's legs and torso. They'd inevitably stick. He dreaded tomorrow, when the warmth of the sun dried it against him. He should be happy, he supposed, he did not yet have a man's thick layer of body hair; there was less to get matted.

Shilara got Milo moving. He'd been covered too, and had taken it much more graciously than either Jasen or Alixa.

Jasen leaned against the wagon's side, watching the village grow smaller behind them, ignoring the bucket stowed next to him—the remaining animal blood and organs, for when it came time to re-coat themselves.

Alixa sat opposite, determinedly not looking at it. Instead, she wrung her hands and gazed at the wagon's floor with a long, far-away stare.

"I always dreamed I'd leave the village someday," he mused.

Shilara said, "Mm?" over her shoulder.

Jasen nodded, though she could not see. "Didn't dream I'd smell of death when I did so, though."

Alixa murmured, "I dreamed that when I left the village, it *would* be when I smelled of death."

Shilara smiled. "Prophecy fulfilled then."

The horse and cart trundled down the trail. It ran along the edge of the boundary for quite some way; close enough that Jasen could pick it out, and the amorphous shape of the rye beyond, whispering in the cool breeze, but not near enough that he would be able to touch it …

Or see any lurking scourge beside it, watching with those dark eyes of theirs.

The boundary did not run the entire way around Terreas. Mountains cupped one side of the village, and this was where the wall gave out. A gate had been erected here; Jasen could not think of a time when it was ever used excepting Baraghosa's visits. Perhaps not even then; the man had peculiar ways about him, could probably use strange magics to cross without needing to touch the gate at all.

Shilara dropped down to open it.

It groaned as it slowly swung wide.

"Rusty hinges," Shilara complained.

She did not clamber onto the cart again, instead leading Milo by his bridle.

Jasen held his breath.

Beyond this threshold lay nearly untrammeled wilderness, rarely crossed. The world stretched beyond, a Luukessia he'd spent his whole life wishing to tread. Now, at last, he was going to.

It should have been a momentous crossing. Yet the cart simply rolled over—and they were on the other side.

Shilara returned to close the gate. Then she climbed back onto the cart, pausing before taking Milo's reins to fish for a spear, which had rolled into the corner where cart floor and edge paneling met. She said nothing, and nor did Jasen and Alixa; she merely repositioned herself, keeping the spear gripped in one hand.

Milo began his canter again—and they were off.

18

Dawn came slowly, spears of pink-red light stabbing through the clouds and brightening the sky by degrees. What had started an indigo backed by a few stars became lighter as the stars faded, blue gradually replacing them.

Light had been filtering into the sky for a good hour now. Perhaps longer. Jasen believed he had slept, though only briefly. Whether Alixa had, he didn't know. All he did know when he blinked his eyes open was that she had taken up position by Shilara's side and the sky was suddenly lighter than it had been.

More surprising, she was asking questions.

"What else is in Wayforth?"

Wayforth? Jasen blinked in confusion. Then he remembered: the village Shilara had promised, where she had found stores of whiskey to pilfer.

Shilara started to give a clipped reply.

Jasen tuned it out. Rubbing his eyes—and then biting back the urge to retch when he remembered his hands were coated in slowly drying blood—he swiveled to look out over the landscape.

Terreas sat near the mountains, on highlands. Though the direction opposite the mountains formed part of the highlands too, it seemed that the other side of the mountain began to descend to lower-lying places. A trail was carved in the mountain's side, or had been once. Shilara directed the horse and cart along it now, gently easing down the mountainside. There was still a way to go, by the look of it; Jasen could see the twisting trail winding below them, turning back and forth like a ribbon.

Up here, the mountainside was not barren, but nor was it particularly rich with foliage. The nutrient-rich soil seemed to have been spewed mostly in Terreas's direction, not down the mountain's edge itself. The ground was rocky, covered in stones. That Jasen hadn't woken earlier was a surprise: the ride was bumpy, mostly composed of small judders but now and again peppered by a larger jolt that sent a bolt of pain up his spine. The little that grew was scrub: stunted trees, spindly bushes. Grasses sprang up in occasional clumps, thin yet tall, eking out existence in the small pocket they were permitted before their roots found unyielding stone again.

Farther down the mountain, the soil was better. A wood was spread out below them. It was a peculiar sight, and one Jasen scoured for long minutes, eyes roving back and forth across. He had seen distant trees, scant few of them springing up along the mountains, and of course Terreas had its own share, carefully tended and renewed now the scourge had rendered the rest of Luukessia inhospitable. Yet he'd never seen them from above, from such a distance. They were tiny and hard to discern, but the strengthening light cast bright patches and long shadows among the treetops, giving them a craggy texture. He imagined reaching out and touching it, and extended a hand to do just that before realizing they were still miles away.

They were probably teeming with scourge.

He hunkered down in the cart, gaze drifting about them and back the way they'd come.

Terreas was long out of sight. Now a mountain stood between Jasen and the place he had lived all his life.

The hairs on the backs of his hands stood up. He rubbed them, and wished he'd asked for a blanket. Shilara would've packed some of those, wouldn't she?

Alixa had a new question: "And there are no people in Wayforth at all?"

"Not one," said Shilara. "Don't you listen? I said as much yesterday."

Yesterday. When Jasen's home had been burned to the ground. It seemed so long ago.

He touched the pendant about his neck, reassuring himself of its presence. Though often cool, where it lay against him and had absorbed his body heat these past hours, it was just slightly warm.

"I just want to know what we'll find there."

"I've told you that, too," Shilara snapped.

"Well, how long will it take to get there?"

"Two days," said Shilara. "If we aren't stopped."

Two days—so a four-day absence.

What would Adem think? Aunt Margaut? The rest of the Weltans?

Would anyone miss Shilara? Jasen squinted at her back, and

doubted that were the case. This had been a trip she had made before; certainly if she did have a friend, someone would have missed her for half a week.

Four days gone at a time, and no one noticed. Jasen felt a stab of pity—then guilt, realizing that in all his time haunting Shilara, lingering at her side and listening to her gripes, *he* hadn't been aware of her disappearances.

He tried to put it out of his mind, as well as the rest of Terreas. The next four days might be difficult for them, filled with fear. But Jasen and Alixa would return, with seed, and secure a safe, well-fed future for the village that did not include Baraghosa.

And Jasen would be welcomed back into the fold. No more whispering, no more heckles. Shilara too, he thought.

"How many times have you been to Wayforth?" Alixa asked.

Shilara groaned. "Cease your bloody questioning, will you? Or I'll prod you in the belly with this spear." And she brandished it. The haft thumped against the cart's edge.

Alixa quieted for a time.

Jasen sat silently too, looking out. The woods were around and behind them—and as the cart came to the spot where the ribbon of a trail curved back on itself, winding down the mountain a little lower than before, he realized it would soon vanish too, as Shilara continued ahead, along a new trail. This was even more uneven that the last, and the vibrations increased.

The sky grew lighter and lighter. The sun still had not risen, but the early morning half light had given way to a softening blue. Few clouds had gathered yet, at least anywhere near to the mountains. But a white puff was growing directly overhead: the cratered mountain continued to breathe its endless plume of smoke. From the foot of it, it looked strangely large.

"Hold these." Shilara thrust the reins at Alixa, then crawled to the back of the cart. "Awake then," she observed of Jasen as she passed. Rooting around for a moment in a sack by the waterskins, she came out with a ceramic jug, stoppered and wrapped tightly with twine to keep the stopper in place.

When she'd taken up her place at the front of the cart again, she drank.

The smell of grain alcohol carried over her shoulder. Mingled with the coppery smell of the bloody bucket, it was less appealing than it had ever been.

Alixa met Jasen's gaze. There was a judgmental look on her face, one that said, *She's starting early*, though neither said a word.

Soon, Alixa began to question again.

"But how many times *have* you been to Wayforth?"

Shilara groaned. "I don't know. Enough."

"Could you make a rough estimate?"

"A thousand. I've been there a thousand times in my life."

"That seems unlikely."

"Of course it's bloody unlikely." Shilara took another swig. "What does it matter if it's two or twelve or two hundred? I've been before. I know where we're going."

"Well, how often do you go?"

Shilara groaned again. Developing into an exclamation, it was louder and longer than the last.

In the pre-dawn light, Alixa's lips quirked up just for a moment.

Oh. So this was it. It had become a game. One did something to irritate the other—being snooty over the idea of socializing with an outcast, for example—so the scorned person retaliated, perhaps by laughing as the other vomited after covering themselves in blood and guts. So then the first party retaliated when they saw an opening—in this case, bombarding Shilara with questions and taking joy in her mounting frustration.

Four days of this? Dread settled in Jasen's belly and a sigh worked loose from lips glued together by animal gore.

When Alixa began her next query, Shilara cut across. "Would you just shut your mouth?"

"I'm only asking—"

"I don't care. I've had enough of it. Scourge have *ears*, don't forget. They won't be drawn to us by scent, but if they hear enough noise, they will come looking. Shutting up is for your sake as well as mine."

This also quieted Alixa, for a time.

Then she whispered, "What did Wayforth do?"

Shilara snapped back, forgetting her own advice entirely, "What do you mean, what did Wayforth do? What does Terreas do? It was a village, not a person."

"But what did—"

Jasen roused, climbing to his feet and pushing to the front of the cart.

"What—?" Alixa began. Shilara shot him a dirty look.

"Is that ...?" he began, staring, wide-eyed.

Then Alixa saw it too. She let out a sharp gasp. Pushing to her feet too, she bowed forward, clutching the edge of the wagon.

A stretch of water had come into view around the mountainside. Jasen hadn't noticed it at first, easing from the left around Alixa. Now it had passed Shilara, and the light of a distant sun had cast hair-thin bars of light across its surface, so it no longer blended into the sky.

That was *water* out there.

That was …

"Ocean," he murmured.

"Is that it?" Alixa asked. "The sea?"

"Yes," said Shilara shortly. "And sit down, would you? If either of you topples over the side, I won't stop to get you."

Jasen lowered himself unwillingly. Still, he watched, transfixed on the ocean.

It was so far away—much farther than Wayforth, certainly. He could not see its edge: the land rose and fell many times between. Distant rises were a dark, dull green, possibly devoured by yet more woodland. Yet they were so distant that Jasen could not make out any of the texture like the one they'd passed. And that sea, that grand ocean, separating Luukessia from the continent to the west, was even farther away.

The enormity of it was not lost to Jasen, not now he'd seen it, nor as it came more and more into view as they ambled around the mountainside. And though he squinted, trying to pick the barest hints out from the horizon, he saw no sign of the distant continent—and west was that way, he was certain of it.

So much water. It stretched so far.

And it was glorious.

"It's only the sea," Shilara griped. She took another drink of alcohol; a long one this time, more than her usual nips.

Yet Jasen and Alixa continued to watch, staring at it with wide eyes as the sun rose, casting more lines of bright light across the surface, short-lived glints that were birthed and died before Jasen's very eyes.

He breathed in, deep, hoping to catch its scent. What *would* it smell of?

For now, he could not taste it. But he would dream of it, he was sure, his mind conjuring answers.

Perhaps, if this jaunt for seed went well … perhaps he might venture out again.

Perhaps he might breathe it in himself.

He grinned and devoured that endless expanse of purest blue.

19

It was mid-morning when Shilara pulled up to a sudden stop.

Jasen had been dozing again, Alixa next to him. Though most of the way down the mountainside, the sun hadn't quite managed to reach them. The long shadow draping them was chilled, and though not as frigid as the night had been, it wasn't much warmer. Combined with their bloody covering, which had mostly dried on their skin but not their clothes, Jasen and Alixa both had come close to shivering. A woolen blanket pulled over them didn't seem to help a great deal, but the body heat from sitting side by side at the wagon's edge was a benefit.

The stop jarred Jasen awake.

"Ssh," Shilara hissed immediately. Her voice was no longer frustrated, as when she had told Alixa to shut up, but tense.

Something was happening. And it made the lingering fog of his fatigue evaporate in a moment.

Alixa perked up beside him. She looked out with round eyes, pupils darting this way and that.

More trees surrounded them now. This was not a woods; barely was it a copse. But there were enough to either side of the bumpy trail, and more spread out beyond, that they were shielded from much of the view up the mountain as well as down it.

What they did not shield, however …

Jasen's breath caught.

Skulking out from between two trees came a scourge.

It was hard to believe it had been … how long since seeing one? A fortnight? That, like the destruction of his home, seemed like a lifetime ago.

The beasts hadn't changed—and of course they hadn't. This was like any other: too long, too grey, too wrinkled, too bare of down except a few stray, over-long and wiry hairs, and black pits for eyes.

Its mouth hung open. Spittle damped its lips, or the place where its lips would have been if it had any.

It crossed the trail—

Jasen watched it move. Though he'd seen several up close recently, most had been in the rye just beyond Terreas's boundary. Only a thin strip of land permitted him to take note of their loping movements.

This one was the first he'd seen move throughout any reasonably-sized stretch of open space. He watched it pick its way across the trail. Its paws, tipped with claws that would run Jasen through in a heartbeat, trod almost carefully—yet it was graceless too, all its movements were. Its body curved upward, rather than running perpendicular to the ground like a dog or cat or fox. And so its back legs came in strange, shuffling sort of movements. The things could put on a burst of speed well enough, that Jasen knew first-hand. But for a sedate pace, they were designed all wrong.

It paused two-thirds of the way across the trail. Its head twisted this way and that.

Jasen felt Alixa tense beside him as its dark gaze fell upon the cart.

But it did not look at it long. A mere glance, the opening of the holes that were its nostrils to scent the air, and then it prowled the remaining distance to the opposite embankment, which was demarcated from the trail itself only by the fact the soil lifted in a small rise. The cessation of this trail's use had otherwise blurred it into the surrounding terrain.

The scourge disappeared in a gap between the trees.

Jasen released the breath he hadn't realized he had been holding.

Still they were silent. Waiting. Shilara would want to let the scourge put ample distance between itself and the cart before moving off.

He was just about to lean forward and tug on Shilara's sleeve, to ask if they were going to move yet, when Alixa tensed again at his side. She loosed the lowest gasp he had ever heard.

He turned to her—and then followed her wide-eyed stare of terror.

Another scourge had broken loose from between the trees, the same side the first had come from. It prowled out, level with the cart.

Jasen's stomach plummeted. It was right beside them, in almost a straight line from where he and Alixa sat. Ten feet of space, plus the cart's wooden edge, was all that separated children and beast.

With unnatural movements, it padded out onto the trail, and paused.

Its head lifted. Its mouth fell open, revealing a maw of teeth, the tongue and fleshy mouth the color of a fading bruise on diseased skin.

And the smell …

The first had been just far enough ahead that the gentle breeze, snaking around the mountain, blew its deathly scent away. The smell of this one, though, could only waft over the horse and cart. It was the smell of rot, of death, musty and rancid, bitter yet sweet. It cloyed, sticking in the back of the throat. One whiff was enough for Jasen to clamp his mouth closed, to tug his smock over his face, trying to bury it with the smell of his own sweat, come on suddenly strong as a wave of fear spilled over him, mingled with the blood from the dead animal guts he'd swathed himself in last night. Yet though that salty, coppery tang was strong, it could not dislodge the scent of the scourge. That had sunk right to the bottom of his lungs and would not be displaced, as though it were oil and he was trying to remove it with water.

Another slipped out—and then another, and another.

Behind, Jasen heard the low, strangled sound of a scourge breathing, and the soft padding of its footfalls as it meandered out of the trees.

They were surrounded.

The smell grew stronger.

Alixa grabbed for Jasen's wrist. Her nails dug in, hard. He let them, sinking his own into his palms the way she did.

If Shilara were fazed, he did not know; he did not dare look. All he could do was stare at the pack that had crossed paths with them, four to one side of the cart, at least one to the other. Five scourge, three people. Poor odds.

He huffed a breath. Oh, it was so rancid! His own smell made it worse, terror on top of rot, on top of death.

He was sweating through the blood. Shilara's camouflage would be rendered useless by the sheer potency of his own body betraying him with preemptive sweat to cool him for the moment he burst off of the cart and broke into a frenzied run from the threat—

No running here though. Running would only get him killed. Get *all* of them killed.

The scourge nearest traipsed forward, gait awkward.

It came to the edge of the cart …

Jasen stared, eyes bugged and wild. The beast was right beside it. If he and Alixa had sat on the opposite side, it would be able to lean forward right now, and press its nose to them, inhaling …

Its nostrils widened. It sucked in a breath. Exhaled.

Ancestors, the *smell* …

Alixa felt it too, Jasen was certain. She had drawn blood, he thought, so fierce was her grip.

If it stopped her from spilling the bile in her stomach, let her, damn it. Let her.

The scourge lifted its head. It sniffed again.

Wants to find us, thought Jasen. *It can tell. Shilara's cover isn't good enough.*

And whose fault was that? His own! His body had rapidly slicked.

He would give them away. He would betray them—he, who had wanted this mission in the first place.

The scourge tilted its head. Its eyes, so black and seemingly unseeing, considered the cart's bulk.

What was it thinking? Wondering what this obstruction was? Perhaps it recognized it as a man-made thing, an object that its meals—or at least its ancestors'—had occasionally accompanied.

Just how long did they live? How long were their memories?

Not important, he thought.

But it could be. For if this one had stumbled upon a cart decades ago, when the scourge had come to infest Luukessia and bring the people inhabiting it almost to extinction, it might well know that carts came with dinner. Lo and behold, a new cart here, where there had not been a cart before ... something must've put it there. Something worth hunting.

It let out a noise from its throat. Like air escaping a confined space, it was more of a sigh than anything. Yet it signaled another, and this scourge wandered over, picking its way across the loose rock scattered across this grassy trail, its walk lumbering and awkward.

People, Jasen suddenly thought. *The way they walk—it's like a person, bent funny.*

And now he couldn't un-see it. For his whole life, he'd thought them like dogs, canines stretched into unnatural, disproportioned bodies. Yet now he saw men, malformed, from some cruel nightmare. They'd been twisted forward, their bodies curved, held in place as if they had been skewered upon a hook.

He felt sick. He was going to be sick.

Don't, he begged himself. *Please. Whatever you do. Do not be sick.*

The new scourge came from the front end of the cart. Jasen turned just a fraction to see it.

It approached the horse.

The horse whinnied softly.

"Hush," Shilara whispered. The word was barely audible, the faintest breath—yet in the stark quiet filled with the breaths and footsteps and awful, strangled noises of the scourge, Jasen picked it up like a klaxon.

The scourge stopped. It twisted its head.

Dark eyes considered the horse.

Milo brayed again.

The scourge began forward—

"Ancestors," Shilara muttered. Gripping her spear, she slipped off the cart's front as lightly as was possible and joined Milo's side. One hand rested upon his flank, trailing along his body as she approached to stand alongside his neck.

Milo shifted, throwing his head to one side. The reins shook, a pair of metal links clicking—

Shilara gripped him. She was not as tall as the horse, but tiptoed so she might whisper in his ear.

"Easy," Jasen picked out. "Easy." She repeated it over and over, slow, and getting slower each time.

Easy, Jasen willed Milo with her. *Easy*.

The scourge that had stopped came nearer … nearer …

It was close enough that it could reach out now—

The horse shifted uneasily—

Jasen clenched his fist tighter. Probably drawn blood himself now too.

The horse could kick, he thought suddenly. It might rear back, thrusting its legs out. Would a direct impact to the scourge's head kill it? Horses were powerful things, Jasen knew; he'd heard stories of boys kicked in the head whilst bothering horses, boys who had never been able to bother them again. But a boy's skull and a scourge skull was not the same.

Could be, he thought. Almost. If they *were* men, once.

He closed his eyes.

If Milo kicked out, there was a chance it would daze the one scourge, maybe even kill it, though it was a long shot. But four more of the creatures—plus maybe a fifth, if the one to their rear was the not the first they'd seen cross—the odds were still too thin. No, he had to hope the scourge passed, and he and his party could continue their passage to Wayforth.

Something was grinding.

Jasen creaked an eye open. He looked on in confusion—

"It's eating the tree," Alixa whispered—or did she mouth those words? No, it was a whisper, deathly quiet; Jasen had not been looking at her and so could not have read her lips.

He turned very carefully in the direction of the noise.

The one that had peered into the cart had gone back to the edge of the trail. There, it gnawed the trunk of a tree. Its head moved up and down, teeth gnashing, as if it were trying to find purchase and failing over and over. The bark must have been hardy, for it withstood the assault without dislodging—but then the scourge pulled away, chewing on thin air for five long seconds, and Jasen saw the wounds it had drawn upon the tree's surface. The gouges were pale yellow. Wood had splintered along the grain, and stuck out. Amber sap trailed down exposed innards.

The scourge resumed its gnawing, lower down now.

The one testing Milo's scent seemed to have given up. It lingered for a long time, staring, now and again cocking its head from one side to the next. Then it whined—like a dog, Jasen thought, just a dog—and departed across the way, stopping on the right side of the trail. There, it stilled, not moving again except for the turn of its head as it stared, unblinking, at the trees along the bank.

Those, Jasen saw now, had gouge marks of their own.

What were they doing? Was food that scarce for scourge now that they had taken to eating bark?

Just how much of Luukessia's wildlife had these beasts decimated?

Jasen did not know. Nor did he care. All he wanted now was to be free of these monsters and the stink of decay that hung around them. Whether that was Wayforth, or back in Terreas, he did not care.

Just let us be free of them.

Yet they did not go. Though Shilara continued to wait, softly patting Milo's neck and whispering on her tiptoes, the scourge had taken up position here and did not intend to move off. They chewed on trees, they staggered back and forth along the trail, slipping in and out of the trunks … but they did not move on.

"When is this going to end?" Alixa whispered.

Jasen shook his head.

The seconds piled up slowly, turning into minutes that went on much, much too long.

The sun had not caught them here. But as it slipped behind a growing puff of cotton white cloud, the temperature seemed to drop yet further. Goosebumps rose on Jasen's skin, the hairs sticking up.

And still they remained.

"Blasted vermin," Jasen finally heard Shilara whisper.

She turned to them. Catching their gaze, she touched a finger to her lips, and made a slicing motion: shut up, at all costs.

He nodded once.

Slowly, very slowly, Shilara began to walk. She gripped Milo's rein, and gently tugged. He threw his head to one side again, shuffling his feet—and the noise was like thunder in the quiet, so terribly loud, so *obvious*. The scourge would come to investigate again, they would, and that would be the end—

Yet for now they did not. Two turned their heads, peering, and Jasen held his breath the way they seemed to, the shallow noises ceasing as they listened and watched with those blank eyes …

Milo was eased into motion.

It was slow. Every step was tentative—but loud.

The cart was worse. It did not creak; no rust on this, like the gate leading out of Terreas. But it carried weight, and the turning of the wheels beneath was constant. It was not a noise Jasen had ever really noticed before, or at least paid much attention to; it became background sound, reaching the ears but filtered out when it reached the brain. This morning though, as it droned, the wheels twisting, metal turning, carrying so much weight …

The scourge turned to watch. All but one ceased gnawing.

Shilara continued.

Jasen froze. Panicked.

Should he call out to her—or whisper, at any rate—to stop their movement?

She's done this before, he tried to tell himself. She has made this journey before. She knows what she's doing.

Then he felt a hot breath on his neck from behind, exhaled in a puff that caused another fog of death and decay to fall upon him, and all thoughts evaporated. All that remained was a hot, black sensation of purest terror.

It's behind me.

It is behind me!

Jasen braced … and as he'd feared, the scourge pressed its nose to the back of his neck.

It was cold and dry, like before … and it felt awful. Icier than the shadows, more frigid now the sun had left them, the chill seemed to be transported directly into Jasen's spine. It ran down like glacial waters. The gooseflesh of his arms became only more pronounced, and he gasped for a breath he could not draw.

The scourge breathed, in and out, nostrils pressed to Jasen's skin …

The cart trundled gently past, separating them.

Jasen clamped his eyes tight, waiting for it to follow.

It did not. But Alixa breathed the slightest, softest breath, and if she had softened at all these last long minutes, she turned rigid again. Her nails dug harder into Jasen's arm, which must have gone numb before this latest squeeze reignited his nerve endings. But the pain was good. It meant he was alive.

It also meant the scourge had pressed its nose to Alixa, and was breathing her in too.

Jasen tensed, waiting. For what, he was not sure. His mind told him that he waited to spring into action—but if the smell of carrion was not enough to put off this scourge, if it did indeed detect a living being it might devour, Jasen would be able to do exactly nothing. The beast would lean forward and snatch Alixa up by her head before Jasen could turn; and in the time it would take for him to grab up one of Shilara's stowed weapons, Alixa would be dead, beheaded by the beast's jaws and torn asunder as the pack descended—

Stop thinking of it.

Yet he could not rid himself of that last conjured image: Alixa's belly split open, and a long cable of intestine stretched between two hungry scourge.

Painful seconds grew, compounding. The cart continued moving. Alixa must be clear now. Jasen did not dare look to confirm it. He simply closed his eyes, breathing shallow breaths—that slightly sweet smell of rot nauseated him, made his stomach twist in discomfort, made him will himself over and over not to vomit—and he waited.

The scourge shifted, shuffling. One made a noise that might've been a haggard breath; another responded from some distance behind.

One began its gnawing.

Shortly, another joined. Then another.

If the rest resumed, Jasen could not tell. Slowly the sounds grew fainter, and in any case three gnawing scourge could easily be four or five, or even ten. Perhaps more, the farther the cart rolled.

Eventually, they were gone, lost to the noise of the cart itself, of Milo, and of Shilara, gently easing the horse along.

Jasen dared open an eye.

The world seemed unnaturally bright now. He squinted against it. The sun was out again, and somehow it had managed to catch a small strip of land here along the mountainside.

Shilara clambered aboard the cart again.

"Remain still," she instructed in a soft whisper.

Jasen did not nod. Nor did Alixa, as far as he could see. No need to confirm anything; he had absolutely no intention of making a sound.

The ride sped up after that, but not much. Shilara was intent on taking things as carefully as possible. If it would spare them from any other scourge that might be skulking these parts, then Jasen was happy for her to progress as whichever pace she saw fit—as long, of course, as she was progressing.

The miles grew.

Eventually, Shilara sighed. "I think we're clear."

Relief settled over them. But it was weak, and Jasen did not feel much better for passing this danger. After all, another three and a half days of this lay ahead. And the route to Wayforth soon split from the mountain—which meant it would divert into even wilder parts of Luukessia, where scourge might tread en masse and unseen—until it was too late.

20

They continued to ride in relative quiet until midday. It was only then that the sun rose high enough to crest the mountains, dazzling them with long overdue warmth. Jasen felt a stab of envy for the people left in Terreas when finally the sun's rays did kiss his skin; they hadn't waited this many hours to be warmed.

He thought again of his father, and Alixa's family. But he stifled the thought: ruminating too long would only make him morose. And in a few days, they would be back to Terreas anyway. Their families' worry would be short-term. The seed the three of them would return with was a long-term solution that would easily compensate for the stress of these next few days.

Still. Perhaps they ought to have considered leaving a note.

No, Jasen told himself. People would only try to follow then.

The excitement provided by the sprawling vistas had deserted Jasen. Alixa too, by the looks of her; she kept her head down and her lips sealed. Little conversation had passed between any of them these past few hours.

The longest exchange had been ten minutes ago, when Shilara said, "We'll stop for lunch. That okay with the two of you?"

"Yes," said Jasen.

Alixa nodded agreement.

Shilara steered Milo to the edge of this trail—though it could scarcely be called that; now traversing the edge of an open field, whatever dirt track had been cut through was long overtaken by grass and weeds. Only a spindly stretch of fence remained as a ghostly reminder of a past when people had ridden through here regularly enough to kick up dust and flick stones and leave a trail of horse manure in their wake.

"Packed bread and meats and cheese," Shilara said. "In the sack by the waterskins. There's not a great deal, so go easy on it."

They dismounted. For Jasen, it was the first time in hours; he'd clambered off once, perhaps an hour before running into the scourge, to empty his bladder. Alixa had either stayed put all night, or at least most of it, perhaps climbing down when Jasen dozed before dawn. How her bladder was not yet bursting, Jasen didn't know.

Then again, Alixa would likely wait until she was a hair's breadth away from rupturing. It would not be very proper to squat out here and wet the daisies—even if only Jasen and Shilara were present, backs turned.

The sack the food was stored in had a dusty smell, like old curtains. It had seeped into the food too, Jasen realized as he took a bite of the sandwich he put together, sitting by the cart's edge. Still, food was food, and musty-smelling food was likely to be as good as he got these next few days.

Alixa considered the sack with a dour expression.

"Go on," said Shilara. She marched around them, carrying a bag of oats for Milo. "Eat up."

"Can I wash my hands first, please?"

"No," Shilara barked. "Don't even think about it. We've a bucket of innards between us to last the rest of this trip. We can't waste it on re-covering any body parts."

"But—"

"No buts," said Shilara. "We had a narrow escape back there. I don't intend to make our chances slimmer by chancing a scourge getting a scent of your knuckles. Now hurry it up. We haven't got all day. This is a quick stop." To herself more than Jasen or Alixa, she muttered, "Bloody scourge slowed us down enough back there."

Alixa sadly compiled a sandwich. She looked as down on her luck as she ever had.

When she bit into the bread, tinged a subtle spot of brown, she retched.

Shilara did not mute her smirk. Nor did she appear to try to keep her smile down as she rounded the cart again.

"Nothing wrong with a bit of blood," she said, squatting to make a sandwich of her own. The bread, she handled roughly, with nary a care for the bloody fingerprints she left on it. "Never eaten black pudding?"

"No," said Alixa.

"Missing a treat then, you are." Shilara slapped another slice on top of the slab of cheese and equally thick hunk of ham she'd laid upon the first. She rose, took a great mouthful, and collected her spear into hand. "I'll keep watch," she said through the half-chewed mouthful, and sauntered off.

Alixa pursed her lips tight, but said nothing. She did not finish her sandwich.

"You'll regret that later," Shilara observed when she came back.

"I won't," Alixa said.

Shilara smirked. "Never felt hunger so bad you'd be willing to eat your own arm, if you could stomach the pain to take a bite out of the thing, have you?"

"No."

"You will," Shilara promised, and she climbed back onto the wagon.

The afternoon ride began in silence. That quiet pervaded, carried through the afternoon.

At around two o'clock—it was hard to estimate; time seemed to have lost its meaning outside of Terreas—Alixa began to fidget. It was subtle at first, but gradually her twitching grew more and more pronounced.

Maybe she'd had finally reached the point where she could hold it in no longer. Time to give it to impropriety and just empty all this backed-up fluid—and there would be a lot—by the trail.

She didn't say anything though. So Jasen asked, "What?" Perhaps she would say something if he offered her the opportunity to; easier to save face that way.

"My legs ache," she muttered.

"Sitting in a cart all day will do that to you," said Shilara from up front.

"How do I ease it?"

"Stretch your legs. Lean forward. Touch your toes. When we've stopped, make the most of it." Shilara shrugged. "It's about the best you can do."

Alixa did as instructed, stretching her legs out in front of her as far as they'd go, and leaning to touch her toes. She seemed to struggle; being cooped up for some twelve hours had done wonders in making her rickety and stiff. Jasen would've followed suit, but then he wasn't entirely convinced he could've touched his toes before anyway, so what was the point?

"Those scourge earlier," Alixa said. "Have you run into them like that before?"

"Couldn't tell you if I've seen those specific ones, if that's what you're asking," said Shilara. "Do run into packs of them from time to time. Just have to take it slow." A pause. "Damned things don't usually hang around for as long as those did though." Another pause. "Might have to take another route home, if they've set up shop there." A third pause, longer, filled with the sound of Milo's hooves and the cart's wheels turning. "Maybe not. Might be even more scourge-filled."

She fell into quiet. Though Jasen could only see her back, he pictured a long frown on her face, eyebrows drawn together and her lips tight.

"Where does the other path lead?" Alixa asked.

"Terreas."

"Does it skirt the mountain?"

"No."

"So how does it get back to Terreas?"

"It's a wider route."

"What sort of—"

"Oh, would you just be quiet, girl?" Shilara said. "I need to think. And keep watch. And listen. A scourge happens upon us, I want to have warning, like the ones we ran into this morning. You talking distracts me."

"I was only asking," said Alixa. Her voice became very small.

Shilara didn't look back. "You like to hear yourself talk too much, is what I think."

"Well, that's rude." Alixa crossed her arms. Turning to Jasen, she began, "Did you—"

"Ssh," Shilara ordered—and this was the same noise as earlier, a tense warning, rather than mounting frustration.

Alixa silenced. Her frown dissolved into a wide-eyed look about the cart.

Jasen pivoted to stare too as Shilara brought it to a stop.

This was not the worst spot to have stopped, in terms of safety from the scourge. Jasen figured the worst was probably the field of rye—or perhaps in the mists clinging to the base of the mountains in the morning. In the rye, you had only the rustling of stalks to give the scourge away before their scent assaulted you. The mists were surely worse: grey and thick, a scourge would easily blend in, only that pair of bulbous black eyes to be seen, stalking ever closer. Jasen hoped to never add that to his growing list of experiences with the creatures.

Nonetheless, this spot was far from ideal. Here, the cart rolled through scrubland. Green grass had given itself over to drier land, most of it dying off as hard, packed earth took over. Hardier plants had found a home here instead, bushes with small, rubbery leaves that clung to a tangled mass of branches. Much of these plants were exposed, and like the spindly trees rearing skyward amidst the carpet of brush, they looked dry enough that a spark would light the entire hillock.

Pressed low, a scourge could stalk the cart with ease.

A whole pack, even.

Shilara listened, craning her neck.

Jasen followed suit. His heart was in his throat again, thudding hard against it. He felt sick.

The tang of death was in the air.

Or was that simply him expecting it to be? Waiting for it?

A breeze came. It rustled the scrub. Dry branches creaked, rubbing together. Knobbled and thin, they reminded Jasen of a frail old man's fingers, laced together, joints bumping together over and over as he swept them back and forth, back and forth. It was a papery sort of noise, that rubbing—and it seemed to come from all directions, terribly loud. When had it gotten so noisy? How had it ratcheted up like this, on just a faint breeze, enough to mute the approach of any scourge lying in wait?

How could Shilara know where they were coming from?

Something rustled behind—

Jasen twisted, a wave of panic washing over him, pumping adrenaline into his veins—

A scourge crept out from between two scraggly bushes.

Jasen's heart skipped. *Damn it.* How many more of the things were there?

The scourge turned in the direction of the cart. It peered through black eyes, turning its head to either side—

It started forward.

Alixa gasped.

"Quiet," Shilara whispered. "You'll attract more of the damned things."

But Alixa twisted back to Jasen. Her eyes wide, she said, "I think that's the one from before!"

"Shut up," Shilara hissed.

Jasen frowned. "What?" he mouthed.

"The scourge we met by the boundary! The one who saved us!"

"Would you shut your damned mouth?" Shilara said. She had a wild look about her. "Do you want to draw a whole pack to us?"

"It doesn't go with a pack," said Alixa, though how she could be sure of that having only seen it the one time, Jasen didn't know. "It's by itself."

And right this moment, it had joined the crew by the rear of the cart—right up against it. It reached over the back wood panel, neck extended, staring. Its mouth opened—the rotten smell about it intensified all at once, strengthened by its breath, as it leaned forward to sniff at the sacks in the back—

"Too far, scourge," Shilara growled. She leapt down, spear in hand. Ducking Milo's reins, she stormed around the edge of the cart.

"What are you—*no!*" Alixa shrieked. And she leapt up and over the side, landing awkwardly, then sprinting.

"You're bloody scum, that's what you are," Shilara told the scourge as she came around. She adjusted her hold on the spear, drew it back—

"*STOP!*"

Alixa threw herself in between scourge and spear, holding her arms high.

"Move it, girl," Shilara said. "That thing'll tear your head from your shoulders just as soon as look at you." And she jabbed out with the spear, feinting around Alixa's side.

Alixa jerked across—not in the opposite direction, but toward the thrust, stopping Shilara in her tracks.

Jasen stared in open-mouthed confusion, stuck to the spot.

"It needs to die," said Shilara, "before it draws even more of them."

"It's on its own," said Alixa. "And it's friendly!"

"No such thing as a friendly scourge. If I've said that once to you, I've said it a hundred times."

"But this one is! Look! I'm right here—and it hasn't touched me." Yet Alixa did not sound entirely sure of herself, and as she spoke those last words, she dared a glance over her shoulder, just to make sure the scourge was not bearing down on her with its massive jaws.

It hadn't. It continued to sniff around the contents of the cart. Alixa might not be there at all.

Jasen watched it, expression drawn. "Alixa, how'd you know this is the same one?"

"It has a scar," she told him.

"Plenty of scourge have scars," Shilara growled. "Stupid things get roughed up all their lives. Deserve it, too."

"I … I just know it is, okay?" said Alixa. "It looks the same. There's something … in its eyes. Right, Jasen?"

Jasen peered into those black orbs, looking for whatever it was Alixa had seen. Whatever it was, he couldn't find it though: all he saw was black, and maybe, if he squinted, the faint ring of an iris almost as pitch as its pupil. Even that, he wasn't sure about.

"Uhm," Jasen said.

"It's the same one," Alixa said resolutely. "I know it is."

"Well, then it's made the wrong choice today," said Shilara. Gripping tight on her spear's haft again, she told Alixa, "Move."

"No!"

"That thing needs spearing before it draws more to us—or changes its mind."

"You can't kill it!"

"It would kill you!"

"No, it won't!" Alixa shouted—because for all Shilara's talk of quiet, this butting of heads had become a full shouting match here in the scrub. "Look!" And to demonstrate, Alixa turned to the scourge, took a deep, steadying breath—and she reached out to touch its flank.

The beast twitched, the way a cat did when taken off-guard by a gentle pat it had not seen coming. It turned to Alixa, twisting its neck to peer down at her. If the scourge changed its mind, it could tear her limb from limb in a moment.

"Alixa," Jasen warned, panic rising—

The scourge bowed its face toward her. Alixa braced, panic washing over her determined expression. She retracted her hand, and Jasen knew in that moment that she had made a mistake, that her pride, her conviction, her desire to prove Shilara wrong in whatever way she possibly could, had done her wrong here—

Shilara reached out to grab Alixa's arm, to pull her clear—the spear rose in her other arm, ready to throw—

Jasen scrambled forward, aware that he could do nothing at all to help—

The scourge's mouth opened—

And before Shilara could intervene, before Jasen could, before the drop of sweat beading on his temple could drip to his eyebrow, the scourge stuck its tongue out, and licked Alixa's hand.

It *licked her hand.*

Jasen stared, gobsmacked.

The scourge's greyish tongue came away, and the dried blood that had been caked to Alixa's palm was almost gone.

It closed its mouth—then gagged. It was a peculiar sound, not like anything Jasen had ever heard. The scourge twisted, coughing and retching in its strange way, till it spat up a lump of something black—then it smacked its mouth, the way babies did, turned back to Alixa—she was frozen in place, eyes bugging out of her head—and licked her palm again.

Then, strangest of all, it lowered to its knees and bowed its head.

What. The hell. Was that.

Shilara's reaction was much the same as Jasen's and Alixa's. She was tethered to the spot, and had stilled in the position she had been in before the scourge's lick. Like a puppet, she had one arm extended, perhaps twelve inches shy of Alixa—not close enough to have been able to save her had the scourge had other intentions—and the other raised, the spear drawn back before she threw it. Only her expression had changed: her mouth hung, and she stared, looking as if the entire world had shifted.

It had, Jasen supposed.

"I told you," Alixa said.

"I don't believe it," said Shilara. Her voice was suddenly quiet, subdued. "It's a scourge. There's no thing as a good scourge."

"This one is. It saved us. You can't kill it." And Alixa turned back, wrenching her eyes from the scourge bowed before her, to give Shilara a very pointed look.

Shilara dropped her spear arm very suddenly, as though either just remembering she held it—or more likely, Jasen thought, because she didn't want to be seen as having been prepared to act to save Alixa.

She watched the scourge. Jasen did too; with Alixa pivoted away like that, it was the perfect moment to dart forward and tear her open at the abdomen, carting her bloody body out into the scrub to feast. Yet all it did was sit there. Like a dog—not a person, as Jasen had seen them earlier. Just a strangely proportioned, docile, somewhat dopey dog.

That's gone grey with disease and lost all its hair, he thought, *and smells like it died a month ago.*

Putting on a casual air, Shilara said, "Fine. You can keep it." She ambled back to the front of the cart, not looking any longer—though by the expression on her face, it took great effort to do so. "But I'm not feeding it." As she clambered onto the front again, throwing her spear down with a touch too much force, she added, "And it's not riding with us, either." And that was that.

Jasen crouched at the rear of the cart. He edged over, peering down at the prone scourge, waiting by Alixa's feet.

"What does it want?" he murmured.

Alixa shrugged. "I don't know." She looked troubled by that.

"Did it follow us?"

"I don't know. I assume so," Alixa said.

Shilara harrumphed from up front, but said nothing.

"Scourge …" Alixa started. "Um. Scourgey?" She lowered a hand nervously, patting it on the head, where wisps of grey-brown hair stuck up. The scar Alixa believed allowed her to recognize this one ran across there, right down the middle of its head. It was wide, the tissue almost pinkish, the way human scars tended to be. Other animals' scars too maybe, though Jasen hadn't seen many chickens or horses or cows with scars in his life thus far.

"I wonder what hurt it," Alixa said.

Jasen said, "Whatever it was, looks like it came close to cleaving its head in two."

The scourge looked up then, dark eyes on Jasen. He felt another squeeze of terror at that, sweat breaking out on his forehead again as it rose, its huge head level with Jasen's—

It leaned forward, and he flinched back—

The scourge nuzzled him.

It pulled away, and regarded him blankly.

"Uhh ..."

"I think it likes you," said Alixa.

Jasen thought its brains had got scrambled, the way it was acting. Maybe it *had* been a dog once, and this was all the dog-ness coming out, instead of the wolf-ness that made the rest of the scourge the vicious hunters that they were.

"Get back in the cart, children," Shilara ordered. "Can't sit out here all day, or its ungelded mates might come along and make a meal out of you two."

Alixa rolled her eyes but said, "Coming." She looked at the scourge—*Scourgey*, Jasen amended—"Follow along, okay? She won't let you ride. Plus, you'll stink up our bread."

When she was sitting aboard the cart, they began to move once again. The scourge hadn't given any indication it understood Alixa's command—and perhaps it hadn't—but it did follow along, taking lumbering footsteps. Though larger than a dog, its proportions gave it longer strides, so it had only to lope along in that unpleasant-to-watch way to keep up with the cart. Its mouth hung open as it followed, tongue bobbing up and down as if tasting the air.

The false breeze generated by the cart's movement flowed from Milo to Scourgey. Not entirely effective at dispelling the rotten stench from the beast, it at least did have some effect.

Jasen watched it. Sitting on the opposite side of the cart, Alixa did too.

She frowned. "Why is this one different?"

Jasen shrugged. "Beats me."

Shilara half-turned. But if she had any thoughts on the matter, she did not provide them; instead, she told Alixa, "Cover your hand with blood from the bucket again. I don't want even an inch of skin more of those monsters could smell."

Alixa was not pleased. But she did it, neither gagging nor retching this time. Then she settled back against the edge of the cart, and watched the scourge follow in their wake.

21

Last night, they'd slept in the back of the cart, but only for a few hours at a time; Shilara kept watch, but then Jasen and Alixa were instructed to take over in turn.

"Not that you could do much if any of those things happen upon us," Shilara had said. "But you see one, or hear one, or even *think* one might be lurking, come back and wake me, you hear?"

Jasen and Alixa agreed they would.

"And that thing isn't sleeping anywhere near us," Shilara added of Scourgey before striding away to empty her bladder.

Scourgey must've understood, because it stalked away from their camp—no fire, for that would only provide a beacon for the scourge to find them—disappearing somewhere in the dark. Only the next morning did it return, and only then after they'd finished their breakfast of hard cheese and salt pork and the cart had set off again.

"Do you think it's a boy or a girl?" Alixa had asked.

"Uhm … maybe a girl," said Jasen.

"Definitely female," said Shilara. "The males have balls."

Alixa's cheeks colored. "Oh. Well, I didn't look to see."

"Can hardly miss them," said Shilara. "Pendulous great things."

The flame burning Alixa's face grew hotter. She mumbled some response, but no more.

The morning passed largely without incident. Except for the run-in yesterday, plus Scourgey tagging along behind the cart, they saw neither hide nor hair of the creatures. They'd not seen much of anything, in fact. Bird calls rang out, but rarely. Shilara remarked that it was a sad thing, as there had been much more birdsong in the days before the scourge. Jasen wondered if their population had been fractioned by the scourge's presence too—or if perhaps birds had learned that safety meant silence. He didn't ask; Shilara had started drinking before he awoke this morning, and she was growing irritable as the day dragged on. Engaging her, especially over something that might set her off on another tirade about the scourge, did not seem wise.

Midday passed, and they stopped to eat. Alixa was hungrier today, and she did eat a sandwich, except for the crusts, which darkened with dried blood. These she gave to Scourgey when Shilara was not looking. The scourge wolfed them down, hacking a few times, but bringing up nothing.

The afternoon slipped by. Open green gave way again to woods, which grew thicker and thicker. A trail had been cut through, but undergrowth had spread over it. Saplings sprang up in places. The cart rolled right over them, firming down two ruts in the foliage that would spring back up again before long; one solitary back-and-forth cart ride would not be enough to turn this trail back to exposed earth.

Then they ran into a problem.

A river spilled over the trail, running across it like a crossroads. The surface glittered in the sun, flashing like a mirror's reflection up at them.

"How deep is it?" Jasen asked.

Shilara squinted. "Deep as the cart, maybe a little less."

"Will we be able to get across?"

Shilara didn't answer.

"Have you been this way before?" Alixa asked.

"Yes. But the river isn't usually this deep. Or fast. A foot or two, yes, but this … the winter's snows must be melting." She cursed, then fell again into silence.

Jasen eyed the flowing water. It made him nervous. A small creek ran through Terreas, and from it splintered off a handful of very shallow stretches, meandering along the side of a lane at a snail's pace. Those were only as deep as the distance from knuckle to fingernail. The creek, maybe eighteen inches at most, was easy enough to wade through.

This river, though, was a different story. The bottom was rendered invisible by a furious current, churning the water's surface as it rushed past, traveling somewhere south-east.

If the river were calm, he might've wondered if it fed directly out to the ocean. Warily watching the torrent now, though, he couldn't care less where it went.

"I feared this would be the case," Shilara muttered. "Warm spring, early summer … ice melts and has to go somewhere. Just our damned luck it went this path."

She dismounted the cart and approached the water's edge. It had overflowed its banks to encroach on the trail, a dangerous rush of water that soaked Shilara's toes as she stepped closer to it.

She moved back. "Too perilous. We ought to turn back."

"No!" said Jasen quickly.

Shilara glanced to him.

"We can't. We need to get the seed from Wayforth."

"And if the current washes us away?"

"It … it won't do that. Right?"

Shilara pursed her lips. "Perhaps. We're weighty enough that …" She frowned, pondering.

"I think we should go on," said Alixa. "We've come so far. We're almost there. How many hours more, after this?"

Shilara thought. "Perhaps four."

"We're so close."

Shilara shook her head. "If we come later in the year, when the melt has finished—"

"If we come later in the year, Terreas will have torn itself apart already," said Jasen. "My home was burned down—that's before we've even started to see insufficient harvests. We have to go on."

Shilara considered him, looking somewhat dubious.

Her gaze shifted to Scourgey.

Then she shook her head again fiercely. "Why would I ask you?" Sighing, she said, "Right. We'll cross. You might want to invite that thing up onto the cart. Blighters can't swim." She clambered on herself, taking up Milo's reins.

"They can't?" asked Alixa.

"Nope. Watched many a few drown with my own eyes." And enjoyed it, by the sound of her voice. Still, that she was inviting this scourge up was a good sign—she was coming around. Perhaps.

Scourgey had held back. Now Jasen and Alixa turned to her, they saw Shilara's words were true. Scourgey padded nervously, legs lifting and dropping without moving it anywhere. Its mouth hung open, its tongue lolling out. Its breaths were heavier than the usual wheezing the scourge produced.

Seeing the children turn, it produced a low whine.

"Come up here," said Alixa, scooting back. She shoved the sacks aside to open a clear spot for Scourgey to sit.

"Get it centered," said Shilara. "Its weight will help hold us down."

Oh. So that was the cause of Shilara's charity.

Jasen helped, shunting empty sacks into piles to either side of the cart's floor. The bucket of viscera he stowed in the very corner, near the rear—as far from them as possible. It teemed with flies. Maggots would appear soon, and the act of smearing bloody guts all over themselves would be even worse than it had that first time.

Alixa patted the cleared space. "Up here, Scourgey. You'll be safe."

Scourgey whined again. But it obeyed, treading carefully to the edge of the cart. Rising, it reached over with one leg. Three enormous claws splayed, reminding Jasen of just how easily this beast could rip them apart.

Its other front leg followed, and the cart tilted back a fraction, rear wheels taking much of the load. Then its hind legs were over, and it lowered into something between a sit and a crouch—the best it could manage, Jasen supposed, with its awkward anatomy—and the whole cart felt as though it had sunk into the earth a good two inches.

Shilara made a noise of disgust. "Foul-smelling thing. Make sure it doesn't touch the food."

Scourgey whined softly.

"There, there," said Alixa. She gently patted the leg closest to her. The joint there appeared to be too high. It protruded, a wrinkled knob, a small number of thick, dark hairs surrounding it.

"Treating it like a dog," Shilara said, shaking her head. "Thought I'd seen it all."

She urged Milo forward.

The horse began to move—then a surge of water spilled the river's edge close to its hooves. Milo whinnied, trying to turn back. He was held in place though, between the two leading beams of wood enclosing him at the front of the cart.

"It's only water," Shilara complained. "Get!"

The shake of the reins Shilara gave was enough to start Milo moving again. He was not very happy about it though, and whinnied again as he stepped into the flow.

Scourgey joined with a sad moan of her own.

"They're scared," Alixa said.

"Too bad. We're crossing." The cart's first pair of wheels had met the water's edge now. "Besides, Milo's done this before. Not as deep, but he'll manage."

"What about Scourgey?"

Shilara shrugged. "No choice if you want it coming along."

"*Her.*"

"Him, her, whatever." Shilara leaned over the side, peering backward. "We're in. Hold tight."

At first, it was smooth. But as Milo descended deeper, and the wagon followed him, the increasing depth gave a larger surface area for the cart to feel the push of the current. By the time the first wheel was half-submerged, the torrent of water cascading at them was strong enough that Jasen felt the cart being pushed.

Milo brayed. He was forced sideways, pushed against the wooden beam on his right. Shilara was dragged in that direction too, reins threatening to go taut. She'd looped them about her hands to keep the leather from dropping below the water's surface.

"Milo! Go!" she roared.

The volume of the river was louder now they were in it, a dull roar in Jasen's ears. With an obstacle to beat against, the already churning surface of the water was split into distinct flows. Water flooded between the wheels' spokes. It splashed under the cart, around its edges. Not quite high enough to reach the sides yet—but as Jasen squinted down the side of the cart and watched Milo push uneasily onward, he realized it would quickly come to meet them.

Opposite him, Alixa looked panicked.

Scourgey whined again. She seemed desperate to avoid looking at the rising waters.

"How much deeper?" Jasen yelled.

"Not sure," Shilara answered. She glanced over her shoulder. "We're not quite halfway, so I'd venture a bit."

Jasen looked back. "Not quite halfway" was an understatement; he'd be surprised if they'd forded even a quarter of the distance yet.

Milo fought on, yet the water buffeted, hard and fast and unceasing, and the horse's progress was slowed.

All at once, the sound of roaring water erupted from behind Alixa with a thunderous clap. She yelped, scrabbling away. Scourgey shrieked, a high-pitched, throaty noise Jasen would never have believed the scourge were capable of.

The water had hit the cart's side panelling.

And still it rose.

Alixa clutched Jasen's wrist, pressed close at his side. The spray opposite was unrelenting, and it sloshed over edge, filling the cart in at the bottom.

Jasen felt wetness seep across his backside.

"Ancestors," said Shilara. "*Milo! Double-time!*"

The horse whinnied a vicious response, one Jasen took to mean, *I'm doing the best I can, here!*

Scourgey quivered. She had begun a ceaseless noise now, and it went on and on, underlining the cacophony of the crashing waters around them. Her legs moved back and forth, claws scratching gouges in the base of the cart. Her rotten scent had gotten worse, whether from fear or the presence of water amplifying the smell, and Jasen could barely keep himself from gagging. Bile threatened low in his throat. He kept it back only by huffing long breaths, reminding himself with every one that if the cart should be swept away, or worse, overturn, the only real hope he had for surviving was the air in his lungs.

The water rose—and the assaulting spray grew stronger.

An inch of water had accumulated in the cart now—

Scourgey scrabbled backward as a particularly violent wave exploded at the cart's edge. The cart shifted, wheels losing purchase—

Alixa yelped, grabbing hold of Jasen—

He braced—

Then a wheel struck something—a rock, some drowned sapling, whatever—and found its hold again—

At the same moment, he felt something in the cart buckle.

The opposite edge of the wagon split open along two wooden boards. How much, Jasen didn't know. All he saw was the cart whole one moment, and then a rushing spray of water jetting in the next.

"The sacks!" Alixa shrieked.

"We've sprung a leak!" Jasen yelled.

Shilara had time for just a momentary glance over the shoulder. "Jasen, get over and block it!"

He obeyed—but the cart had canted sideways, and so it was like dragging himself up a slippery hill. He snatched up a sopping sack on the way, one of the empty ones they'd use for seed.

Scourgey howled as he passed.

"Calm down," Jasen said. "You're spooking me."

He gripped the opposite edge of the cart. It was soaking, and the tumult of water surging upward every second fought to shove his fingers clear. He held firm, counting seconds.

The spray bursting through the side was violent. Jasen tried to shove the sack in front of it. But the sheer force battered his fist, shunting it from left to right, as though the water did not want him to stop the cart from filling with water.

He grunted, coming from the side instead.

The first time, his hand was forced away before he could get a hold.

The second, he caught the split in the wood with a finger—he thought.

"How's it going back there?" Shilara called.

"Working on it!"

"Well, work on it a little faster! All this water filling us up will send us downstream!"

Jasen gritted his teeth.

The cart shifted again below him, losing purchase. This time it regained it almost immediately.

He did not trust their luck to hold out.

Mustering all the steely force he could, he thrust a hand into the flow of water again. This time he managed to catch his fingers in the open seam. The wood had split sharply, and he felt the biting sting as it jabbed into the skin above his knuckles. But he'd found it, and hooking an elbow over the edge instead, he awkwardly used his free hand to fight the sack into the opening, stuffing it full—

The sack burst away. A new torrent blasted through—

Jasen yelled. The wave slapping the edge of the cart dislodged him, and he tumbled sideways. He staggered as the world turned, trying to avoid slamming into Alixa—

Wood crashed against his ribs. The other edge of the cart, he thought.

At the same time, Alixa yelped.

Had he hit her after all?

Then he made out words amidst the thundering rapids:

"The bucket!"

He turned, looking for it—

The blast of water that had ruined Jasen's makeshift plug and forced him back to the opposite edge of the cart, had spilled over and inside. The flow rebounding from the cart's bottom, it had snatched up anything it could: and Jasen saw them floating away now, half a dozen waterskins ejected from a sack's tear, and the bucket. It had gone overboard sideways, spilling its contents in a crimson cloud.

And in the second and a half it took for Jasen to find it, already the bucket was far out of reach.

"What happened back there?" Shilara cried.

"The bucket went over!" Jasen shouted back.

Shilara swore. Gripping the reins between wet, bone-white knuckles, she yelled a command to Milo, urging him on.

Scourgey whimpered. Still planted dead center, she was braced awkwardly against the side of the cart with one extended leg. Jasen wouldn't be surprised to learn the claws underwater had dug footholds into the cart's base to help keep it in position.

"We should be past the worst of it now!" Shilara called back. "Plug that gap though, Jasen, would you?"

"I'll try," he said.

He scrambled over again. His ribs ached where he'd slammed the edge of the cart—a bruise, to be sure, and a damned big one at that.

But in spite of the pain, and the floods intent on stopping him, he did somehow manage to stuff an empty sack into the split in the cart's side. Maybe because of willpower, or maybe because Shilara was right: they were easing out.

He remained there to keep it in position, an arm hooked over the side. He turned away from the spray, panting hard.

Slowly, the spray softened. The water level dropped.

The water in the cart itself began to drop with it, spilling out of the front.

Milo quickened. The riotous noise dropped, as the cart's side panels lifted clear. Then the water was lower and lower down the wheels, passing the axle, lower still . . .

Milo was clear. He was muddied, body almost up to his head coated and soaked, and his face was flecked with foam. But he was past: and with him came the cart, finally easing free.

"Easy," Shilara ordered when they were a suitable distance clear.

Milo stopped gladly.

Shilara hung her head. Then, groaning, she pushed herself off the cart. She landed heavily, with a sopping thud.

She, like Jasen and Alixa and the scourge, was soaked to the skin.

She stood for a long time, sucking in breath after breath, facing the dirt.

"Are you okay?" Jasen asked after a while. He fingered his pendant, reassuring himself that it was indeed still there, that the water had not whisked it away.

"Just getting my wind back. That's all." Another in-out suck of air. "Okay. Let's see this damage. This side, is it? Get out, both of you. That thing too."

Scourgey followed willingly. It was a trembling wreck of a thing, nothing at all like the vicious hunters that Jasen had heard them to be—had *seen* them to be, as he fled in the rye field a whole lifetime ago. Now it was more like a dog—a fat, grey, pathetic dog.

"It's okay," Alixa said softly, gently patting its shoulder. "We're safe now."

Jasen followed Shilara around the side.

The split in the wood was not as bad as he had feared. Touch had made it seem larger. The sack protruded, black and coated in a thick layer of mud. It hadn't entirely stopped the flow, but it had done enough to keep them from being dragged downriver.

"Okay," said Shilara. "Nothing a good carpenter can't fix. And if we can't salvage it, well, we're bringing the village seed. They'll take the loss of a cart happily."

"The loss of a cart?" Alixa asked.

Shilara frowned at her. "What?"

"What about the loss of *us*? We could have died back there!"

"But we didn't." Shilara was businesslike. Maybe a touch callous.

"But we—"

"But nothing," Shilara cut across. "We survived that. It wasn't even that bad."

"*Not that bad?*"

"Aye, that's right." Alixa opened her mouth, cheeks flaming red, but Shilara carried on before she could say anything. "When you've fought in a war, you learn to be practical about things, not emotional. We lived. We have a damaged cart to deal with, one which Terreas will want back, if we can return it in one piece. A hole that small is fixable."

Alixa fumed. "And the bucket?"

"*That*, on the other hand," Shilara sighed, "is a great loss." She looked into the cart's bed, squinting at the remaining sacks. They were sopping wet—bread ruined, for certain, although the cheese would likely be all right if a little worse for wear. The meat would be practically unscathed; dry it off and they'd never know they'd gotten into trouble. Waterskins, several lost, but they could be refilled easily enough from another water source. Wayforth might even have a well they could use.

But the bucket … that was their only camouflage against the scourge. Now it was gone—and on top of that, the water had washed away most of their bloody coverings.

No one said anything. But they all thought it, Jasen could tell, looking from Alixa to Shilara. They weren't yet at Wayforth, and had two days of return travel after arriving at the village. Two more full days in which they might attract the scourge—

And no camouflage against them at all.

22

The afternoon passed.

There was no conversation. No one had much of anything to say at all. Like yesterday, after they had made their escape from the pack of tree-gnawing scourge, the grim reality of their situation seemed to settle heavily upon them. Alixa, who bore it most heavily, sat opposite Jasen with her knees drawn in close to her chest. She had linked her arms around them, gripping herself tight about either wrist. Her knuckles were pale. Jasen wouldn't be surprised to see a row of crescents imprinted into the skin of either arm when she did finally move.

Shilara was more reserved. Or perhaps her worry was less obvious simply because she sat back to them. She'd not had anything to drink since crossing the river.

Even Scourgey seemed subdued. She seemed to sag as she followed the cart, and her face pointed earthward.

Strange, Jasen thought, how something so outwardly menacing could look so worn down.

The woods had broken about an hour ago, spilling them out into sunlight again. The trail had more or less vanished by now. It gave way to a series of hillocks, steep and rolling up and down, up and down. Each one they crested presented a view barely farther than the next rise of overgrown green.

"Roll those sacks out flat," Shilara told Jasen and Alixa, "so they can dry. And toss the bread out behind us."

"Won't it attract scourge?" Alixa asked.

"Soggy bread like that won't attract *anything*. Let alone one of those poxy, disgusting things."

Jasen and Alixa obliged, splitting the task quietly between them. The sack of waterskins, they draped the top of over the edge of the cart. Ditto the sack of meat and cheese and—ugh: a mound of wet pulp. Alixa scooped it out with a squeamish look on her face. No wonder; it wasn't very pleasant to touch. Still, between them they rid the sack of it, hanging the top of that one over the edge too. Scourgey considered the plappy lumps, and sniffed, but did not taste.

Milo's oats were half-ruined, coagulated into a soggy mess. Shilara was not pleased by this, but said thinly, "We'll restock in Wayforth." When Jasen asked if the abandoned village would have any oats to its name, Shilara didn't say anything.

The rest of the sacks were laid out, some overlapping. After that, the sun could do its thing.

Up and down, up and down ... the hillocks bounced them, the ruts in the ground finding each wheel and rocking them. Jasen accustomed himself to the bumps, though his tailbone began to ache, and he shifted in search of a more comfortable position.

Then, as they hit the top of a particularly large rise—

It was as if a veil draped over Luukessia had been pulled away. With only smaller crests to block it, Jasen caught sight of a faraway village. It was spread atop a hill some miles distant, looking almost like a crown.

"Is that it?" Alixa asked.

"Aye," said Shilara. "Wayforth."

Jasen watched it, unblinking. A well of hope filled his chest—yet there was an undercurrent of fear there too, whispering against his spine, carving a dark hole in his stomach.

What if the granary was empty?

What if the seed was no good?

What if scourge had come to haunt those buildings, creeping through it the way they'd woven through the trees yesterday, the way they slunk through the mists and the rye surrounding Terreas?

What if this whole trip was a waste—or worse, ended in bloodshed?

He swallowed, but his throat had gone dry.

No, he told himself. *Don't think of that. Do not curse yourself.*

It was easier said than done.

They rolled down a hill—and now the pressing fear grew heavier, settling over all of them. The atmosphere had shifted from one foreboding quiet to another, and this one felt somehow worse.

Another rise came. Milo pulled the cart easily through the knee-high grasses. A handful of bushes sprung up, and trees, spindly ones that could not have been many years older than Jasen. He wondered if perhaps these hills had been used for some purpose, in the days when Wayforth had prospered; farms of their own perhaps, or a network of trails leading to other villages dotted across Luukessia. If that were the case, just how long had it been since Wayforth's people had died or deserted it? Had it been since the coming of the scourge? Or sometime after?

Shilara would know. But Jasen decided he did not wish to, and so said nothing.

The next hill flattened, then descended sharply—

Shilara hissed. She tugged the reins, bringing Milo to a sudden stop.

"What in the ...?"

Below, in the valley formed between this rise and that final long slope leading to Wayforth's outer reaches, was a span of woods—or at the very least the remains of one. The trees had been stripped bare: not a leaf clung to any branch, though they should've been thick and full as the summer drew on. There were few branches for leaves to cling to anyway. Most of the trees had been reduced to their trunks—and each and every one bore the telltale wounds of gnawing teeth.

"The scourge," Alixa muttered, touching a hand to her lips.

Shilara said, "This was not like this last time I was here." Frown deepening, she wondered aloud, "Why would they tear all of this up?"

"They hate life," Jasen said.

They all turned to him, Shilara with a blazing look, brow furrowed deeply across.

He paused, mouth open before he carried on. Where had he got that idea? His mother possibly? Someone else in the village? It was Hanrey's sort of wisdom, but Jasen didn't remember him saying it, nor had he been conscious of even thinking such a thing until the thought fell from his lips.

Scourgey came around the side of the cart, behind Jasen, leaping her paws up the side to brace herself against it. Craning her head over, she ogled him with one black, empty eye, and licked his back.

Jasen stared. Alixa watched too.

"Um ... good scourge." Jasen patted the beast awkwardly. Her rotten smell was worse so close to him—but he'd smelled a lot of rancid things these last days, and her scent no longer filled him with the same revulsion as it had before. Which was very peculiar, he thought.

Shilara had cocked her head over her shoulder. "Hate life, do they?" she griped. "Explain that one."

"I don't know."

Shilara's look at Scourgey was disgusted and disdainful in equal measure. Turning back and urging Milo down the hill again, she said,

"I heard those things are the dead. Dead and damned, souls of the ancestors of the westerners of Arkaria, for worshipping strange gods and doing magic." Her voice was scornful. "Load of old tripe."

Scourgey's head had been displaced by the movement of the cart. She walked alongside it now though, and Jasen looked into her face, mulling over Shilara's words.

"Are we going through that?" Alixa asked, pointing over Shilara's shoulder to the stripped woodland down the hill.

"Have to. No point wasting time going around."

"How will we get through?"

"Milo will manage."

The trees became visible only when the valley between the hills flattened. They'd approached under a dark, foreboding stormcloud—metaphorically; the sun was cheerily bright, which it absolutely should not be over a sight such as this. Now, the cart passing through, that uneasiness turned into a smothering anxiety that made Jasen's chest tight.

On the hillock, he had thought the trees' destroyed limbs had formed a thick carpet underfoot. Yet now, rolling through, he saw that he was incorrect. The grass had been torn up too. Earth was turned over, heaped, troughs formed beside the tree trunks. Exposed roots were ghostly white—and terminated short, ripped into shreds wherever the scourge had uncovered one.

The place stunk of decay. It was a sick odor: the lingering, haunting mist of scourge, and the musty scent of rotting wood, water and insects filling the wounds the scourge had left, softening and fraying the tree's grain, returning it to the earth by the inside first. The smell turned Jasen's stomach.

And everywhere it was the same. Saplings had been torn up, battered down, broken as low to the ground as they would go. Trunks were carved open, like disemboweled pigs. Bark scattered the dirt everywhere, great chunks of it as though the scourge had come to first flay and then tear asunder these trees.

Jasen turned a wary eye to Scourgey. She followed along, stinking of death all by herself.

Her kind had done this.

He tried to remind himself that Scourgey was different, and he believed it ... but not entirely.

23

Jasen had never experienced a dead village before.

It was as haunting as he had imagined it to be.

The silence hit him first. It came from all directions, the absence of noise somehow frighteningly loud, burrowing into his ears and digging deep into his brain, settling there. The rattle of the cart, Milo's hooves, Scourgey's footfalls—all these things ripped clefts in that quiet, but they could not dispel it.

Nature had begun to reclaim Wayforth. In the years since it was emptied, the stone pathways had become so overgrown as to be rendered mostly invisible. Only small mosaics remained here and there, where something had uncovered them. The stone had been cracked though, and what Jasen presumed were once grey oblong cobbles had fractured into many disparate pieces.

Without maintenance, the houses had suffered. Thatch roofs had rotted away in the elements. Holes had opened, and twine mesh had given way, spilling damp material earthward. Walls sagged from water damage, and close to the ground, more rot had split open dark spaces where water could seep through.

Even those buildings that had survived these years without great decay did not appear lived in. Jasen could not put his finger on why. Perhaps it was the darkness in the windows; perhaps the pervasive silence gave away the village's lack of inhabitants, even if he had not known prior to arriving. Perhaps it was the lack of smoke coloring the sky. Terreas had plenty of that as the afternoon wore on. It brought a smell with it too, one Jasen hadn't really been aware of until now he was absent from it. A soft, subtle tang of burning wood, undertones of cooked meats or warm bread—it lingered in the air, growing heavier as the sun lowered to fall behind the mountains and vanish into velvet night.

Wayforth did not have this scent. It smelled only of rain, and the faintest, softest hint of the decay that would eventually strip these buildings, the way the scourge had destroyed the woods down the hill, returning it all to the earth.

Alixa cradled herself as the cart rolled down the main street. "I don't like this at all."

"It's unnerving," Shilara said—rare agreement with Alixa. "We'll be quick."

They rolled on.

A house passed. It looked not unlike those in Terreas. A few touches that made it unique to Wayforth—the timber was a slightly different color, with twisting curlicues in a handful of places. A sign above the front door had once hung by two short chains, but only dangled on one now, the other rusted and snapped. The words had faded, leaving only a faint black ghost of whatever had been written upon it. Names, probably. Whoever had owned the place was long gone. A side wall had given way, spilling brick into an alley between houses.

Jasen squinted into it as they passed. It was dark though, impossible to make out what was inside.

"Have you ever been inside these buildings?" he asked Shilara.

"A few times," she said, and she sounded uncomfortable admitting it. She'd probably avoid his gaze if they were face to face, frowning uneasily. "They're not places you'd want to wander into."

"Why?"

"Plenty of dust, for a start. Dust that thick gets in your lungs and doesn't want to get out again."

Whatever her other reasons for warning Jasen off, she did not elaborate. He did not ask her to, and instead went back to watching. Maybe when they stopped, he'd peek in one. Just to see.

Shilara must have known where she was going, for she directed Milo throughout the outer reaches of Wayforth. Jasen wasn't sure whether he longed to delve farther into its center or not, to see the more built-up parts of it. They intrigued him, seeing another human settlement beyond his own. But the disquiet felt as if it would only grow more unpleasant as they pushed deeper.

Not to mention the fear of scourge. Putting more buildings between them and the open hills only gave more places for the beasts to hide.

A series of compact storehouses had been erected by a roadside, once wide enough for two carts to amble past side by side. Two were open. One was practically empty. In the other, he caught a glimpse of barrels.

"Your whiskey?" Alixa asked.

Shilara grunted. "That'll be it. I'd offer you a nip, but I doubt you'd take it."

"I wouldn't," Alixa said stiffly.

"Thought not. Shame, though; it'd loosen you right up. Almost make you bearable." Shilara tugged Milo's reins, pulling him to a stop. Then she dropped onto her feet, ducking the jutting wooden beam and making for the next storehouse. "Seed's in here. Those sacks dry yet?"

Jasen felt over the fibers of those laid out nearest him. "Not entirely."

"Doesn't matter. It'll do. Anything wet will dry—or if it's ruined, it'll ruin by the edges and protect what's in the middle. Go on, grab them up and come over. Every one of them. No, not the one you used to plug the hole with; it might need to be there on our way home."

"Won't the river wreck the seed?"

"Possibly," said Shilara with a *nothing-we-could-do-about-it* sort of shrug.

The door was closed, but not locked. No need, Jasen supposed. So Shilara just yanked it open. Grass had grown thick around the door's base, and so impeded more than the first half-inch opening. She tugged harder, grunting, tearing tufts up and smearing mud into a flat, exposed streak as the door obeyed.

Jasen and Alixa followed, arms loaded with sacks between them.

Inside were rows of barrels. The building was not particularly deep—some eight feet perhaps, and only about four wide. It was loaded with shelves though, and tall. A set of ropes dangled from the ceiling, presumably for bringing down barrels from the higher shelves.

Labels were stuck to the front. In the dim light coming around the half-opened door, the faded words written upon them were even harder to make out.

Shilara found a discarded metal bar and used it to pop the lid of one of the barrels by the door.

Inside, packed to the brim, were pale green seeds. Grain, by the look of it.

"That's the summer dealt with," said Shilara. "Start loading up," she told Jasen and Alixa, pointing at it.

"What about you?" Alixa asked indignantly.

"There are winter squash seeds somewhere back here," Shilara said. She was bowing already to squint at labels, wrinkles starkly pronounced under the strain. "I'm fairly sure, at least." A moment later: "Got it." She cracked open that lid too.

"If you knew there was all this seed here," Alixa said, "why haven't you brought any back before now?"

Shilara shrugged.

"It would've helped with Baraghosa," Alixa started hotly.

"I helped the village," Shilara snapped back, turning on her and jabbing out with a finger. "I fought for Terreas. I *still* would fight for Terreas. I got shunned for that."

Alixa's mouth had fallen open. At Shilara's last words, though, she clamped it shut.

"You are fighting for Terreas," Jasen said. "We all are."

Shilara pursed her lips. "Hmph." She didn't say anything else and set to easing the barrel out bit by bit, gripping it in around the top and rolling it back and forth to bring it out.

Jasen and Alixa set to filling a sack. She held it open while he took handful after handful and poured them in—"You've got bigger hands," she said. That was slow going, and soon he found a scoop that had fallen into a corner, speeding the process. After a few minutes of this, Shilara came over and watched, frowning.

"This is a waste of time," she said, and Jasen stared blankly at her. She seemed to be calculating, and then, abruptly, she was done. She gave a barrel a shove, and it tipped, just slightly. "Nothing for it, then – we'll take these and forget about filling the sacks."

"But—" Alixa started to say.

"But nothing," Shilara said, already positioning herself, bracing to lift one. "Come on, then, children. We don't want to be scooping all day, caught here with our breeches down when the scourge come to eat us." Scourgey, who was meandering around at the entry to the storehouse, looked at her. "Not you. You're housebroken, though I struggle to understand how that happened."

Scourgey made a low, whimpering noise. To Jasen's ears, it almost sounded like approval.

They set to work as three, dragging the barrels out and loading them onto the cart together. It was not an easy job, not even close to it, and it made Jasen ache in his muscles, all the way down to his bones.

But they were doing it. They'd come all this way. And though it caused Jasen's muscles to moan, made his arms feel as though they were creaking and ready to give out, he felt a swell of relief with every barrel he loaded, for each one brought Terreas a little closer to being saved.

All they had to do was get them home.

24

The last barrel was the hardest. Jasen groaned, breath hitching. He couldn't suck the air in properly, and the little he could manage was right at the top of his lungs only, filling only a few inches' worth of space. But up it went, up, up …

He groaned as it finally touched down atop the cart.

Releasing a white-knuckled hold, he sagged.

"Jasen?" Alixa asked. "Are you all right?"

"Just a … minute," he panted. "Get my … wind back." Sweat clung to his hair, wetting his curls into thick bands that stuck to his forehead. Salty liquid had run down into his eyes and left them burning. He'd tried to blink it away then. Now, he gave up, just closing his eyes and focusing on refilling his lungs.

Damn it. Why had this exhausted him so much?

"Are you sure you're all right?" Alixa asked warily.

Jasen nodded. He forced himself to look up and grin, a wide show of teeth that wasn't very much in line with just how exhausted he felt at this moment. "Thought I was … fitter than this," he said. "I guess these years of not having a trade to labor at have made me soft."

"It's these last few days, more like," Alixa said. "They've made us tired, harried all the worse from the ride and the worry. My body aches." She made a show of rubbing her shoulder. Yet though she had a sheen of sweat damping her body, Jasen suspected it was mostly that: a show. She didn't wheeze the way he did, wasn't struggling for breath. And he didn't think she'd skimped on taking her fair share of the weight.

Must be something about sleeping on wood that doesn't agree with me, he thought. He'd have to ensure he didn't get into a habit of it, breaking it with a nice long stay in his bed as soon as they were back in Terreas—

But he didn't have a bed anymore, did he? It had burned, along with his house. The thought sent a small dart of shock through his body, from the top of his skull where it rippled like goosepimples beneath his hair to the bottom of his feet. Well, there wasn't anything to be done for it now. He'd have a bed again. Along with the greetings and many thanks bestowed upon them when they rode back into town would come gratitude. This amount of seed would help feed the village for many years to come, allow them to plan more carefully. He looked around the storehouse. And if this cartload wasn't enough for years, they could come back, as many times as needed.

Yes, he'd have a bed again. And a house. And a life, really, because this—this journey, the one he'd undertaken to Wayforth, had been like an opening of his eyes after a long slumber. He'd need to change, of course, and he could see the direction of it, now.

For the first time in...ever...he could see a future for himself.

He thought fondly of it—

The earth rumbled.

He grabbed out for the nearest sturdy object—the barrel they'd just pushed onto the cart—and held firm. Eyes wide, he stared at Alixa, confusion flooding him as the earth shook for long seconds—

A house across the way gave in. It crumpled, wood cracking over the top of the rumble.

The vibration underfoot grew soft and gave up. The house was left moaning alone, clattering into a heap of rubble. Dust and airborne fibers from the splintered wood plumed up in a fine cloud.

Jasen and Alixa exchanged an alarmed look. "What was that?" she asked.

Before Jasen could tell her that he didn't know, Shilara came running from—someplace. Another storehouse, most likely; something she'd forgotten, she'd said, abandoning them with this last barrel between them, seeing as it was only half-full.

"Are you all right?" she called—and then saw both Jasen and Alixa at the front of the cart, sweaty but not much worse for wear. Milo was still tethered where they'd left him. He shuffled nervously back and forth, whinnying and shaking his head. Her concerned expression softened. "Oh."

"We're okay," said Jasen.

"What was that rumble?" Alixa asked.

"Don't know," said Shilara. "Don't much care. We're all set, aren't we? Barrels loaded?"

"Yes," Alixa said, a little flat. She gave Jasen a sidelong look, apologetic. He wondered just how much of a state he actually did look right now.

"Good. Clamber up then. We'll be off."

"Now?"

"Afternoon isn't yet over. If we make good time, we could shave some hours off this return trip."

"I just thought …"

"What?"

Alixa rolled an uncomfortable shrug. "That we'd stop to catch our breath. Or that we could sleep, you know, in a proper house, in a proper bed."

"Dusty houses and beds do not make for a good night's sleep," said Shilara. "Trust me." And she untethered Milo, walking him to the cart. "The swifter our return, the better."

"What about catching our breaths?" Again, Alixa cast Jasen a sidelong look. She wore a concerned frown, drawing lines across her forehead. "We can have a little pause before moving off, can't we?"

"We're not walking to Terreas," said Shilara, tying Milo back into place.

"But—"

"Listen," Shilara cut across. Her thin patience had been exceeded. "Look at the both of you. Look at me. Loading the cart has been strenuous. We've sweated, all of us, and gotten soaked. And in doing so, we've lost our camouflage."

She was right. Jasen couldn't know his own face, but he could see his hands and arms. They were almost the color of his skin again. Only a faded brown coating was left. Alixa was the same. Shilara too. Between their jaunt through the racing river, and the sweat pouring off them as they loaded eight barrels into the rear of the cart, their protection had been reduced to a fraction of what it had been when they set off in the early hours of yesterday morning.

"Scourge will smell us," said Shilara. "From a mile off, the way we probably stink at the moment. And seeing as we lost our only cover against that, I'd rather like to head off sooner rather than later. All right?"

"Yes," Alixa mumbled. "Of course."

Shilara smiled smugly. Then she looked about, frowning as she craned her neck. "Where's your...hanger-on?"

Alixa and Jasen peered.

"Scourgey?" Alixa called.

"A scourge with a bloody name," Shilara mumbled, shaking her head. "It's not a pet. It's overgrown, murderous vermin."

Alixa ignored her and called for the scourge again.

It wandered out from between two buildings back up the road. Head hung, it cast their cart a sad sort of look as it came, walking piteously slow.

"Scourgey?" Alixa said. She approached, reaching out to touch it. Pressing a hand against its flank, she asked, "What's wrong?"

Shilara looked less than impressed. "Get up on the cart, girl. We're leaving."

Alixa shot her an annoyed look. "I have a name."

"Get on the cart."

Alixa huffed. Patting the scourge gently, she obeyed, returning to the cart and climbing aboard. Jasen followed, and together they settled into their usual spots on either side of the cart's bed. Shilara dropped heavily onto the front and wound Milo's reins around her hands, and with a snap of them, the horse sprung into motion.

It was not particularly quick motion.

"See this pace?" Shilara said to Alixa. "This is another reason why we're moving now instead of dallying. Those barrels aren't feather-light."

"I know." Alixa rolled her eyes. "I helped load them."

"Then you know Milo's struggle. Only he's pulling eight times more than we were at a time."

"Seven and a half," Alixa muttered, voice just loud enough for Jasen to catch. "Plus however much whiskey you managed to bottle and slip into your pocket."

"What was that?"

"Nothing."

"Hmph."

Wayforth slipped away behind them. Jasen found he didn't care as much to look into the windows as they moved now. He still hadn't quite managed to fill his lungs. Though he could not see a reflection of himself, he knew color blazed in his cheeks, as he felt its heat riding high in his face.

He'd do more to keep himself in shape when he got home, he thought. Start by finding a laboring job to assist with. Build up his arms, his shoulders, so if ever—whenever—they needed to come to Wayforth again and raid its abandoned stores, he'd not find himself so beleaguered.

The village faded behind them, cart and scourge descended the hill. Shilara took them sideways along the slope, charting a longer, shallower path so the weight of the barrels would not cause the cart to lose control, ploughing Milo down by rolling over top of the horse as its momentum allowed it to overtake the horse in the only way it possibly could.

"Ancestors protect us on this return trip," Alixa said as they went. "May the spirit of our mothers and fathers gone before ride with us and keep us safe from harm."

Then it was quiet again.

"We'll avoid the woods," Shilara said as they neared the bottom of the hill. "What's left of it."

"In case of scourge?" Alixa asked.

"And the ground. Extra weight will dig us in."

She kept watch all the while—a thorough watch. Her head turned and turned. When it twisted in Jasen's direction—back up the hill toward Wayforth—her forehead was covered with lines. Her lips were downturned, pressed incredibly thin.

"What is it?" he finally asked.

"Nothing."

"It's not nothing, surely."

"It is," Shilara said, tense. "Very much nothing. There don't seem to be any scourge in this area. Not compared to before."

"There's one," Alixa said.

Shilara turned sharply—then realized Alixa meant Scourgey. Grimacing and waving her off dismissively, she continued to Jasen, "We've run into almost none. One pack in less than two days—that's nothing. And then it was only a small one. Not at all like the masses I've encountered on other journeys here."

"There must've been a lot here to chew up these trees like that," said Jasen, gesturing.

Shilara followed his gaze into the decimated woods. "There must have been," she agreed. "But they're not here now. It's strange. Very strange indeed."

She said no more of it. Jasen was not sure what to think. That the scourge were not present was a good thing; they'd not greatly impacted their journey thus far, and if the same held true as they returned to Terreas, it was only to their good fortune.

But that begged the question: for an island so utterly overrun by the beasts, its inhabitants run almost to extinction, left to eke out existence in remote safe havens—if there were any others beyond Terreas—then …

Where had the scourge gone these past days?

25

They'd ridden well past dark. Shilara had refused torchlight, picking out their route by eye. Jasen followed, squinting into the darkness. The moon was out, casting enough light that he could see some of the way. Whatever landmarks she was using to navigate, though, he could not make head or tail of. It all looked the same in the milky darkness.

Shilara had directed them a different way home. It had involved crossing the river again, but downstream, where it been both slower and much shallower. The land there was open too; no fear of scourge lurking. Scourgey had crossed the waters nervously, whining softly—but the flow was barely more than three inches deep; not the drowning hazard for her that Shilara no doubt wished it were.

They had ended up in a stretch of woods again just after night fell. Another cart trail, or the wide ghost of it, was carved through, brush growing across it as nature worked on reclaiming it. The cart's wheels pushed it flat, and Milo and Scourgey stamped it down further, but Jasen knew their imprints wouldn't last long. Unless the scourge were beaten back, these trails would not stay wide and clear, the way they once had woven throughout the landscape. Even if the scourge were somehow defeated, it would take untold generations to rebuild Luukessia. Less time if people from the continent to the west came—but what if that too had been swallowed by scourge?

What if Terreas's people, and Baraghosa, were all that remained?

Jasen wondered it again, the way he often did, turning over and over. But he did his best to force it away. Why should he fixate on depressing things? They were heading home, with seed that would allow them to carry on without Baraghosa's trade. Terreas would not regret their choice, the way he had said they would.

They did not need him anymore.

That thought alone should have filled Jasen with joy.

Yet for some reason he couldn't quite focus on that. Other thoughts crowded his mind. The strangely ominous lack of scourge. His sudden fatigue. The rumble of the earth underfoot this afternoon. He didn't know what to make of any of them, save his exhaustion. But even that was strange. It had come on while shifting the barrels, an all-encompassing sort of fatigue that refused to leave, settling in his bones.

Maybe he'd caught something out here, some pox that the mountains shielded Terreas from.

Never mind. Not long and he'd be home. He could rest.

The trail widened in places, passing points where, way back in time, carts could slip into so that another rider and his horse could trundle past. Now they were just as overgrown as the rest of the world had become without people to tame it.

Shilara stopped at one of these. "It's not ideal," she said, "but we'll smell scourge before we see them, and mount up again if we need."

"Couldn't we just ride on?" Alixa asked. She shot furtive glances about the woods. These trees did not bear any of the gouge marks the scourge had dug in others—a good sign, Shilara said. Jasen wanted to believe her, but with dark descended upon them, every little noise in the darkness—a vole scurrying through the undergrowth, an owl striking out at its unlucky victim as the rustle it created gave it away—made him jerk his head around and squint into the murk.

"Could," said Shilara. "Would like to, in fact. Milo needs a rest, though. And I need to sleep for at least a couple of hours."

"What about after that?"

Shilara groaned. "Fine." She tugged out a blanket and one of the empty sacks. Dry at last, they made a decent place to lay now the cart's interior was piled high with barrels. Chucking them down roughly beside a wheel, and stowing her spear to her side, she landed heavily and pulled one of the thin blankets over her. "Keep watch. Wake me if you hear scourge. Otherwise, don't disturb me." And she rolled over, back to them: conversation finished. If that weren't message enough, her snoring was; it started less than a minute later.

Jasen and Alixa couldn't build a fire; light out here would only draw unwanted attention. A shame; Jasen needed energy, and what he craved was a hunk of meat cooked over flames, oils sweated out, thick enough to coat his mouth and throat with. A good crisp edge—he'd kill for it.

He swallowed, wishing he weren't salivating so much.

"Go to sleep, Alixa," he told her.

"You sure?"

"Yeah. I'll keep watch."

"I can sit up. We can sleep once Shilara is awake again, in the back of the cart."

"It's a bit awkward with all those barrels. And the motion."

"It's only a night."

Shilara loosed a particularly loud snore. She seemed to half wake herself, and jolted slightly. A few steadying breaths later, she was slumbering easily again.

"Go on," Jasen whispered. "I've got Scourgey for company."

Alixa shook her head. "I'll stay up."

She did. For hours they sat there—or perhaps it felt like it—listening to the noises of the dark. Only a little conversation passed between them. Alixa tamped down yawns, and Jasen felt a stab of regret that she had not listened to him. It had been a difficult day for all of them. They deserved the respite. Maybe Alixa most. She had come this way, risking herself being shunned by the village for daring to endanger their lives—that was how Hanrey had put it, back when this whole thing started, wasn't it? To cross was to endanger their lives. It was terribly improper, and doing it that first time had driven a wedge of anger between them.

Yet here she was, in spite of all that.

"Why are you here?" Jasen whispered.

Alixa stirred. She'd been still for—fifteen minutes? Twenty? She didn't seem to have fallen asleep; her breathing had not slowed in that telltale way. She had simply quieted, and now his question roused her.

"What do you mean?" she whispered back.

"Why have you come out here? Past the boundary. Only days ago you would have rather died than cross it."

"To help save Terreas."

"Yes, but why?"

Alixa frowned in the dark. "I don't ..."

Jasen twisted toward her. She was fuzzy in the darkness, and so too was he, he supposed. But maybe if she saw his face better he could convey exactly what had occupied a corner of his mind for this whole trip.

And *before*, really.

"I know that you've come to save Terreas," Jasen said. "But *why*? You're so worried about being proper, in everything you do. Something like this—they'd shun you." Lower, he added, "You'd be like Shilara. An outcast, on the edges."

"They won't do that," Alixa said. "Not when they see what we've done."

"They might." He didn't believe that, but he didn't see how Alixa couldn't have considered it. That was all she did, consider what others would think, worry about what was *proper*.

"They won't."

"You sound so sure."

"I am. We're doing Terreas a great service. We're saving our people's lives. And if I have to … to be *improper* to help do that, well, then I will. I have." This last sentence came after a moment's pause, as though she were reminding herself of it.

"And before?"

"Before what?"

"I was shunned," Jasen said. Suddenly he couldn't look at her—it embarrassed him, although he had been there with her almost every moment of it. Clasping the pendant about his neck, taking comfort in its edges, he carried on quietly, "They didn't treat me like Shilara. But they treated me close to it. And—you saw what happened to my home."

"They were cruel."

"You associated with me," Jasen whispered. "You stayed by my side." Blinking away unexpected tears—where had they come from?—he looked up to her. "Why?"

"Because you're my cousin," she said. "And it is proper to stand by your family."

He nodded. His throat had constricted, gone tight. Averting his gaze down to his lap again, he managed to force out a wet, "Thank you." It was not enough, nowhere near a fraction of his appreciation conveyed in it.

"Why did you come? After the way they treated you?"

Jasen shrugged. "They're scared. And I know what that feels like."

"Do you?"

"Of course." His eyebrows knitted. "Why wouldn't I?"

"You always seem so fearless." In a small voice, Alixa added, "Not like me."

"I'm not fearless. I just … try to have courage, I guess. It's important to be courageous, Mother said. Nothing wrong with being scared—just have to be brave in the face of it."

Alixa nodded. "I'm trying to do that."

"You're succeeding."

"It's hard."

"I know."

They were quiet for a while, listening to the noise of the forest. There was little of it; just the quiet shuffle of small animals. A sweet, leafy smell was carried on the cool air. No death, no decay, no rot; Scourgey had gone, loping away into the darkness when it was apparent Shilara was stopping for the night. Sleeping? Prowling for any stalking beasts roaming the woods? No way of knowing. Didn't truly matter, as long as they remained safe.

"When we get back," Jasen said slowly, "do you think we might be treated as heroes?"

Alixa stared.

"What?" Jasen asked.

"Is that why you came?" she hissed. "So you can be a bloody hero?"

"Uhm ..." He was an inch away from telling her that she had adopted Shilara's way of saying things—but her eyes were wide, blazing with a fire that was obvious in the darkness, and he decided that maybe he didn't need to tell her that after all.

"Is that why you came out here?" Her voice was rising.

"No," Jasen said quickly, hoping to head off an explosion. "Just ..."

"Just what?"

He licked his lips. "It ... might be nice ..."

Alixa did not get to say a word, for from the direction of the wagon came a splutter.

Jasen and Alixa twisted. His heart hammered in his chest—

"Sorry," said Shilara, turning toward them in her makeshift bed. "I've been listening a while. But that one ... that tickled me." She pushed the blanket aside, and got to her feet. She gave a little groan as she went, clutching the spoke of the nearest wheel to help herself up. "Damn these bones."

"How much did you hear?" Alixa asked hotly.

"None of your darkest secrets, so don't worry," Shilara said, waving her off. She leaned back against the edge of the wagon.

"What was so funny?" Jasen asked.

"You talking about being a hero."

"What's funny about that?" A little of Alixa's hotness bled into him there.

Shilara gave a thin little smile through the dark.

Jasen held himself from asking, "Well?" That would've made him an even closer reflection of his cousin.

"Let me tell you a story," Shilara said, and she came to join them, sitting opposite the cousins in a loose triangle.

"About what?" Alixa asked.

"War," Shilara said—and the woods seem to grow quiet around her, their clearing becoming strangely claustrophobic.

"We were just like you," she said to Jasen, "back when the war began with the scourge. I marched into battle with the men, see, because we'd already lost many in a war with our southern neighbor, Galbadien—have you heard of them?" She didn't pause for them to nod in the starlight. "We were low on troops, low on men, even before the scourge came. So when Briyce Unger, our king, called for help, I put aside the foolishness of spinning and sewing and all that twiddle and answered his call. I did things and went places I was never supposed to—and all of them, all the men there, like you, longed to be heroes. They came from villages, just like yourself"

"Who were they?" Alixa asked.

"They were countless; names don't matter. Point I'm making is: in the same way you hadn't seen the world before, none of these boys had seen war before.

"Like you, Jasen," she continued, looking him hard in the eye, "they had no idea what they were walking into.

"Droves of people came—because it's not just soldiers who march to war, but their families, entertainment, merchants. I wasn't attached to anyone, but I blended in, hoping, wishing all the while that I could be a part of the war myself."

"You did fight," said Jasen. "Didn't you?"

"Oh, aye," Shilara said. "I was a part of it, all bloody right."

"What was it like?"

"Brutal," she said, her voice blunt and melancholy, almost haunted. "Whole armies were slaughtered. The villages we tried to blockade, to protect, were overrun anyway as the scourge broke through our defenses, whittling us down, killing every person we staked our lives to protect. They flooded in en masse, packs the likes of which you'd never hope to see in your darkest nightmares, and left—devastation.

"Most of my comrades perished. For a long time, I envied them, for they never got to see the bloodshed grind to its end. They went on to be with our ancestors, free of all...this." She made a gesture to the air around her. "They were done happening upon half-living men or women, or worse, children, whose sides had been split open, innards torn out. They didn't have to taste iron in the air anymore, so heavy and thick it choked you, worse than the scent of a thousand of those verminous beasts who'd spilled so much blood.

"Frightening, isn't it?" she asked Alixa and Jasen, looking between them in turn. "To think that you'd think the dead *lucky*, for however grisly their fate, it was better than surviving. Surviving to see the land of Syloreas, of Luukessia...turned into this." She gestured again, more harshly this time.

Quiet. And then, softly, from Alixa: "You feel guilty."

Shilara didn't answer, not with a word, nor with a nod or shake of the head. She only continued.

"When I realized how hopeless things were, I retreated. It was a hard battle, fighting my way to Terreas, and one I almost lost many a time. But I got there, pursued by them, a hair's breadth away and on my tail. I was crawling then, bloodied, damn near dead myself. They could've had me, easy."

"They left you at the boundary?" Jasen asked—then: "Wait. You ... didn't you *discover* the boundary in the first place?"

Shilara lowered her head in a sage nod. "Aye. Wasn't a wall there, decades ago, when I crossed it. I was dragging myself by the end, horse dead miles back, battles fought that I'd won, all the way up to a mile outside the village. I left dozens of their dead behind me, but they'd struck true—got me here." She patted her leg. "They were almost upon me, a pack of them. But just as they came to finish me—and they would have—something out there made them stop. It was as if an insurmountable hurdle, totally invisible, lay in their path. And so the scourge let me crawl away."

"But why?" Alixa asked.

"We're the favored of our ancestors," Jasen answered for Shilara. "They watch over us. That's why the scourge don't cross the boundary." It was an explanation he had heard many a time—from his mother, from Aunt Margaut, and over and over from the assembly, past and present. Hanrey had been particularly fond of that one for many years, back before he'd truly soured.

"What about the other villages?" Alixa asked. "Why didn't their ancestors protect them?"

"They were undeserving," said Jasen.

Alixa frowned, turning her nose up at his answer. "That doesn't seem very likely to me. Why wouldn't they be deserving?"

"They just ..." Jasen began, then found he had no further words. Exactly why *hadn't* the other villages scattered across Luukessia been deserving of salvation? He'd never thought of it before—and now he tried to source an answer, all he found was an enormous hole.

"Whether our villages' ancestors failed them or not," said Shilara, "it's enough for me that the scourge did not pursue that day. But—"

Some distance off, twigs snapped—hard.

Then more.

A branch cracked in two.

The smell of rot seeped into the air on the night's breath.

"Damn it," Shilara whispered, rising.

Scourge.

26

Shilara moved into action, footsteps swift. She made for Milo, who was tied off barely four feet from the cart; quicker to jump into action that way, should they need to. He was awake already, in no need of prodding; someone else struggling with a sleepless night.

"On the cart," Shilara barked—or a whispered approximation of it anyway. "Now!"

Jasen and Alixa did not need telling twice. They clambered up and onto it.

"Where's Scourgey?" Alixa whispered.

"Don't know, nor do I care," Shilara said.

"We can't just leave her."

"It'll catch up if it wants to."

"*She*," Alixa said.

"I don't have time to care." And with that, Milo reattached to the cart, Shilara climbed aboard. She got the horse moving with a whispered, "Yah!" before she'd even settled her backside.

Milo pulled. The cart was slow to begin moving, weight of so many barrels holding it in place. But once those wheels began to turn, they turned quicker, building speed as the cart returned to the trail proper, leaving this passing place they'd tucked into.

"The sacks you slept under!" Alixa whispered to Shilara. "They're still back there!"

"Oh, aye? We'll go back for them then." Shilara shook her head violently, twisting over her shoulder to shoot Alixa a dirty look. "I couldn't give a goat's anus if the scourge are making jackets out of the ruddy things. I don't miss them, and neither will Terreas once we're back with all this seed. So shut your know-it-all mouth for once in a—"

"*Scourge!*" Jasen cried, pointing—

Shilara turned—

Milo had jerked sideways as a pair padded out from behind the trees on the left, just ahead. The horse made to dodge, looked like it wanted to turn and gallop deeper into the woods—

But scourge were certainly in that direction too, and in any case, there was no traversing these trees. Milo could pass if he were unshackled, but the cart would never follow.

They'd fall prey to the beasts roaming the woods.

The scourge leapt forward—

Shilara yanked on the reins to steer Milo around them, keeping him on course rather than making for the nearest getaway between two tree trunks. A moment later she'd swung her spear around. Rising, she stabbed out as the cart thundered past in the night. One of the scourge leaned forward to snap, the maw that was its mouth wide as it loosed a bestial roar—

Shilara stabbed it in the throat.

"Take *that*, you scum!" she cried, already past.

Jasen rose to squint over the top of the barrels.

The stabbed scourge had stumbled sideways, and it coughed a spray of dark blood. But its partner was already surging past—and from another parting in the trees came another, and another, wrinkled heads pointed in the direction of the cart hurtling away from them on groaning wheels.

"Sit back, Jasen," Shilara said. "And get a blade. Alixa, you've yours?"

"Yes," she said quickly and patted down the small sack of possessions she'd brought. Her daggers were out in an instant, clutched in hands whose knuckles were surely bone white under the force of her grip.

Jasen retrieved one of the blades Shilara had brought along. It was perhaps ten inches long, not even a foot. Not quite the size of the one on her belt, but long enough, Jasen hoped, that a biting scourge would feel the tip drive through the roof of its mouth and back away before snapping down with its jaws and taking his forearm off. Or worse.

Sweat oiled his palm. He squeezed tight, but it made the hold of the hilt feel far from secure. Releasing it, he wiped his hands hard on his trouser leg, and retightened upon the blade's handle. Not perfect, but solid enough—for now.

"What are they doing back there?" Shilara asked.

Jasen rose.

"Following," he said, voice strangled and dry. "They're gaining."

"How many?"

"Six. At least."

Another burst from the trees at the cart's side.

"Seven!"

It leapt forward in a great bound—

The cart was already past, but it caught the back wooden panel. For an eternity that could have been only a quarter of a second, it hung there, both forelegs hooked, trapped between the barrels of grain and the rear of the cart—

It struggled upward, teeth gnashing. The smell of death was rancid, the strongest it had ever been—

It was going to vault the barrels and descend on them.

Then the wooden panel snapped off. One moment the scourge was there, hanging from it; the next Jasen saw a glimpse of its belly as it was left behind, a wooden oblong tumbling with it; then its brethren had overtaken.

"We lost the back of the cart!" Jasen cried.

Shilara swore.

"The cart is open?" Alixa peered into the dark.

"Calm yourself!" Shilara barked. "Now they'll have a devil of a time clambering on."

"But the seed!"

"If a barrel clouts one of them in the face, that's a good thing."

"But Terreas needs it!" And before Jasen could do a thing, Alixa had risen, and throwing herself around the row of barrels.

"Alixa!" he shouted, standing too.

"Would you bloody well sit down?" Shilara cried.

Alixa had woven into the gap. She sidestepped, pressed impossibly tight down a space Jasen knew he would never manage to slip into. He could not follow—but he could grapple her to safety—

He staggered toward his cousin—

The cart bounced. He felt his feet leave it for a moment, and cried—

He landed hard on his back. His head collided with the side of the cart. Whether his eyes had instinctively closed or not, he'd never know; the darkness made it damned hard to tell, and the explosion of white hot stars across his vision made it even more troublesome to tell.

"—you stop being so bloody stupid?" Shilara was shouting.

"The barrels moved!" Alixa cried back.

"Forget the bloody barrels!"

"But they're what we came out here for!"

Jasen forced himself back to sitting. Oh, but he hurt so bad. Heat spread about his midriff, seeping around ribs back to front. Were they broken? Probably not—but then, the pain in his chest was contending with a violent headache now, so how could he really be sure?

"At least make yourself useful and tell me how many are behind us!" Shilara barked over her shoulder.

"Six!" Alixa replied.

Six? Weren't there seven a moment ago? Where had the last gone?

Jasen had a confused image of one seeming to dangle in the air, clutching something long, with splintered edges—

We lost the back of the cart, he remembered, and jerked upright. The world gave a dizzying sway.

The cart. It thundered through the woods, wheels turning the fastest they must have ever gone. Breeze kissed his face—and yet it could not seem to force back the awful taste of rot that had marred the air, filling it, unrelenting, fighting to sink into his throat, take hold of his lungs—

He squinted ahead. Dark, of course—but there were so many trees still, a tunnel of them that led to some infinitely distant freedom.

And the trees, Jasen realized with dawning horror, were steadily becoming more and more tattered. Limbs were missing from those they past and those hurtling in a parallel line toward them; not all, but enough that they had a misshapen look about them. Long gouges were torn in the trees, milky against the dark, charcoal color of the trees themselves.

The scourge owned these woods. Like the trees before Wayforth, they were in the process of stripping it down to death.

And now the cart was surging deeper into the eye of the storm.

He felt sick—

The cart bounced hard again—

Alixa screamed.

Jasen's head snapped around.

The lurch of the cart—over some small rise, Jasen guessed, or the cratered trail where the scourge had delved for the trees' roots—had caused the barrels to jolt backward. One teetered. Alixa must have grabbed for it, because she held tight—

Then the barrel of grain tipped over the cart's edge. Alixa tilted with it—

"ALIXA!"

She screamed, loosing her hold on the tilting barrel. Her legs swayed as she fought to correct, trying desperately to bring her center of gravity over the cart's base again—

Jasen leapt over the barrels, sword thrown aside to free both hands for purchase—

But Alixa canted, unable to stop herself.

Her daggers disappeared behind her, lost to the scourge hurtling behind.

She flung a hand out, both—

"What's happening?" Shilara cried.

"I'm coming!" Jasen shouted, Shilara forgotten. The barrels were high, awkward to vault, but he thrust over, hoping—

"*Help me!*" Alixa cried.

She was still on. Good. But as Jasen pushed over the last of the row of barrels, right to the cart's edge, he saw how treacherous his cousin's grip was. She'd managed to force herself forward, grabbing out with one arm. Now she clung to the thin sliver of the cart she could hold, one arm and one leg, as though she was lying alongside it and wrapping in it a hug from behind.

It would take just one more energetic bounce to send her to her demise.

"Hold on, Alixa!" Jasen ordered. His heart hammered in his chest, hard, thudding against his throat. Ancestors, he was going to be sick. His whole body was cold, but oiled in sweat—and that scent of scourge chasing them, infesting the woods, these creatures' domain as they destroyed all the life here too ... it clogged his throat, nauseatingly thick.

"Jasen," Alixa moaned. Her eyes were shut tight, her face screwed up. She'd managed to keep her head this side of the cart. Her cheek rested on the base, a third frantic gripping point. It juddered against the wood, surely needling her with splinters.

"I'm here," he said. He looked for a place he might clamber down, where he could pull her back on—but the barrels had shunted too far back, making it difficult. Even Alixa, with her smaller frame, would struggle to squeeze into the free space remaining at the back of the cart. The little that did exist was occupied by her arm and leg thrown over. He could hardly ask her to shift them; if she lost her grip, or the cart gave another shuddering vibration at the wrong moment—

"Help me," Alixa said, face pale like moonglow in the night.

"I'm going to," Jasen breathed—but how, damn it? He was stuck atop these barrels, and even lying flat as he was, his arm would never stretch far enough to grab her hand, let alone pull her back on board.

Think, would you? There's got to be some way of saving her. Think!

He racked his brain—

"Jasen, be ready with that sword!" Shilara cried from behind.

Huh?

He looked up—

The scourge had closed in. Alixa's scent must have lured them enough to put a frenetic burst of speed on, because the gap was closing even now.

"Swipe at them, Jasen!" Shilara boomed.

Alixa screamed.

"I—I don't have it!" he cried back, voice high and strained. "I threw it down back there to get Alixa!"

Shilara swore again, a whole ream of curse words.

The closest scourge opened its jaws wide—

It bounded forward, teeth deathly white, pointed and sharp and capable of tearing through flesh and muscle and bone—

"Alixa—!" Jasen cried, reaching out—

She screamed as if she knew—

And then Scourgey leapt through a gap between the trees. She rent the air with a keening roar and crashed headlong into the scourge just inches away from tearing Alixa's throat out. They tumbled, and so did others alongside and behind, a cascade of dominoes all toppled at once as Scourgey leapt into the fray—

"What in the blazes was that?" Shilara cried.

"Scourgey," Jasen breathed back. He stared, not daring to believe his eyes as the tumble of scourge limbs and gnashing jaws receded behind—

Then a shuddering breath from Alixa brought him back down to earth.

"Hold tight," he ordered—and was that his voice shaking? To Shilara, he said, "Can you stop?"

"The scourge still behind us?"

"A way back," said Jasen. "Scourgey jumped in. She saved us."

"Well, I'll be." Shilara muttered something Jasen didn't catch. "Can't stop; this thing'll take too long getting up to speed again if they change their mind. But I'll slow." She was already doing it in fact, and Jasen felt the rumble of wheels diminishing as Milo eased his pace. The barrels beneath Jasen vibrated less and less, and their weight quickly sapped the cart of momentum.

When it was slow enough that he felt steady, Jasen slipped into the spot between where Alixa's left arm and leg held her to the back of the cart. It was a tight fit, but he held a barrel with one hand, trusting its weight to keep him from tipping the both of them over the edge. He half-squatted, and gripped Alixa's arm in his other hand.

"I've got you," he said.

She whimpered again. Her eyes were still shut firmly, so tight Jasen wasn't convinced they would ever open again.

"I have you," he promised—at least, he hoped he promised. Things might not be their direst if Alixa tumbled off now—the scourge were far behind now, impossible to see in the darkness, though their scent seemed to have scarred the air permanently, their rotten stink low but easily overriding what otherwise might have been the cool sweetness of foliage and the earth.

Looking back, once it was over, Jasen wasn't entirely sure how he managed to bring Alixa back onto the cart. It took so very long, and he panicked at every moment that she would go over the back where the rear panel had snapped off. Yet she did not, and somehow, miraculously, Alixa was aboard again. Sometime a little later, she was once again sat in her usual spot by the side of the cart, where she cried, and Jasen slung an arm over her, telling her that it was okay, that she was safe. Even Shilara offered words of comfort, though they were sparse.

Sometime even later still, the cart rolling at its full speed, they broke out of the woods. Alixa's tears had dried before then. She had instead lapsed into quiet.

The moon was sinking toward the horizon when they came out. Hours away still from departing to the dawn, but it was not overhead, or even close to it. Its fierce light outshone the surrounding stars, leaving it the single glowing orb in a pool of ink.

"How long until we're back at Terreas?" Jasen asked.

"We could arrive by dawn," said Shilara, "though it'll be close. It means running Milo ragged, but … I'll do it. I want to be back across that damned boundary before anything else goes wrong."

"What if he tires before then?" Jasen asked. "Before we reach it?"

Shilara said nothing.

Jasen did not need her to. He knew well enough. With no more animal innards to hand, and the sweat of their fear and this pursuit having helped shed the last of their covering, they were not just unprotected; now their bodies were actively working to thwart them, to raise a voice to the heavens that screamed, "Human meat this way!"

And if any closed in before they passed over the boundary …

Things did not look good.

27

It was an hour of riding in near silence before the scent of death filled the air again.

Jasen tensed, as did Alixa. Shilara moved for her spear, twisting to squint an eye about her—

But there was something different about this smell, something familiar. And so Jasen said, knowing without being entirely sure of *how* he knew—for other scourge surely smelled the same as this one—"Scourgey's back."

Alixa hadn't moved much at all since her sobs had died on their way out of the woods, merely sitting in a stunned silence, face morose. Now she did shift, rising so she might look over the barrels. Jasen mirrored her, peering into the dark landscape, the features of this gentle rise indistinct.

"Scourgey," Alixa breathed.

"You see her?" Jasen asked.

Alixa nodded.

Jasen frowned. "Where?"

His cousin pointed.

He squinted into the dark, unable to discern the scourge from it.

Just as he was wondering if perhaps she were seeing things, Scourgey finally came close enough that he could pick her out. She loped to the cart, mouth open, head turned down, the way a dog might wander behind its master, sniffing the ground beneath its feet and relishing every one of the myriad smells that touched its nose.

"Can we stop?" Alixa asked.

"Why?" said Shilara.

"So I can thank Scourgey."

"You going to hug it?"

"She saved me."

Shilara pursed her lips. "I'm not stopping. Thank it with your voice instead."

"Here, Scourgey," Alixa called—whispered, really, though a louder one than before. She stood up, leaning forward against the nearest barrels. Her hair, Jasen noticed, had spilled out of its braids, and fell to either side of her shoulders. It must've been like that for a long time—a long time that she had not bothered to swipe it back into its usual place.

Scourgey picked up her pace, and eventually lumbered alongside the cart.

"Thank you," Alixa whispered. She reached out and touched the scourge's flank—then, as it tilted its head closer, she leaned forward as far as she would go and wrapped arms about the creature's neck.

It could kill her, Jasen thought.

No, not "it." Scourgey was a "she." And she wouldn't harm Alixa. Nor would she harm any of them.

Scourgey was different.

How, Jasen didn't know—*couldn't* know, he suspected, unless he learned to speak scourge. But for some reason, this one had fought off its brothers and sisters, to protect them. Scourgey had appointed herself guardian to Jasen and Alixa and Shilara—because … why?

He took her in once Alixa had moved off. She did not look greatly worse for wear. A few new wounds along her body, oozing black blood. There was a coppery sort of tang to that, like rust gone furry and strange in the rain, but it was not what made Scourgey's scent any different to the other scourge. If indeed it was different. Jasen suspected that perhaps there was nothing remotely dissimilar between Scourgey's rotten odor and the fog that surrounded the other scourge; it was something in his mind, and his mind only.

Alixa stepped aside, and looked to Jasen expectantly.

He took her cue, and carefully climbed to his feet. Using the barrels to guide him, he joined Alixa's side.

Reaching out, he pressed a hand to Scourgey's cold, leathery skin.

"Uhm. Thank you."

Scourgey looked back at him with one black pit of an eye … or at least Jasen thought she did. It was difficult to tell, honestly.

"You want to say anything to her?" Alixa asked Shilara—or demanded.

Shilara glanced at Scourgey sidelong. Her expression was tight, but perfectly readable: the last thing in the world she wanted to do was thank this creature. It was, after all, one of the beasts that had overrun Luukessia. She had fought them, tried to drive them back, and been almost broken by the horror of what they'd done.

Jasen recalled what she'd said way back at the beginning of all this, when he'd saved Tery Malori out in the rye spread beyond Terreas's boundary: "The only good scourge is a dead scourge."

Yet though he expected nothing to come from her mouth—or, more likely, a harsh, snipped response—she averted her eyes, watching Milo and the path he led the cart upon, and mumbled, "Appreciate it."

And then she was quiet.

They all were. The noise between them became only the rumbling of the cart's wheels turning, turning, and Luukessia falling behind as they approached the mountain, and with it, Terreas.

At some point, the gentle slope became the dirt and stone of a mountainside trail. It wended higher and higher, and began to turn back in on itself.

Jasen closed his eyes, and it passed.

Then a judder, and he was awake. The sky was different, brighter with the approaching dawn. Only a lone star remained that he could see, winking against a lightening purplish-blue.

"—nearly there," Shilara was muttering.

Jasen roused. He swiped a balled fist across one eye, then the other.

"... much farther?" Alixa asked.

"Just around this bend."

Jasen tuned into their conversation. Only he couldn't quite get his brain to focus entirely upon it. There were other things vying for attention, not least of which was his fatigue. Nights of poor sleep had piled up, and though he had never been the swiftest person in Terreas to get up to speed in the mornings, on this particular one he was already struggling like never before.

The impact last night, maybe? Had that rattled his head?

What impact? he thought, confused.

Scourgey's smell washed over him, heavy, a dense fog.

Fog. That made Jasen blink, take in his surroundings properly.

Usually fog condensed around the mountains before dawn, staying put much of the morning, till the sun made its way high enough that its blinding glare and brilliant heat could dissipate the mists. That they weren't surrounded by it suggested they'd come from another direction though—and as Jasen peered up, he found empty sky where he'd anticipated seeing the mountains themselves.

Just where—?

On the opposite side.

He frowned. The confusion ratcheted up higher inside of him.

"Why did the mountains move?"

Shilara and Alixa both turned his way, the former only briefly. She had a grim look on her face, and that set off another confused fragment of Jasen's mind, spinning wheels madly to catch up and place him in the world again.

"You're awake," Alixa said.

"We came in from the other direction," said Shilara.

"Why?"

"Scourge on the road," she answered flatly. "Managed to see them far enough off that we could change course. Could've been back an hour ago if we hadn't, but Milo's making good time. Damn near run himself to death, but …"

"Poor Milo," Alixa whispered. "You'll rest soon, boy."

Jasen squinted at the mountains. He'd never seen them from the wrong direction, and never from this vantage point, beyond Terreas, which still lay out of sight—though the remnants of this trail forked left maybe two, three hundred feet ahead. Hadn't Shilara said the village lay just beyond the bend? If that were the case, he was just minutes away from seeing the home he'd left behind—how many days ago now? Three? It was hard to keep track; the excursion had blurred into one long, endless trip, filled with sleepless nights and fuelled by pure adrenaline—

Something was burning.

Cookfires.

Jasen's stomach rumbled.

But even as it did, another flash of confusion crossed him. It was usual for Terreas to start up their fires early, before the sun crested the horizon beyond the mountains … but should the smell be so heavy when they were still so far away?.

"Are the cookfires usually this strong?" he asked of no one in particular.

"No," said Shilara, short and terse.

Jasen looked skyward. Clouds had settled in above the village, blotting out the sky—and they were dark, close to the mountains. Stormclouds? Perhaps; storms were not uncommon in the summer. And the temperature had been hot these past days—although maybe that was from all their desperate fleeing, and Jasen had only felt hot as fear made him ooze with an apparently ceaseless oily sweat. Not changing his clothes for days had only made that worse.

Scourgey whined.

Jasen eyed her. She loped close to the cart—yet there was a reluctance to the way she stepped. Her head was turned down as low as it would go, eyes focused on the earth passing underfoot.

"What's wrong with her?" he asked.

Shilara shrugged. "Been whining like that for the past couple of hours."

Alixa looked worriedly at the scourge. "Do you think she knows she won't be able to come into Terreas with us? That she'll have to stay beyond the boundary?"

Any day before this one, Shilara would surely have called that idea a load of old tosh, and mocked Alixa for having it. Scourge were not capable of intelligent thought, after all; they were just mindless creatures, alive to kill, to rip, to tear, and nothing more.

But she said nothing, so Jasen had to answer Alixa's question for her. "Maybe."

Scourgey moaned again.

Peculiar.

The cart rounded the last bend. Milo was heaving now, pace slowed. How fast he'd been going during the hours when Jasen slept, he didn't know, but the last he remembered, Shilara had pushed Milo as fast as he could manage. They'd been going up a gentle slope then. It would've grown only steeper as they ascended the mountains to where Terreas lay. Tugging the barrels and maintaining such a pace was a serious undertaking, especially for a horse accustomed to barely any slope, and pulling barely any weight, in the small haven that was Terreas and its tiny slice of surrounding, unmolested land.

Alixa was right when she called Milo a "poor thing." He'd worked harder than any of them.

That thought quickly dissipated, though—because there was Terreas. It was still a couple of miles away, the boundary at least another few minutes' journey from where the cart rounded into view. Up the last of the hill to where the village lay nestled under the mountains and presently shadowed by the brewing stormclouds above it, blotting out the brightening dawn, Jasen saw a faint dusting of lights. Tiny amber dots, they illuminated windows smaller than a pinprick from so far.

Somewhere among them was his father, his aunt, uncle, cousins.

A swell of hope filled his chest.

It had been a trying excursion, one that Jasen had feared he would not make it back from. But here he was, returning to a Terreas that had tried to shun him in its fear—and he would save them, he and Alixa and Shilara, with this bounty of grain they had managed to return. One barrel lost was not so many, for they still had plenty enough to last—and never, ever would they need to deal with

Baraghosa again.

That was the sweetest thought of all.

At least, perhaps the sweetest after getting to see his father again, to look into his face and see the pride there when he knew that Jasen was safe, that he had survived and kept his head about him—and that Jasen had done the unthinkable, leaving the village after a lifetime of warnings never to do so. And then, to top it all off, to have not only lived to tell the tale, but returned with provisions that would sustain Terreas's people for decades, never needing to trade with Baraghosa again.

Tears bit Jasen's eyes, unbidden. He blinked them back.

"We did it," he murmured to himself. "We saved Terreas."

A smile lifted the corners of his lips, wider than he'd grinned in a long time—

The world rumbled.

There was just enough time for the smile to slip from his face as his eyebrows tightened in confusion—

And then the cratered mountain exploded right in front of him.

28

The noise was world-ending. There was no describing its volume; the explosion was a roar unlike anything he had ever known, like a thousand—a million—scourge, all loosing a bass note as one grotesque, enormous cacophony—

And it did not end. It went on, as the earth quaked and the mountainside split. Jasen slammed his hands over his ears before his eardrums burst, and his entire head went with it—

In the space of a fraction of a second, the time it took to blink, the cratered mountain split asunder, the one that had smoked so regularly that Jasen and Alixa had joked between them—whose joke was it, now?—that someone built a cottage there—

That cleft in the mountain that had sometimes spilled over with molten rock had ruptured. Rock there, countless tons of it, so much and so heavy that it would take thousands of years of work to carry it down the mountainside, blew off the mountain like dust. The shattered stone was flung through the air—but Jasen saw it only for a moment, for the mountain belched a noxious cloud of deepest grey smog. It was as if the earth had taken a great lungful, holding it the way Jasen had seen the elderly sucking on pipes and keeping the smoke in their chest for as long as they possibly could. Now it plumed out, a relentless billow—

And rolled across Terreas in an instant.

Jasen had a second to cry something—Alixa and Shilara had too, for he was certain he heard their voices amidst the rumble, even though he surely couldn't have; the cacophonous noise had drowned them out—and then the smoke swept over them.

It was hot, so damned hot. Jasen's skin warmed some twenty degrees as it flowed over him. He clamped his mouth shut, and held his eyes tight—but too late. An acidic sting had already set in, and he screamed as it burned him, blinding, surely wrenching his sight away from him forever—

And *still* the explosion roared in his ears!

Someone was clutching him. Little hands.

Alixa? Must be.

He groped for her in his blindness, catching her wrists, tightening his hold.

I'm here, he tried to convey, broken into a deep sweat. *I'm still here.*

What about Shilara? Milo? Scourgey?

Still out there, surely. Unless a wayward rock had careened this far—and Jasen could not be sure of that, because how would he ever feel the impact of a nearby rock, given that the world shuddering underfoot with such unbridled, relentless force.

They'd survived the blast.

But Terreas ...

His eyes jolted open, and he sucked in a panicked breath.

It made him cough. Disgusting, acrid, it was sour and hot and tasted of bitter ash—

The world was cloaked in grey. It was as if the mists about the base of the mountains had spread across all of Luukessia, only a hundred times thicker, and so damned hot on his skin.

Yet despite its denseness, it could never blot out the horror Jasen's eyes found.

From the split in the mountain poured a river of magma. A roiling stream of vibrant orange, Jasen watched it with wide, terrified eyes as it oozed like water down the mountain. It blackened as it went, the molten rock cooling and hardening at its edge—but new cables, the color of bright embers, flowed over the top, or the tubes split open, new magma renewing the flow. Its vibrant whiteness was sapped with so much smog clouding the space in between, but even so it made Jasen squint harder than the fumes did.

He opened his mouth to scream—

"*FATHER!*"

But it had already come too late. The explosion had rained destruction down in an instant. The exhumed side of the mountain had been thrown forcefully over Terreas like hail. The cloud would have been suffocating, so hot skin would blister instantly as it rolled over the village, the surrounding air granted insufficient time to cool it.

And the flow of lava was spilling toward Terreas.

Alixa was screaming—

The mountainside gave way under the intense pressure that had been building for—how many years? Had this been fated before Jasen was born? Before the scourge defiled Luukessia? The smell was overwhelming. There were no comparisons Jasen's mind could find. He knew the smell of bonfires, from the rare times that Terreas held one. And just days ago he had witnessed his home go up in flames, engaging in a futile effort to save it as it was turned to ash and cast up into the sky.

But nothing could have prepared him for the intensity of this fire. The heat and smoke flowed not just into his lungs but beyond, filling his blood. Every magic little piece of biology that carried oxygen throughout him now was filled with black soot, hard, burned rock, superheated halfway to glass. He was leaden with it, and he coughed—

Flesh burned too. He could smell it, taste it—like burning pig, well past charring as it twisted on a spit—

People. Those were Terreas's people, burning under the lava.

His father was among them.

He screamed and made to leap from the cart—

"GET BACK!" Shilara yelled. She grabbed him from behind—he had forgotten she was here at all—and he saw, through the corner of his eye, that she held Alixa too, pinning her into place so she could not leap over the edge, could not hurtle for Terreas as it was buried deeper, deeper below molten rock, rivers of it, burning white hot—

"We have to go back!" Alixa was screaming. "We have to—"

"There's nothing we can do!" Shilara cried.

Their voices echoed from far away.

There's nothing we can do …

There had to be. Had to be something. If Jasen could just get a breath, a real breath, and clear the painful shrieking in his head—if he could climb over the side, if Shilara would just let him—

"They're gone!" Shilara shouted—and there was pain in her voice, pain like Jasen had never heard from her, had never thought he *would* hear from Gressom.

"*They can't be!*" Alixa screamed.

"*They are! Alixa, they—Alixa—stop fighting!*" Shilara shook the girl, and Jasen sagged, all the fight going out of him, realizing that he knew the truth of Shilara's words before she'd said them. Before Alixa heard the awful reality, before her heart was ripped in two as she acknowledged the truth of it.

"No one could survive that," Shilara said. Her cheeks were wet with tears beneath the ash, Jasen saw, seeming to condense out of the air into smears like snow stained with streaked charcoal. "Everyone back there is dead, Alixa. I'm sorry."

Alixa's mouth worked up and down, finding words.

She found one:

"No!" And she flung herself forward, fighting against Shilara's arm to be freed, to leap from the cart, to bound toward the village—

Yet there was no village left to run to. It had been buried, the cloud of dust and smoke rising, billowing where once it had stood.

His father was gone.

"No," Jasen whispered.

"Can you hold her?" Shilara asked him.

He blinked, dazed.

"Please," Shilara said—and she was not talking down to him, the way she sometimes did, but on his level, one person appealing to another.

Jasen nodded shakily. "What will you do?"

"I need to turn us around."

He blinked, not really understanding. "And go where?"

Shilara's brow was furrowed, the ash covering it smoothing out the lines in her face. "Anywhere but here."

Shilara eased away from Alixa. Alixa looked like she might bolt and Jasen half expected her to as he slipped across to her. He kept his arm about her midriff but it mattered not: she did not fight him.

"Haw, Milo!" Shilara said.

The cart began to shift, turning. Terreas swiveled—

That's not Terreas anymore, Jasen thought. *That's just rock.*

Your father is dead.

Why do I feel …

Nothing?

Shock. His body was protecting himself from collapsing into a mess when it mattered most. Later, surely he would turn into Alixa.

For now, he held her.

"What's happening?" Alixa asked. Her voice pitched up, high. "Why are we leaving?" No answer, yet Terreas kept swinging around, so it was almost behind the cart's stack of barrels—utterly, totally pointless barrels. "*Why are we leaving?*"

"Because if we stay here, we'll die with them," Shilara said. Then: "Yah!"

And they were in motion again.

Alixa screamed, a wail to compete with the eruption in sound. It shook Jasen's eardrums, and he tightened his hold as she fought against himself, desperate to go—

Terreas, or what had once been Terreas, slipped behind.

She screamed for a long, long time.

Jasen's lips were clamped closed. Inside, though, he screamed with her—for Terreas was gone, his father was gone, his aunt and uncle and cousins and every person he had ever known in his entire life. The lone stronghold remaining against the scourge, the only place in this land that had endured and survived all these years …

… All of it had vanished in an instant, buried under rubble, and there was nothing they could have done to stop it.

They three were the last people left.

… save one.

The name tasted bitter as Jasen's lips formed it soundlessly.

Baraghosa.

Jasen recalled the way the reedy, slithery snake of a man had stood before the Assembly. Stickly as he was, his voice just a touch too high for a man, he should not have cowed any of them … yet Terreas fell at his knees, this loathsome, vile, wandering man, stalking the forsaken earth of this isle.

Jasen hated him.

And every echo of those last words intensified that hate until it was a burning fire in his chest:

"You will regret this."

He had done this. He commanded his strange magic, slipped past the scourge where normal men could not.

He had promised that Terreas would regret their decision not to agree to his deal this year.

And this was what he had done.

"Murderer," Jasen muttered.

Baraghosa had killed Jasen's only parent. He'd slaughtered Terreas's people … all because they had refused him one boy.

You will die for this, Jasen thought, lips tight and eyebrows knitted. His breaths were short but heavy, pants of rage as it pulsed through him, that sickly blackness, that fury—that promise.

I will kill you, Baraghosa.

I will kill you.

29

Farther from the mountain, the air began to clear. Dense fumes still clung closely to the ground, but the wind blew and forced it to yield. It thinned, and the temperature dropped to that of a warm spring day. Jasen could see well enough to take in Alixa's stunned expression. She had a far-away look, as though her brain had shut down. Another self-preservation mechanism, perhaps?

Did any of them even have any left worth preserving?

Another distant rumble shuddered the ground beneath them.

"Is it erupting again?" Jasen asked. His voice sounded alien to his ears; croaky, as though he'd been shouting. He had, of course—but not long enough to have exhausted his vocal cords like this, surely?

You screamed back there, he thought.

Oh. Well, that explained it.

Shilara pivoted. She was tense, face etched with deep, dark lines. Ash clung to her; clung to all of them. Shilara had tried to swipe it off, but had only ended up smearing it worse.

"Blast," she said.

Jasen turned, expecting to see another billow pouring forth from the erupting mountain receding behind—

What he saw was, somehow, even worse.

The scourge streamed through the ashen mist.

As if summoned by the terrifying, tumultuous roar of the mountain's explosion, they'd come, a seething mass. It must be every single beast that had lingered around Terreas, waiting for the day they somehow realized they could cross the boundary by merely stepping over it. Dozens and dozens of them, all running as one, all teeth, all clawed limbs, all fury and thirst and hunger for death wrought upon their faces and in whatever wicked souls the beasts possessed.

They ran through the woods, their black eyes seeking one thing, one target—

The cart.

"What do we do?" Jasen asked. "Where are we even going?"

"To the sea," said Shilara.

"But it's days away!"

"Not the eastern coast," Shilara answered. She whipped the reins, urging Milo to go faster—and the poor horse fought on, whinnying in pain. Scourgey, approximating a gallop alongside the cart, quickened her pace too. "We can get there by nightfall, so long as we keep our speed."

"And what do we do when we get there?"

"I've a boat," said Shilara.

Jasen rounded wide eyes, switching them from the scourge pursuing them down the mountainside, to Shilara's back. "A boat? You have a *boat*?"

"Call it insurance," said Shilara. "It's my escape plan, should I ever need it."

"For how long have you been planning this?" Jasen asked.

"Long enough. Does it matter? The scourge can't swim, so we just sail away." With a haunted backward look, Shilara added, "Nothing left here for us anyway."

Jasen followed her glance. The scourge were much too many in number for Scourgey to fight off.

Worse—

"I think they're catching up."

Shilara cursed. "I thought they might. Bloody barrels are slowing us down."

"What should we do?"

Shilara paused to think

"Chuck them overboard."

Jasen began an automatic protest: "But—"

"'But' nothing. The seed is worthless to us now. It might as well come in useful in buying us time and speeding our journey."

Jasen considered the barrels sadly. They'd come so far, endured so much, for them. He and Alixa had smeared themselves with animal guts to slip past the scourge without detection. They'd fought rivers, dodged scourge, and—

All of it was for nothing.

His stomach felt hollow.

Damn it all.

"All right," he said wearily, rising onto unsteady feet. "How should I do this?"

"Can she help?" Shilara asked, nodding backward to Alixa.

Jasen knelt beside her. "Alixa?" He gently touched her shoulder.

She didn't move; just carried on that blank stare into the earth. Nor did she flinch when Jasen lifted a hand in front of her face, wiggling fingers just a couple of inches from her eyes.

"She's not going to be able to help," said Jasen.

"Thought not," Shilara said tensely.

"Will she be okay?" Jasen asked nervously. His cousin couldn't have broken entirely, could she? She was the only family he had left in this world. If she were gone …

"Seen it before," Shilara answered. "Shock. People shut down."

"But they're okay afterward, aren't they?"

"Some of them, yes."

Shilara tied the reins into place. "Ride on, Milo," she instructed—and then she clambered up alongside Jasen, weaving through the barrels.

The scourge were closer now, maybe a hundred feet back. They'd cut the separating distance dramatically.

Well, time to address that.

"This one," Shilara said. She and Jasen lay atop the barrels for now, as there was barely any room to stand side by side at the rear of the cart. "This'll clear some space."

"What do we …?"

"Push the top," said Shilara. "Won't be easy, but between us …"

Jasen nodded nervously. "Okay."

"On three. One … two … three."

They heaved. At first the barrel did not want to yield … but slowly, gradually, it tilted.

When it had tilted far enough, gravity did the rest. Jasen and Shilara released their hands—and down it went, flying from the end of the cart. It slammed into the earth, rebounded, splitting from a fracture—and then collided head on with one of the scourge. A cracking sound punctuated its fall—the barrel, the scourge's skull, perhaps both—and the beast fell away, taking another with it in the tumble.

The rest closed ranks.

"You'd do better to just stop chasing," Shilara called to them. "Plenty more where that came from."

Over the next one went … and Jasen watched as it spun, then a second later crashed into the pursuing pack, knocking two scourge hard. It exploded in a shower of grain—pretty, almost, if bittersweet now the seed, and all their work, was entirely useless.

With floor space open to them, Jasen and Shilara clambered down and one by one unloaded the rest. The scourge did not learn, for though their numbers dwindled they did not relent. They pulled into a tighter pattern directly behind the cart, making it all the easier to bombard them with barrels of grain.

"Last one," Shilara grunted. Closest to the front of the cart, it was an undertaking by itself to maneuver it into position. Between her and Jasen they just about managed though—damn, but this took it out of him; he was covered in sweat again, and heaving great, unsatisfying breaths—and, after lining it up with the remaining scourge following behind them, they let it fall.

Jasen watched sadly as it bounced. It survived the impact though, no splitting open like the others had—

Like the mountainside, he thought—

And then it smashed the final pairing, sending them to the ground in a cloud of shattered wood and a hail of grain.

It was all gone.

His father.

Terreas.

And the seed they had sought to save them.

Just three people, a horse, cart, and their faithful scourge.

All of it had been for nothing.

Shilara must have detected what he was thinking, because she reached up and squeezed one shoulder.

He turned sad eyes to her. "We failed."

"Didn't fail." Her eyes were inscrutable as Jasen stared at her. This must have been the Shilara that fought in the war; grim, unyielding, no hint of drink on her breath. To the front of the cart she went, untying Milo's reins and settling herself into place again.

Jasen stood, one hand around the cart's edge, holding him in place. Milo's pace had picked up, but he was flagging, and Jasen could not pretend otherwise. The fact they were plummeting down a miles-long hillside toward the eastern coast was keeping them going more than Milo was.

Behind them, and mostly shielded by the mountain, Jasen could just make out a hint of Terreas. It was hard to pick out under all the smog, and the hellish tower of smoke filling the sky ... but the glow of magma and pillar of black cloud was all too clear.

Home was gone.

His father was gone.

Damn it all.

"They'd have wanted you to survive, you know," said Shilara from up front.

Jasen glanced to her. She hadn't looked about; he got a glimpse only of her back.

She said no more. Neither did Alixa, who still stared unblinkingly into the distance.

Jasen had no words of his own to add, no argument to give.

And so he did the only thing he could: he returned to his usual spot at the side of the cart, leaning his back against it … and he waited.

Though whether he was waiting to be saved, or to die, he did not know.

30

"What do we do once we get to the sea?"

That question came from Alixa. It was the first she had asked—the first thing anyone at all had really said—in hours. And it was good that she was speaking again, had come to life when she had been practically shut down since the mountain exploded … but her voice was sad, and weary, and desolate.

For a long time, they'd traveled in stunned silence. No one had found the words to say much of anything—and how would they? What exactly could any of them say at all? Terreas was gone, as were every man, woman, and child in it.

Adem was gone.

Jasen had gone over and over it for hours, that stark thought. His father was gone, dead, buried under ash and the magma flowing out from the mountain.

He'd wondered what his last moments would have been like. The rumbling had been terrifying in its power from where the cart approached Terreas. The village itself lay closer to the cratered mountain, so there was no question that it would've been felt. Even the deepest sleeper would have been awakened by that vibration, shaking the whole world madly like a dog shook a weasel. So Adem would have known. He'd have known, for at least a few minutes, that something was happening, that his world had just changed irreparably—

Jasen had seen fear on his father's face just once: when his wife, Jasen's mother, finally succumbed to the illness that had eaten away at her for so long, turning her into a ghostly replica of herself. When Adem had been told she was gone, he had looked scared, the way a little boy might, not at all like the man Jasen had always known.

Would he have worn that expression when he woke to the world shaking so violently beneath him? Or when he realized that the mountain had exploded, side ripped in twain, as superheated rock poured out in a great explosion?

Would he have had time to panic, to fear, as it rolled over him?

Would he have had time to contemplate escape?

Would he have had time to think of the son who had slipped away into the night without so much as a goodbye?

Round and round in circles Jasen went. And he would continue to go round and round. As long as he lived, he would wonder, would think.

He cried silently, face turned down. Alixa, opposite, sobbed too, more loudly, even though Shilara told her, as kindly as she could, to keep quiet. They had outrun the scourge, after all; it would be madness to call their attention to the little cart once more.

But then, what did it even matter if they did? Everyone they had ever known and loved was gone, buried under molten rock, turned to ash. What was the point in living a second longer?

Jasen clutched his mother's pendant, tight.

He would never let it go.

And he would lament, always, that he had nothing of his father's.

That set off a fresh wave of tears. And so he cradled himself, crying, chest heaving with every wretched breath he sucked in.

Yet eventually his tears gave out. They should have continued forever, but his body could not keep up. He was exhausted, thirsty, hungry; he had little left to give, and certainly nothing to be funneled into crying. So he fell gradually into a dull silence, staring deep into the recesses of the world, face red and eyes puffy, and heart broken.

Shilara had pushed Milo on. What reserves he drew on, Jasen did not know, and maybe there were none; maybe he was carried forward simply by gravity as the cart rolled down the slope that led to the nearer shore, around the side of the mountain, the one Shilara where promised a boat, and salvation.

Salvation. What point was that? Let the damned scourge get them. Let them get *him*. This whole thing had been his idea, going to get the seed. Now he was alone in the world, when he might have at least died with his father.

He hadn't said goodbye.

Damn it. Damn it all.

He thumbed a tear away.

The morning transitioned to afternoon. Not once did they pause.

They rode downhill, and there was no sign of scourge.

Once, Jasen would have taken in this world with wide, excited eyes.

They rode through rolling meadows lined unevenly with hedgerows that must have, once upon a time, been a neatly groomed line. Trees sprouted in close formations, somehow nothing like the ones in Terreas: their bark was white, mottled with dark spots, the leaves light and small. A stream cut through the landscape, and they trundled beside it for at least an hour. Willows grew along its edge, trees Jasen had seen in the lone storybook he possessed and which his mother read aloud before kissing his forehead and bidding him a goodnight, telling him that she would see him in the morning …

Now she was gone, as was his father, and he had not one person in the world to tell about the willows, the way their boughs hung down to kiss the water's surface. It was just the three of them in a green, patchwork blanket world that would never excite or interest Jasen again.

And now, as afternoon turned into evening, Alixa asked her question again: "What do we do once we get to the sea?"

"I have a boat," said Shilara quietly.

"And where do we take it?"

"The land to the west. Arkaria."

"How do you know it's even still there?" Alixa's eyes were red and dry. "What if it's overrun by scourge?"

"It's there," said Shilara, steady and certain. Jasen wondered how she managed that after watching their whole world end.

"How far?"

"I don't know."

"Do you have provisions?"

"No."

"Then how will we survive on the sea?"

Shilara pursed her lips. "We'll fish."

"And water?" Alixa was dogged, not letting go. "You can't drink saltwater. That's what the ocean is, isn't it? It'll make us sick. We'll die."

"Saltwater makes you thirstier," Shilara responded wearily, but said little more.

Quiet again.

The cart rumbled on.

Scourgey followed. She was nervous, Jasen could tell. Her mouth hung open, greyish tongue licking at the air. Now and again a low whine would come from her throat, like a sad dog. Alixa looked at her morosely. In better spirits, she might have comforted the scourge, or at least tried her best to. Now …

The other scourge would be back. There was no question of it. The land was overrun, and the last bastion holding out against the creatures had been buried under a layer of glowing magma. Even now, if Jasen twisted to look back, he could still see the glow, the huge billow of smoke still pouring from the mountain's wrecked side.

He would not turn. Would not look. Would not see the tiny smudge where Terreas had once lain.

He looked anyway, and his heart splintered even more. A single tear burned the corner of his eye, dribbling down his face.

He sniffled.

What point was there in going on?

Scourge. They were coming.

So?

Around and around he went.

The seconds compounded far too slowly. One minute was an age. That hours yet remained until they reached the sea was madness. How would they ever get there without the scourge happening on them again? How would they not get overrun? How would they endure a flood of the beasts? Like Terreas under the flow of magma, there was no hope. The scourge had mobilized en masse. They would bury Jasen and Alixa and Shilara, and extinguish the last living people on Luukessia.

The land of Luukessia would be theirs.

Let them have it, Jasen thought. *There's nothing left here for us now.*

So why didn't he just leap off? Why did he not just run into the trees, looking for a scourge to set upon him and take the pain away?

For this, he had no answer. All he knew was that he could not do it … and that the thought of scourge was both inviting, and frightening.

They were coming, though. Soon, they would be back. And the cart would need to quicken, Milo dragging it faster than he ought to be able to, so they might stave off death another day.

Jasen felt sick. So damned sick.

The shadows lengthened.

The sun lowered.

Ahead, the sea beckoned.

Just days ago, that stretch of water had been inviting.

Was it now? Now it repulsed Jasen as well as drawing him toward it, for it offered survival, it offered escape, which he both longed to take and abhorred. There would be no sense of adventure in touching those sands, in stepping out into the water, as he had imagined a whole lifetime ago when he set out on this journey—or multiple lifetimes ago, before Baraghosa had visited, before Jasen had crossed the boundary to save Tery Malori.

He should die here, and finish things. Not live another day.

"Milo is slowing," Alixa said.

"He's tired," Shilara answered. "I've run him half to death."

"Will he make it to the shore?"

Shilara's answer was clipped: "I don't know."

"But the scourge …"

Quiet, but for the rumble of the cart down the hill.

Minutes ticked into a quarter of an hour, then half. That doubled, tripled …

The sun lowered. The sea came closer and closer.

"Another half hour," Shilara murmured. "We're almost there."

"We'll make it?" Alixa asked.

"Mm."

Jasen spared a sad look behind him.

The mountain's noxious spewing cloud was increasingly difficult to make out against the darkening skies. Sun dipped low enough to cast the mountains, and Terreas, in shadow, turning the sky into a bruised sort of twilight.

The magma, though … Jasen could see that. It still glowed hot orange, like forged metal, burning bright against the darkness. From here it was slow to change, but Jasen would never forget it up close, the way the molten rock moved, glowing reds and yellows turning to black as it hardened, then cracked and spilled a fresh wave of heat through.

That it was still aflame now, and visible from so far, stamped out any lingering hopes that Jasen might have. The village, and its people—it was all gone.

Goodbye, Terreas, he thought.

Goodbye, Father.

He closed his eye on a fresh wave of tears—

And then he smelled it, the scent flooding into the back of his nose, shoving its way into his throat and nearly making him gag:

Death and rot.

The scourge were back.

31

"Scourge," Jasen warned. His voice rose with a note of panic he didn't realize he felt, one which the smell of them had brought on—

And then he saw the thing, and that panic reached a new plane entirely.

They *flooded* out of the landscape behind them. A woods had not long passed, short, but it had given the scourge plenty of cover as they picked up the scent of their targets again.

It had also given time for more of them to mass.

The things must've had some way of communicating, some shared language between the beasts that they could use to corral themselves into groups, for this … this was ridiculous. It was as if every scourge alive on Luukessia had collected into one huge, surging wave. And perhaps they had. Terreas had fallen. Now the only people left alive here rode this cart, the last three humans remaining on Luukessia … and the scourge meant to have them, meant to snuff out all three. Decades of destruction, and now the job would finally be finished.

The roiling mass was like a wave. It flooded down the hillside, this final stretch of open terrain, dotted with only a few bushes and trees in the run of unkempt fields laid out before the beach, and the shore, and the boat and all the promise it held. And Jasen very much *wanted* to take up that promise, now he saw the things again, now he saw so *many* of them, leathery and wrinkled and awful, smelling like a thousand corpses piled high and gone to rot in the summer sun, alive with maggots and flies, worming their way through rancid flesh—

He had to live. Being eaten by those things was not the way to go.

Alixa and Shilara must've turned, for Alixa shrieked a cry. At the same time, Shilara cursed.

"Blasted things," she griped. Then: "Blasted—*Milo!*"

The horse must have caught wind of the vile scent of the hundreds of scourge surging behind them, for he tried to bolt sideways. Without the weight of the barrels any longer, he might well have managed—but the horse had been run so hard and so long, up the mountainside and down again, fleeing these beasts for how many hours now? Eighteen? Twenty? That he had any strength left was a miracle.

Shilara tugged the reins, trying to pull Milo under control. "Hold, damn it! We're almost there!"

"Ohh," Alixa said. "There are so many of them …"

Scourgey cast a look back along her flank. Weighing up whether she might fight them off, maybe. Unlikely—and however her mind worked, she must have come to the same conclusion too, for she whined and picked up her pace to hurry alongside the cart rather than lagging as she had done much of their journey to yet.

"Will they catch us?" Jasen asked.

"Shouldn't," said Shilara, "if Milo could just keep—pace—*would you stay on course, you bloody dumb beast?*"

"He's tired!" Alixa moaned.

"He'll be minced meat if he doesn't point where I want him to—oh, oh—no, no, no—"

Milo slowed. The cart juddered along behind, carried as its wheels kept turning on this last little slope leading to the sea. It caught up with Milo, knocking him in the backside—which should have incited him to speed along. But he only slowed further, and Jasen watched in horror as—

Milo collapsed.

The cart rolled across him—

Alixa screamed.

The horse's body acted as both a weight and a hurdle, arresting the cart's speed in a moment.

"Noooo," Shilara said. It was a distinctly Alixa sort of noise, and for a confusing moment Jasen was not entirely sure that his cousin hadn't made it. But Shilara had climbed down from the cart, squatting beside the downed horse. Side on to Jasen, he could see: those were her lips moving. That whine had come from her.

"Is he dead?" Alixa stammered. She was close to tears, perilously so.

Shilara shoved at Milo, the way Jasen might try to rouse a particularly deep sleeper. Or, perhaps, the way a put-upon wife might fight to wake her drunken husband at a time when she truly needed him. They were hard, forceful shoves—and Milo did not move an inch.

She pressed a hand to the horse's midriff.

"Yes," she said. "He's dead."

"Then what do we do?" Alixa demanded.

"What do you mean, what do we do?" Shilara spat back. Her hackles were up, and she flashed a fiery glare at Alixa.

"I mean, *what do we do?*"

"What do you *want* us to do? I'll just put the bloody horse on a set of strings and puppet our way to the shore, shall I?"

"Don't be ridiculous!"

"Then don't ask stupid questions!"

"Please," Jasen began—

Everything had broken down. Here, on the hillside, this last stretch of land before the shore that promised a way off this forsaken land, Shilara and Alixa were going to pieces with the scourge just minutes away—and closing in every damned moment.

"Well, what do we do then?" Alixa asked. "Do we run?"

"Do you think you can outrun those?" Shilara demanded, jabbing a finger back up the hill.

"*Then what do we bloody well do!?*"

"Please," Jasen began again, holding up hands—

Shilara opened her mouth to the heavens. "*I DON'T—*"

Scourgey leapt into the space between them, cutting her off.

Shilara rounded as if stung, ready to defend herself. Her face contorted, and Jasen knew exactly what she thought in that moment: that this scourge was an intelligent one after all, and it had led them on to trap them, to give the scourge a hunt. She had been outwitted, drawn into trusting a beast she had sworn she never would, and now, here, this dastardly monster's plan had come to fruition—

But then Scourgey sunk low. Worming her head across Milo, she opened her mouth to bite at the reins. Gently, eyeing Shilara, she pulled them.

"She wants to take us," Alixa murmured.

"Ancestors," Shilara said. Her voice was far-away. "I don't—"

Scourgey made a breathy, strangled sort of noise.

"Quick," Jasen said, suddenly leaping down and into motion. He grabbed at the reins, ripping them out from where they'd become tangled under Milo's head. "Hook her up."

Shilara unstuck herself. Squatting on the other side, she, for that moment, forgot all the disgust she felt at the scourge. Her hands flew, fingers prying at the reins, loosing them from Milo. Then she slung them about Scourgey, rearranging as best the strange beast's elongated, misshapen anatomy would allow.

The scourge almost fastened, Shilara ordered Jasen, "Up on the cart. I've got this. Now!"

He obeyed, clambering aboard.

Without the mass of barrels obscuring him, and the rear panel of the cart broken and lost, he had a clear view up the gentle rise leading inland.

The tidal wave of scourge—that was what they were, Jasen thought, a grand wave the likes of which he had never seen, enough to displace probably half the ocean in its thunderous swell—was less than a minute behind them.

"They're almost on us!" he cried.

Shilara leapt up. "Go, beast!" she yelled.

Scourgey broke into motion. The reins went taut, and the cart jerked under the sheer, sudden force of it. Alixa yelped and toppled—Jasen caught her before she fell over the edge in a repeat of last night, only a thousand times worse—

Then they were hurtling down toward the beach.

The cart bounced violently. Something about Scourgey's body shape, and the way she imitated Milo's gallop, made the whole wagon judder up and down in a sickening, unpleasant wobble. It seemed to be in the air more often than its wheels touched dirt. Every impact slammed a bolt of pain up Jasen's spine. The cart groaned, rattling madly under each impact—

"Can't control this damned thing," Shilara grumbled.

"She's not a horse!" Alixa cried.

"She'll break the bloody cart in two at this rate."

"Let me do it!"

The look on Shilara's face said she considered a retort. But then she said, "Fine." Thrusting the reins at Alixa, she moved aside, crawling backward over the cart's base. "You'll get better results anyway. Jasen, with me. You've a sword?"

"Uhm …"

Shilara had already found it, thrown haphazardly among the scant possessions they had left. She held it out for him, and he took it as she rooted around for her spear—

"What are we …?" Jasen started.

"Rear of the cart with me," she instructed.

"But why—?"

"If a horse with a cart can't outrun scourge, then this scourge can't, either, not with a cart weighing it down. They're gaining."

Jasen's stomach flipped with panic. She was right. The army of grey beasts flying in their wake was closing in. Unlike Scourgey, they were unencumbered; they could speed without weight on their backs. In fact, the mass was a slave to its own staggering swiftness. The rear pushed the front of the army forward, and if those scourge there were to trip, it mattered not; their bodies would be carried forward until they finally rolled under the feet of those behind, and a new front line formed.

"Speed her up, Alixa!" Jasen called behind.

"I'm trying!"

"And get her to run a bit bloody smoother while you're at it, will you?" Shilara griped.

The cart shuddered violently in apparent response. Shilara bit off a curse word, grunting to herself.

The scourge onslaught drew nearer, and nearer …

Jasen cast a frightened look over his shoulder. The sea had to be a good two miles away yet.

We'll be overrun before getting there, he thought.

The knot in his stomach tightened.

He had to buy them time as best he could.

Leaning forward with Shilara, belly pressed flat to the cart, he steeled himself as best he could. Gripping tight to the base's rear, ignoring the splinters needling him where the back panel had been so violently ripped loose, he squeezed the handle of the blade Shilara had thrust at him. His palms were both sweaty—but it would have to do.

Ten meters of space between them now.

The thundering of their feet was terrific. So vast in number, the footfalls of the pursuing monsters were so loud that the rattles and bangs of the crashing cart disappeared into the fray.

"Ready?" Shilara asked.

Jasen swallowed. Nodded. "Ready."

He took deep, calming breaths—but the scent of rot was overpowering, so many of them surging all in one seething, roiling mass—

"*DIE!*" Shilara shrieked—and she thrust out with the spear as scourge drew within stabbing range.

Jasen followed. His movements were clumsy; he'd had practice with daggers, same as Alixa, but he never took it as seriously as she had, and in any case he didn't think any amount of practice would have adequately prepared him for this. But he thrust out again and again, stabbing the blade at anything within reach—an eye, an open mouth, the exposed neck of one of the wrinkled beasts. He nicked them, and they flinched away, roaring—

Ancestors, their *breath*!

—and he had to tighten his slimy hold to prevent the blade from being yanked out of his hand by the scourges' movements. It did not go, but it did try, and every tilt of the blade that Jasen did not command sent a pulse of fear through him. If he lost this sword …

A particularly voracious scourge with ebony eyes leapt through the throng of its fallen comrades. Its teeth were bared, and Jasen was again reminded of a dog, snarling, on the attack—

Shilara stabbed for it—

But the beast was faster, would reach her arm before the spear spun around.

Jasen yelped. He swung the blade sideways, hoping, closing his eyes though he knew he shouldn't—

It sunk into flesh.

The scourge hissed, and recoiled—

The blade was jerked out of Jasen's hand. He almost followed with it, arm almost wrenched from its socket—

He dared open his eyes.

The scourge had fallen back … and with it, again like a chain of dominoes, the marching army collapsed. Onslaught slowed by the tumult of fallen bodies at the front finally amassing enough weight to cause problems, the scourge began to fall back—and as if she knew, Scourgey picked up her pace, widening that gap.

"Yes," Jasen breathed.

He turned to look over his shoulder at the sea—

"We're close," he said.

Shilara nodded haggardly. "I think maybe a mile—"

The cart slammed the earth hard. It rose skyward, sailing in an arc through the air, Scourgey leading the way with her body—

It landed on its front wheels only, and hard—harder than any impact before.

The front axle snapped.

Jasen had a moment to register the force of the impact, and the snapping sound that came with it—

Then he was thrown into the sky, over the cart, over Scourgey—and headfirst into packed, unyielding sand.

32

Pain overloaded every one of Jasen's senses. It came from everywhere, an all-encompassing roar. His back, his ribs, legs, arms, head. There was no choosing which of these things was most painful, because it all felt like fire, burning its way back into his consciousness as the woolen feeling in his skull began to dissolve.

Grit had gotten into his mouth. There was a metallic taste to it, dull and unpleasant.

Two realizations came to Jasen at once as he burbled, spitting it out. First: the grit was sand. And second, the metallic taste did not come from that sand, but from a split bottom lip.

Doesn't matter, he thought at almost the same moment. His body was a broken heap and he'd never get up. *Let the magma find me; I'm dead anyway.*

Except all this pain was testament to the fact that he was *not* dead, not yet—

And there was noise behind him.

Someone was shouting his name.

His eyelids twitched, the way they did when his father roused him from sleep and he did not want to go.

Father, he thought dully.

But Adem was dead, along with everyone back in Terreas.

And Jasen was alone.

"*Jasen!*"

No. Not alone.

Alixa. Shilara. They were here too. They'd survived.

The beach. That was where Jasen had fallen. Less than a mile from the shore, if that, the waters promising salvation from the scourge, from the ruined hellscape that was Luukessia.

They could still get out of this. They could still live.

It just meant moving first.

Jasen forced himself into motion. It was slow, and the pain seemed to ignite, swaddling his being, increasing as he stretched. But his body obeyed. He untangled the pretzel shape he'd fallen into. Newly formed bruises screamed at him, and muscles groaned in agony.

But the pain in his head was worse, he decided. It swam and a dense fog filled it. Every thought came just a little too slow, not properly attached to the one before it, terminating instead of leading smoothly into the one after.

Was this what drunkenness was like?

Someone cried his name again.

He pivoted toward the sound, blinking in confusion.

Alixa. She staggered to her feet. Tears streaked her panicked face.

The cart had tumbled some way back. Jasen had been thrown the farthest. How, he wasn't sure; Alixa and Shilara had been downed right near the front of the thing. It lay diagonally, fallen to one side toward the front where the axle had snapped. A spray of sand had been thrown up from its violent loss of momentum, and the fallen corner had embedded itself in a fine mixture of sand and dirt, the last feet of which blended into the beach.

Scourgey had fallen too. She was half crumpled in a heap, sprawled to one side where the cart's sudden cessation had tugged her around in an arc. One of the beams she was affixed to now jutted across her body, pinning her to the ground.

But they were all trapped. The scourge were not far behind. The flatlands were open enough to see the way Luukessia rose all the way to the mountains that cradled Terreas—or the ruined slag that remained of it. An army of the things drove this way even now. Not deterred by the lead Scourgey had been able to provide, they surged toward the beach—how far away?

Shilara was slower to rise than Alixa, who lurched for Jasen. Her face was tight, and she winced as she found her footing.

"Jasen!" Alixa cried, and she slammed to her knees at his side, spraying up more sand. She gripped him. "Are you okay?"

"Hurts," he moaned.

"Is anything broken?"

"I don't know." His head, most likely. It wasn't working right at all. "Ohh …"

"Help him up," Shilara told Alixa. Her voice was hoarse, as though she'd spent half a day shouting at the top of her lungs.

"Where are we going?" Alixa asked.

"The sea. Quickly!"

Alixa obliged, taking Jasen by the wrist and helping him to his feet. Damn, it was so painful … and he was so tired, damn it.

I'll sleep in my bed soon, he thought, and he looked forward to it for five full seconds before remembering that his bed was gone, had been gone since the day before he left on this mission to save the village.

"We'd saved it," he moaned, clutching at that stray thought. It should have felt comforting, but it was cold instead.

Alixa frowned down at him. "What?"

He looked her in the eyes, blinked slowly. "We'd saved Terreas."

She stared back for a long moment before she nodded. "I know."

Shilara made her way around the cart. Their belongings had been thrown off in the fall, and most lay strewn across the beach, dug into small craters of sand. She sifted through them, one hand pressed to her side, lumbering awkwardly.

Her spear. Finding it, she bowed low—the expression on her face was terribly pained—and then, staggering back to the cart, she raised it over Scourgey's head—and sliced through the reins holding her in place.

"Get up," Shilara ordered the scourge. "You're loose."

Scourgey didn't need telling twice. Now freed from her shackles she could scramble free from beneath the wooden beam pressing her to the ground, and she did, with a flailing of limbs that dug pits in the sand and flung it out behind her.

Jasen was up too. He closed his eyes, arm slung over Alixa's shoulder for support. Each breath was labored, shallow; too deep and his ribs felt as if they would penetrate a lung.

Perhaps they would. No way of knowing for sure what was intact in there.

Doctor can look me over, he thought.

He frowned. No doctor anymore.

No one left on Luukessia at all, save for them. Just three people desperately running to the sea.

The sea. They were right on it. He twisted back to look at it—and there it lay, a sight he'd wished his whole life to take in with his own eyes, shimmering waters golden and alive with the dancing rays of a setting sun. Salty air filled his lungs, and it was a rich smell unlike any he had ever known.

If only he could separate it from the taste of blood.

"Move," Shilara barked—or wheezed. She was limping already. "Go."

Alixa obeyed. She pulled Jasen into motion with her, granting her shoulder for support.

At first his feet were unwilling. And that was confusing, because when Jasen looked down his legs still reached the ground in straight lines, but his brain told him they'd become utterly tangled. Yet as they limped on, they moved more easily, lurches becoming gentler stumbles.

Scourgey followed, whining.

Alixa threw a glance behind her. "They're gaining."

Shilara pursed her lips. "We're not going to make it." She'd taken to using the spear as an over-large cane. It left soft impressions in the sand behind her.

"We will!" said Alixa frantically.

Shilara turned, squinting across the flatlands that met the beach. "We won't," she muttered. "We're all of us injured. We've no boat."

"We have to do *something*," Alixa said. "We can't just ... just lie down and wait to die!"

No? But it sounded so good to Jasen at this moment.

They staggered on, a loose line, three broken humans and their friendly scourge. All limped, this final short leg of the race reduced to an agonizing crawl.

And still the scourge came closer, closer ...

"What do we do when we get to the water?" Alixa asked.

"I don't know," said Shilara.

"What? I thought you'd planned for this for years!"

"My boat is tethered miles from here. We'll never reach it in time."

"We could...swim?" Jasen asked, the memory of days spent crossing the deepest part of the creek with careful strokes coming back to him, the rite of passage all the boys of Terreas crossed. He could swim, if his hands and legs could remember how.

"I suppose we have to," Shilara said tautly. Blood and sweat streaked the ash on her face.

Crossing the creek, he could do, the dozen or so paces where it grew too deep to touch bottom. But swim for miles?

He couldn't. Body in full working order, maybe; alien though it was, he would try his hardest. But now, a wreck ... treading water was about all he could do, and the part of his brain that still worked was dubious about even that.

He wouldn't last long, whatever the case.

On they went. The shore came nearer and nearer. The sand had been blown into small dunes, no more than a few inches high, arrayed in softly undulating waves along the beach. They'd not been touched by human feet for years, decades, and there was a strange beauty in the way their footprints broke that untouched landscape. How that could be, Jasen was not sure. Was it the fact that humanity still lived, still fought on, even despite the odds stacked so deeply against them? Or perhaps Jasen's brain still was not operating at full capacity, and his sense of beauty had gone askew.

Must be the latter. After all, beyond those soft divots were the scourge.

Closer. They were so much closer than when last he'd looked. He could smell them.

"We won't make it," he murmured.

"We will," Alixa said—but there was a tremor in her voice, conviction sapped. "We have to keep going."

"I don't know that I can," he breathed.

"You can!" Alixa said. She grabbed him by the arm again, pulling—

Shilara gripped him too. "Go," she ordered—

For a long moment, the world was frozen. Jasen met Shilara's gaze, his eyebrows knitted low on his red, wheezing face … and he saw her for the first time perhaps since this whole thing began, saw just how tired she was, how far this had pushed her, the great distance they had come together—

That order shone in her eyes, desperately:

Go.

Where?

He opened his mouth to ask, ask this woman who had led them, endangered her own safety for a village that had shunned her—

Then she shoved him ahead of her.

Maybe it was his own momentum carrying him onward now, but damn it, he went. His bones ached, his body moaned, threatening to break under so much duress … but the shore was close, its waters so inviting, for he had longed so long to do this, to step into them—

Salvation.

The single word floated through his mind.

They were three hundred yards away … two hundred and fifty … two hundred …

Scourgey loped on, keeping pace. She limped least of all and could've outpaced them easily. Yet she kept close, whining, throwing her head from side to side the way Milo did.

"She's scared of the water," Alixa breathed as though reading Jasen's thoughts. "It'll be okay," she whispered to Scourgey.

Scourgey whined back.

Jasen turned around, saw—

"Shilara?"

He stopped, and Alixa was forced into stillness beside him—

Shilara was not with them. She stood back a hundred yards or more, on her own. She just stood there, waiting. Coming toward her, implacable, racing across the dunes—

The wave of scourge.

"*Shilara!*" Alixa cried.

"Get to the water!" Shilara boomed without looking back—and her vocal cords had found some last store of power to draw on, for there was nothing papery or thin about the way she shouted now. "I make my stand here, so you might live on!"

"*Shilara, they'll kill you!*" Alixa screamed.

Shilara lifted her spear to the sky. "Then I will take as many of the bastards with me as I can!"

She turned to face the scourge, less than thirty seconds away—

"Hear me, vermin, and know my name, for we have met before! I, Shilara Annabella Gressom, stand to fight you once more—one last time! In the name of my ancestors, those who came before me, and those I ward now, my descendants, I stand before you!"

"*Shilara!*" Alixa screamed—

"Go," Jasen said, eyes wide. "Move!" And he yanked her into motion again—toward the lapping shore.

"But Shilara—" Alixa cried.

"For too long you have sullied these lands! You have slaughtered the kind, good, noble people of Luukessia, now to the last of them. I will not fail my ancestors. Meet me in battle, you scourge, and know that I will not fail the next links in the great chain that stretches from my ancestors unto me and now to—"

And then they were on her.

"*SHILARA!*" Alixa cried.

Shilara swung the spear, stabbing out madly. She ducked backward, avoiding the snapping of jaws as the beasts surged around her, all focusing on their sole target. The flurry was mad, chaotic, and for the first time Jasen understood how she had survived the war when so few of her compatriots had managed the same. She was a warrior, honest and true, fighting swiftly, with finesse the likes of which Terreas could have learned from as she jabbed and thrust and pivoted, battling back the tide.

It was the only time Jasen would see it; for though she stayed them valuable seconds, the scourge overcame her, scrambling over the corpses of their own to snap at her with relentless jaws. One moment she was there, fighting the mass—then next they had overflowed her, blotting her from sight. One last skyward bob of the spear—then it was gone.

"*NO!*" Alixa screamed. She fought him—

"We're almost there!" Jasen wheezed. She was strong and he was weak now, and it was all he could do to drag her onward. "Please, Alixa—don't let her death be for nothing!"

With that, Alixa stopped fighting him. She looked back, one last time, and then followed along as he pulled her forward, across the shores—

Water splashed Jasen's ankles. Alixa's were wet a moment later—

Scourgey whined at the shore—then, with a cry of abject terror and purest pain, she followed, stepping out into the sea close behind Jasen.

The waters rose—

"They're coming again," Alixa said, dull and flat, all life seeming to have left her.

"Move," Jasen breathed.

The water covered up to their knees now. Scourgey's whining was shrill, pausing only for a breath to refill her lungs. Her rotten scent had turned up a notch, salt taking over in the brisk air, and Jasen realized, idly, that this was what fear did to all creatures. It had made him and Alixa and Shilara sweat on the road to and from Wayforth, when their lives were threatened, and it made Scourgey's odor intensify too.

All animals, he thought. That was all they were when it came down to it: animals.

And this desperate march into the sea was proof of that basest instinct of all: the need to survive. Even when everything had been lost, and Shilara, their guide, was gone, when they had nothing to live for and nowhere to go—still they waded through the waters, up to their waists now …

The scourge had found the ocean's edge.

Do not follow, Jasen willed. *Do not follow* …

One leapt out—

It screamed as it landed in the water. Footing lost immediately, it crashed down into salty sea. No deeper than half a foot, but the noise the beast loosed was like a rabbit caught in a trap. Its head plunged under, cutting the sound off; then it was up, and it staggered back to the sand.

"Yes," Jasen breathed.

"Should we stop?"

Jasen was tempted to say yes, they should … but the scourge clearly did not learn from the efforts of the rest of their pack. Others followed, whining away. One turned back; another suffered the same fate as the first, head going under as its legs gave way. A third overcame the terror, though, and it lumbered after, deeper—

"Keep moving," Jasen said.

The water was up to chest height now—

"I have to swim," Alixa said. The water sloshing about her was deep enough to spill into her mouth. It made her words burble.

"Swim," Jasen told her—and he did the same, feet leaving the packed sand below. He thrust his arms out—

Scourgey latched hold of him from behind.

He cried out—the force of it bobbed him under for a moment—then he was spluttering. Saltwater stung his eyes, filled his nose and mouth—

"I'm not a raft!" he moaned, her weight pulling at him.

"There are more coming," Alixa said. She was close to crying again. How she'd held it in this long …

Jasen longed to look over his shoulder, to assess. But Scourgey made that impossible. So he said only, "Swim farther out!"

They did. And it hurt, oh ancestors, did it hurt … but the deeper waters were the only thing keeping them safe.

Something thrashed behind them.

A wave of panic swept over him. "What's happening?"

"They're drowning," said Alixa.

Jasen closed eyes, nodded. Small relief—but not enough of it. "Good. Go deeper."

"What about Shilara's boat?"

"I … I don't know. She didn't say where it is."

"So what do we do?"

"Just … just swim."

And they did, kicking legs until they were a hundred and fifty yards out, far enough that their feet would never touch the bottom …

Far enough that the scourge would not follow.

There, they ceased.

Jasen turned back. It was awkward, Scourgey clinging to him. Her claws dug in, making him hiss with pain.

No scourge followed. The sea was flat behind them again, ripples from Jasen and Alixa and Scourgey shrinking to nothing long before they reached the shore.

The scourge waited there, an army of wrinkled, leathery, grey beasts. They watched under the setting sun. It was reflected in their black eyes, a fiery orb sinking lower and lower as they watched—and waited for Jasen and Alixa to return.

33

Shilara was gone. Terreas was gone. Their families were gone.

And now Jasen and Alixa bobbed in the water, just treading. The shore teemed with scourge as far as he could see, waiting, watching for them.

"What do we do?" Alixa coughed.

Waves pushed at them from behind. They were not so large as to spill over Jasen and Alixa's heads, pushing them under—but they did force them ever closer to the shore. Both kicked their feet to remain back, but they could only keep it up for so long. The salt in the water kept them buoyant enough, even with Scourgey clutching Jasen's back, whining and struggling … but they'd not slept last night, had been through hell today. How long could they truly keep it up?

"I don't know," said Jasen. "Keep swimming."

"I can't," Alixa said, breath coming in short gasps.

A harder wave rushed at their backs. This one curled over, and a salty spray soaked Jasen up to his ears. Scourgey shrieked, using him almost as a ladder to keep herself above the water's surface, and Jasen felt the sting of a claw slicing the skin of his arm.

"Relax," he hissed. He'd have added, "Please," but did not. The scourge did not know the meaning of the word, and he needed to save his breath. Already his lungs were aching. If they had any hope of outlasting the scourge arrayed on the beach, he needed to make the most of every lungful of air he could manage to take.

They'd lost everything today, everything except each other. But what more was there to say?

His arms ached, legs ached, head ached. He was fighting the currents with everything he had, but his strength was flagging, and now he wondered …

What was there even left to fight for?

Luukessia was overrun. The last haven had been turned to ash, magma spilling over it. Only the scourge remained in this land, and they waited on the beach for their last prey to return, to come back as the sky turned darker and darker.

One thing Jasen knew in his very bones: they could not survive in those waters for much longer, kicking desperately to keep themselves afloat under the towering mountain of smog pouring out of the cratered mountain over the horizon.

There was nothing left.

No hope.

No one to save them now.

And nothing to go back to.

The realization sunk into Jasen like a heavy ball of metal dropped into water. It rolled through him like he'd taken a drink of the stinging, salty water, coming to a stop in the pit that had once been his stomach.

They had nothing to go on for.

All was lost.

If one of these waves should rush over their heads now …

He closed his eyes, swallowing hard, not daring to acknowledge the rest of that thought.

"Alixa," he croaked.

She was but a shadow in the growing dark. "Jasen?"

He wanted to say—so much. Where to begin? He wished to apologize, first, for dragging her into this. But then, if he hadn't, she would be dead anyway, buried under a flow of magma back in Terreas with the rest of its people. Though, perhaps that would have been quicker …

He wanted to commend her for her bravery. She had flown in the face of everything she believed these past days, everything she held dear. She had faced terrors the likes of which she would have never imagined she would face even a week ago, defied all convention and her nature. She had called him courageous and brave less than twenty-four hours ago, and said she wished to be more like him. But now as he floated here, taking stock—she was better, so much better.

He'd always longed for adventure, to cross beyond the border. She never had. Who had been braver to go on this journey? Certainly not he; he was just heeding the call of his nature. No, it was Alixa, who had defied her own to come along … she was the brave one here.

There were so many things to say—

"Jasen," Alixa said, voice picking up with sudden life. "Look!"

He turned in the direction of her wide-eyed stare.

There, against the twilight—burned the light of a single torch.

"Something is out there," Alixa said—and there was desperation in her voice, raw, determined, so utterly hopeful—for this light, whatever it was, wherever it came from, might yield the promised salvation they'd sought in the race to the sea, might offer escape, might offer *life* when it had seemed theirs was to be stripped away from them once they finally succumbed to fatigue or dared to embrace it.

And she began to shout.

"*HELP! HELP US!*"

And then Jasen was adding his voice to her own. "*PLEASE! NEAR THE SHORE! WE'RE BY THE SHORE!*"

"*HELP US!*" Alixa waved frantically. She bobbed up and down, and her face dipped under the water, flooding her mouth. But she rose as high as she could each time, flapping her arms above her head madly. "*HELP!*"

The light had been drawing a slow line level with the horizon. But now it seemed to turn, curving slowly—toward them.

"It's coming," Jasen wheezed. "It's coming this way!"

"*WE'RE HERE!*" Alixa screamed.

"Wait," Jasen said suddenly. "What if—"

Scourgey whined as another wave washed over them. Saltwater spilled into Jasen's mouth, grit floating in it. He coughed it out and grunted, wishing a log had washed out here for the scourge to cling to instead of half-drowning him instead.

"*THIS WAY!*"

"Alixa! What if—what if it's not help?" Jasen asked. "What if it's something else? Something bad? A spirit of the sea? Some—some monster, like them?" He thrust a hand quickly back toward the shore, now vanished in the dark. Still, he knew the scourge waited out there. He could smell them over the salt air, barely.

Alixa clamped her mouth shut, thinking. "It's—it's not," she whispered, strangled. "Oh, ancestors … did we just … did we just lure it over? No …"

It came closer and closer every second, growing from a flickering pinpoint.

Noises drifted too—chatter, in strange tongues.

The hair on the back of Jasen's neck rose.

It *was* a sea spirit, bearing down upon them.

Only … the water was moving too, around it; he could hear it breaking, cleaved into channels. Sea spirits floated above the waves, didn't they? They couldn't affect the way the water actually flowed.

And then Jasen saw it:

Wood.

The prow of a boat.

Alixa must've seen it at the same moment as it came closer, because suddenly she was screaming again—and Jasen was too, doing his best to wave one-handedly, because this was it, this was their survival, the promise fulfilled. This was how they made it out of here alive, intact, escaping the scourge when all seemed lost—

The boat was grand, the sort of thing Jasen had dreamed of one day seeing. Under other circumstances he would have been excited to see it, to catch sight of its sails pulled skyward, blotting the stars not obscured by the cratered mountain's devastating belch of acrid smog.

This?

This overjoyed him.

Figures stood upon the deck, looking down as the boat pulled up alongside Jasen and Alixa and Scourgey. They were dark in the night, shadowed.

One called something down, words Jasen and Alixa did not understand.

"Please help!" Alixa cried. "The shore is overrun!"

More words, chatter between the figures above. One voice rang above the rest, deep and sonorous.

"Help us!" Jasen yelled, and the instruction was ragged in his throat. "Please."

More voices … and then something was tossed into the water. Jasen caught sight of it falling, and flinched away as it landed not far from him—then he realized, blinking off the spray that had wet his face, that it was a rope ladder.

"Alixa," Jasen ordered. "Go."

She paddled to it. Hands groping, she found the rungs and began to pull herself up.

Jasen swam behind.

Close to the ship, Scourgey leapt off of his back with a shriek. The force of her jump thrust Jasen underwater for a moment then, when he broke the surface again, and coughed away the water in his lungs, he saw the scourge scaling the side of the ship as though it were the easiest thing in the world, her claws driven into the ship's hull.

When Alixa was high enough, Jasen gripped onto the rungs himself.

Someone on deck called something, two hard syllables.

The rope ladder was pulled up, both on it.

Jasen stopped climbing. He simply closed his eyes on threatening tears, and let them lift him and Alixa aboard.

There, they collapsed onto the deck, wood beneath his fingertips, the rough grain of the wood beneath his palms.

"Thank you," Alixa was crying. "Th-thank you."

More talk.

Jasen blinked at it in confusion, looking up at his saviors. Men, by the looks and sounds of their voices, which were low and talked so quickly that Jasen wasn't sure he could have kept up even if he had understand the language.

Shadows, he thought, looking at them. The night makes them shadows.

Then he realization: no. No light was capable of silhouetting these men. That was their skin Jasen was looking at: a deep, rich ebony. He stared, their eyes on him, curious. His relief was overwhelming, muting anything but his gratitude. "Th … thank you," he managed to get out.

Where had they come from?

But these thoughts turned to mush. Jasen sagged, falling low against the deck. The fight that had driven him all day was finally gone, and he could give himself over to his exhaustion.

He was alive.

They both were. Somehow, they had survived.

As they lay there on the deck, dripping with water, Jasen's mind spun in a daze. Voices washed over him, foreign words, not unkind, but entirely alien to his ears. Yet even if he could have made them out, they would have passed through one ear and out the other without him taking them in.

Only one train of thought was clear—and it echoed over and over and over.

He had lost his home today.

Lost his family.

Baraghosa had caused that.

No matter the cost, no matter where it meant going—Jasen would find the spindly devil who had taken everything from him.

And when he did, whatever it took …

… he would make him pay.

Jasen and Alixa Will Return in

A RESPITE FROM STORMS

Ashes of Luukessia
Volume One

Coming 2018!

Author's Note

Thanks for reading! If you want to know immediately when future books become available, take sixty seconds and sign up for my NEW RELEASE EMAIL ALERTS by visiting my website. I don't sell your information and I only send out emails when I have a new book out. The reason you should sign up for this is because I don't always set release dates, and even if you're following me on Facebook (robertJcrane (Author)) or Twitter (@robertJcrane), it's easy to miss my book announcements because...well, because social media is an imprecise thing.

Come join the discussion on my website:
http://www.robertjcrane.com!

Cheers,
Robert J. Crane

ACKNOWLEDGMENTS

Editorial/Literary Janitorial duties performed by Nick Bowman, Sarah Barbour and Jeffrey Bryan. Any errors you see in the text, however, are the result of me rejecting changes.

The cover was once more designed with exceeding skill by Karri Klawiter of Artbykarri.com.

The formatting was provided by nickbowman-editing.com.

Many, many thanks to my illustrious co-author, whose name is not actually Michael Winstone. You know who you are, and you do magnificent work. Thank you.

Once more, thanks to my parents, my in-laws, my kids and my wife, for helping me keep things together.

Other Works by Robert J. Crane

World of Sanctuary

Epic Fantasy

Defender: The Sanctuary Series, Volume One
Avenger: The Sanctuary Series, Volume Two
Champion: The Sanctuary Series, Volume Three
Crusader: The Sanctuary Series, Volume Four
Sanctuary Tales, Volume One - A Short Story Collection
Thy Father's Shadow: The Sanctuary Series, Volume 4.5
Master: The Sanctuary Series, Volume Five
Fated in Darkness: The Sanctuary Series, Volume 5.5
Warlord: The Sanctuary Series, Volume Six
Heretic: The Sanctuary Series, Volume Seven
Legend: The Sanctuary Series, Volume Eight
Ghosts of Sanctuary: The Sanctuary Series, Volume Nine* *(Coming 2018, at earliest.)*

A Haven in Ash: Ashes of Luukessia, Volume One
A Respite From Storms: Ashes of Luukessia, Volume Two* *(with Michael Winstone—Coming 2018!)*

The Girl in the Box

and

Out of the Box

Contemporary Urban Fantasy

Alone: The Girl in the Box, Book 1
Untouched: The Girl in the Box, Book 2
Soulless: The Girl in the Box, Book 3
Family: The Girl in the Box, Book 4
Omega: The Girl in the Box, Book 5
Broken: The Girl in the Box, Book 6
Enemies: The Girl in the
Legacy: The Girl in the Box, Book 8

Destiny: The Girl in the Box, Book 9
Power: The Girl in the Box, Book 10

Limitless: Out of the Box, Book 1
In the Wind: Out of the Box, Book 2
Ruthless: Out of the Box, Book 3
Grounded: Out of the Box, Book 4
Tormented: Out of the Box, Book 5
Vengeful: Out of the Box, Book 6
Sea Change: Out of the Box, Book 7
Painkiller: Out of the Box, Book 8
Masks: Out of the Box, Book 9
Prisoners: Out of the Box, Book 10
Unyielding: Out of the Box, Book 11
Hollow: Out of the Box, Book 12
Toxicity: Out of the Box, Book 13
Small Things: Out of the Box, Book 14
Hunters: Out of the Box, Book 15
Badder: Out of the Box, Book 16
Apex: Out of the Box, Book 18* *(Coming February 1, 2018!)*
Time: Out of the Box, Book 19* *(Coming May 2018!)*
Driven: Out of the Box, Book 20* *(Coming July 2018!)*

Southern Watch

Contemporary Urban Fantasy

Called: Southern Watch, Book 1
Depths: Southern Watch, Book 2
Corrupted: Southern Watch, Book 3
Unearthed: Southern Watch, Book 4
Legion: Southern Watch, Book 5
Starling: Southern Watch, Book 6
Forsaken: South Watch, Book 7* *(Come Late 2018—Tentatively)*

The Shattered Dome Series

(with Nicholas J. Ambrose)
Sci-Fi

Voiceless: The Shattered Dome, Book 1
Unspeakable: The Shattered Dome, Book 2* *(Coming 2018!)*

The Mira Brand Adventures

Contemporary Urban Fantasy

The World Beneath: The Mira Brand Adventures, Book 1
The Tide of Ages: The Mira Brand Adventures, Book 2
The City of Lies: The Mira Brand Adventures, Book 3
The King of the Skies: The Mira Brand Adventures, Book 4* *(Coming Late 2017/Early 2018!)*

Liars and Vampires

(with Lauren Harper)
Contemporary Urban Fantasy

No One Will Believe You: Liars and Vampires, Book 1* *(Coming Early 2018!)*
Someone Should Save Her: Liars and Vampires, Book 2* *(Coming Early 2018!)*
You Can't Go Home Again: Liars and Vampires, Book 3* *(Coming Early 2018!)*

* Forthcoming, Subject to Change